# THE *Heart* STEALER

BOOK TWO
NOLAN
U

*Katy ♡ xoxo Archer*

# KATY ARCHER

Archer Street Romance
www.katyarcher.com

# CHAPTER 1
## RACHEL

"What am I doing here?" I whisper under my breath as I grip the steering wheel and stare at the house I'm supposed to be aiming for. Hopefully I've got the address right. Hopefully I'm looking at Hockey House right now.

I laughed so hard when Mikayla told me the guys she was living with had *named* their house. Who does that? And who picks a lame name like Hockey House?

I'm not laughing now, though, am I?

Tears prick the back of my eyes as I gaze at the two-story home that seems to sprawl across the property. There's a big front yard with neatly trimmed edges and a wide driveway that currently has no cars in it, but I bet it's usually loaded with cool pickup trucks that scream Jock City.

Mikayla's painted a pretty clear picture over our weeks of video chats and messaging.

The house has six bedrooms, lots of guys, and my little best friend. She probably fits in just fine with a bunch of rowdy hockey players.

Me? I'm gonna be a fish out of water. A gasping, panting, about-to-die fish out of water.

Biting my top lip, I then swallow, and it hurts. I'm not sick, my throat's just aching.

Probably from all the tears. I feel like my entire body is one big bruise.

How am I supposed to knock on that front door feeling this way?

Are any of them even home right now?

My gaze flicks from the empty driveway to the light above the front door. It's illuminating the steps like a homing beacon.

Except this isn't my home.

Nowhere is home anymore.

"Shit." I close my eyes, desperate to keep the tears at bay. Panic is making my heart race, threatening another sobbing meltdown. I need to clamp this down. I can't fall apart again.

And I can't walk into Hockey House with a blotchy face. Mikayla will take one look at me and start an inquisition... and I can't tell her what happened to me last night.

Was it only last night?

I rest my head against the steering wheel, exhaustion hammering me from all sides.

I've had like two hours of sleep in a truck stop outside Vegas and have spent the entire day driving. I can barely see straight. And I'm turning into an ice cube sitting here.

"Come on, Ray. Move your ass or freeze." Gritting my teeth, I reach for the door handle and force myself to breathe.

There are lights on in the house—a soft amber glow

is coming from what I assume is the kitchen or dining room. Maybe it's the living area.

Hopefully Mikayla's in there, ready to give me a hug. Because, shit, I really, *really* need a hug right now.

With a little sniff, I step out into the crisp night air.

*It's frickin' freezing!*

Hugging the jacket to my body, I wrench open the back door and wrestle my suitcase out. Thankfully, it's not my big one. I just grabbed the first one I could reach from under the bed and threw in what I could. I have no idea what I packed. I probably forgot underwear and half my clothes, but it wasn't like I was thinking straight.

A shudder runs through me, my lips trembling as a tidal wave of tears threatens to take me out again.

*Pull it together! Don't freak Mick out. Just don't!*

My reprimand seems to work, because by the time I reach the front door, my eyes have dried enough to notice the light sprinkling of snow dancing through the air.

*Great. Snow.*

Yes, that was sarcasm.

But I'm cold.

And I don't care if it's pretty.

My fingers are aching, and my internal organs are starting to shiver.

That's why my hand is shaking when I ring the doorbell. That's the *only* reason.

I frown, fisting my fingers and praying that Mikayla's home, that I have the right freaking house, that the disaster my life has become somehow has an out.

The handle clicks, and I hold my breath as the door swings open. It's impossible to keep my gasp in check when a shirtless guy who looks like he's from the cast of *300* opens the door.

*Holy shit.*

He's carved from stone. Big, broad, and beautiful. It's impossible not to gape at his pecs, the shape of his bronze muscles, and... yep, I'm pretty sure he's got an eight-pack. Not six, *eight.*

*Stop staring at him, Ray!*

I glance at the ground. "Um... uh... hi."

"Hey." His voice is cheerful, relaxed, and it gives me the courage to check him out again.

I know I shouldn't be ogling him and obsessing over his muscles, but those perfectly shaped ridges are making my belly dance. He's gorgeous. Even his face is beautiful. All cut jaw and defined lines. He's got this protective soldier look about him, and—

*Stop being attracted to this man! You've just left your boyfriend less than twenty-four-hours ago.*

The thought of Theo makes my belly stop dancing. Instead, a tight fist forms beneath my rib cage as I battle memories of our fight last night.

Blinking to ward off any signs of how horrible it all was, I force a polite smile before looking to the safety of the ground again.

"Can I help you with something?" he asks.

"Maybe." I rub my forehead, no doubt messing up my bangs before flicking them out of my eyes. "I'm looking for Mikayla Hyde. I think she lives here?"

"Oh yeah. She does." This wide smile stretches across his face, and I can't help drooping with relief. I've got the right house. Thank God.

"She's not home right now."

And there's that fist in my stomach again.

"But you're welcome to come in and wait for her." He smiles again, and for a second, he comes off like a cheesy salesman, until I look into his eyes and sense a genuine kindness.

Although, I've been fooled before.

"I don't think she'll be too much longer. She's out with—"

"Ethan," I murmur, this soft laugh coming out of me. It's wooden and seriously lacks any humor. How can I ever laugh again?

I cross my arms and look over my shoulder, spotting my car on the road and wondering what the hell I'm supposed to do now. This guy is probably going to invite me in, but... do I go?

Can I trust him?

"So... do you want to come in and wait for her?" He steps aside, gesturing for me to walk past him. To enter Hockey House.

My heart rate spikes.

*Who else is in there?*

*A bunch of guys? Are they drunk? Will they—*

"It's perfectly safe."

My eyes dart to his face. He's smiling again.

"I'm a gentleman, I swear. I'll set you up in the living room with a coffee or hot chocolate, and I'll leave you alone if you want me to... or I can sit and keep you company. Whatever you need."

He seems so sweet and sincere. I seriously want to trust him.

But I thought Theo was sweet too.

Shit, I'm such an idiot.

Tears spring into my eyes before I can stop them. Covering my mouth, I try to hide them, but then a sob betrays me. It makes my body jerk, a weird sound coming out of me that I fail to smother.

Before I know what's happening, two strong arms wrap around me, and I stiffen.

*What's he doing?*

*Is he going to drag me inside?*

*Is he—*

"I'm not gonna hurt you," he whispers. "I promise."

Why do I believe him so easily?

Am I just being a fool again or...

For some reason, my body goes. With a little nudge from him, I'm walking inside. Warmth immediately envelops me as the door swings shut behind us. It's so nice to be out of the cold and snow that I just stand here, allowing this to happen.

His hand is on my elbow now—a light, undemanding pressure that would be easy enough to shrug off.

"It's gonna be okay." His voice is so gentle, his expression so tender.

I want to stare at him.

Believe him.

But he doesn't know.

How can it ever be okay?

After what went down? What I did?

I clench my jaw, fighting this onslaught of tears that wants to take me out.

"I'm Liam, by the way." He touches his chest, and I somehow manage to rasp a reply.

"I'm Rachel."

His lips rise into yet another smile. They seem to come so easily for him.

"You're Mick's friend from California. She talks about you all the time."

It's hard to see through the building tears. I try to smile, but I'm not really sure what my mouth is doing. "Hopefully good stuff."

"Always good stuff. You're one of her favorite people. Top five... in fact, you're potentially number one, although you might be tied with Ethan now. You'll have to ask her." His wink is adorable. I manage to catch it after a quick blink that causes tears to spill down my cheeks.

I want to laugh and smile at him. He's kind of adorable.

But my jaw is trembling again, and I'm sucking in a ragged breath that has hints of sob riding beneath it.

His expression crumples, this pained look crossing his face before he opens his arms wide. "C'mere."

I hesitate, stepping away from him. "Why?"

"Because you look like you could use a shoulder to cry on." His voice has dropped to a husky murmur. "My shoulders are big, and I'm not gonna be some slimy creep and make a move on you. I know we've only just met and you might not be able to trust that, but—"

"Liam," I whisper, the name finally conjuring up past conversations with Mick.

"Yeah, sometimes they call me Padre. Mick might have told you about me? Ethan and I grew up together. He's my best bro." He says "bro" with this little grin that's obviously trying to win a smile out of me.

I nod, remembering a few odd stories. Mick raves

about Liam. And she does sometimes call him Padre, because he's like the protective bear of the group, always looking out for his teammates.

*You can probably trust this guy.*

The thought makes my belly tremble, like after twenty-four hours of a living nightmare, I can take a second to breathe. To not be scared anymore.

My chest heaves, my belly jerking as I suck in a breath, and then the tears start in earnest. There is no stopping this flood. I don't even bother covering my mouth, just let out this aching moan and lurch into his arms.

They wrap around me instantly, strong yet gentle, and my body buckles.

I can't carry this weight anymore. My legs won't hold me.

And before I know what's happening, he's scooped me into his arms and is carrying me to the couch. Lowering himself onto it, he settles me on his knee. My long, gangly legs curl into the cushions as I swivel my body and rest my head against his shoulder.

He's right.

His shoulder is big. And solid.

It catches my tears, holding me steady while I finally let myself weep without trying to fight it.

His hand lightly cradles my head, his thumb rubbing circles on the back of my scalp as I mourn what I thought would be a love to last forever.

Theo was my guy.

And now he's not.

And I ache in so many ways.

# CHAPTER 2
## LIAM

Rachel's tears are soaking into my skin. I absorb each one, hoping to make her feel better. I have no idea what went down or why she's here. She looks kind of scared and cut up, which is killing me.

Nothing rips me apart more than a broken woman.

When her face flashed with fear before, I felt the old memories stirring. They're not that old, and it doesn't take much for them to come to life in an instant. Mama weeping at the kitchen table, dabbing her swollen lip and trying to tell me that the lump beneath her eye was no big deal.

"Bruises heal, *mijo*."

Anger burns, my stomach automatically clenching.

Rachel sniffs, and I will myself to relax. I don't want her picking up on my black vibes. I'm trying to make her feel better.

It'd be great to know what the problem actually is, but I can't quite bring myself to ask. It feels like prying, and she's in the sob stage of her recovery. I just need to give her a minute.

I need—

The front door swings open.

"Hey-yo!" Ethan calls into the house.

"'Hey-yo'? Seriously? Where did that come from?" Mick loves to hassle my boy, and I can't help a little grin when he laughs.

"I'm trying something new, Shorty. I like it. Hey-yo. It's gonna be my new greeting from now on."

"Not around me it's not."

"Okay, lil' mouse, I'll save it up, real special-like... just for you."

There's a small scuffle, and then laughter floats into the living room as they playfully tussle their way toward me. They're both laughing, and Mick lets out a screech when he hits her ticklish spot, but Ethan quickly swallows the sound with his mouth, lifting her off the floor so she can wrap her legs around him.

Rachel's gone completely still on my knee, like if she turns to stone she might, in fact, disappear.

I loosen my grip on her, and she slinks off my lap while Ethan lets out this gravelly moan that tells the entire room what he has in mind for his girlfriend.

Yeah, that can't happen just yet.

So, I clear my throat nice and loud.

It takes three coughs for the sex-crazed couple to finally register other people in the room. They pull away from each other, their lips swollen and glistening, their expressions dazed. And then Mick's eyes bulge, her mouth popping open.

"Ray?"

"Hey, Mick." She brushes a finger under her eye, then forces a smile, but it doesn't really help.

Her face is blotchy, her eyes rimmed red. She's so obviously been crying, and there's nothing she can do to hide it.

Mikayla wriggles out of Ethan's arms, jumping around me to plunk down on the couch. "What's wrong? What are you doing here? How did you get here? I..." She brushes Rachel's bangs aside with her small hands, her eyebrows wrinkled with worry. "What happened?"

Rachel's face bunches, and then she lets out this shaky sigh, her body deflating against the cushions. "Theo and I broke up."

"Aw, babe." Mick slumps back against the cushions, taking Rachel's hand and squeezing it against her chest. "What happened?"

Rachel shakes her head, a small, stiff movement that says it all.

Thankfully, Mick doesn't push her. Instead, she cups Rachel's cheek, her thumb rubbing back and forth as they share a look of pain. "I'm sorry it hurts right now."

Rachel sniffs. "I just needed to see my bestie."

Pulling her into an instant hug, Mikayla rests her head on Rachel's shoulder and squeezes the life out of her. Rachel's quick to pull away, like she doesn't want a big fuss to be made.

"I'm sorry to just show up like this. I should have called ahead, but I've been running on stress and tears and—" Her voice catches as her eyes start to glisten again.

"Hey, that's totally fine. You are allowed to show up unannounced, *anytime*. I'm always happy to see you."

Mick grins, excitement taking over her expression. "I can't believe you're here!"

She dives in for another hug, and Rachel manages a weak smile... although she does seem lighter now that Mick's arrived. It's obvious how close these two are.

I share a quick look with Ethan, who's grinning down at them before giving me a questioning frown.

He points to my bare chest, a glint forming in his eyes as if he's about to smirk but isn't sure if he should.

I roll my eyes. *As if.*

The poor girl has obviously had her heart smashed to pieces. Like I'd make a move.

Jumping off the couch, I mutter that I'm going to take a shower, but then the front door pops open and the rest of the guys pile in the door.

I instantly worry that it's all going to be too much for Rachel and shift without thinking, blocking the guys' view of the couch.

"'Sup, bitches!" Casey swans into the room, his swagger confident and just a little drunk. He always has one too many.

"Hey-yo." Ethan raises his hand in greeting, not even fighting a grin when Mick groans from the couch.

Asher gives him a weird look before dumping his keys on the kitchen counter and shedding his coat, which probably cost more than my entire wardrobe. He dumps it on the bar stool and goes to the fridge while my body tenses.

Casey wanders toward the couch, no doubt set on starting up a late-night gaming session.

"Bax, you in, man?"

A distant voice replies from down the hallway, "Yep, set it up!"

About the only time Baxter will voluntarily hang out in the living room is when he and Casey are gaming together. And I mean *only* Casey and him. The guy's not a socialite, and if he walks in and finds Rachel in his spot, he's not gonna be happy about it.

He already struggles living with Mikayla, although he still voted to let her stay. The guy's got a good heart, he just likes to keep to himself. And I think he's scared of girls.

The thought makes me grin, but then Casey's nearly at the couch and—

"Hel-lo."

*Shit.* I clench my jaw, crossing my arms and firing a warning look at him, but he doesn't even notice.

He's already jumping around Mick, a broad smile taking over his face as he perches on the coffee table and extends his hand to Rachel.

She's obviously eyeing up the tattooed beast with caution, sharing a quick glance with Mick before shaking his hand.

"You must be Casey."

"That I am." His chest puffs out, and Mick sits forward, slapping her palm against his shirt.

"Okay, peacock. Put those feathers away. She's not interested."

Casey glances at lil' mouse, feigning offense. "How the fuck would you know? She's probably sitting here lost for words because she's so taken with my beauty."

Rachel's lips twitch as Mikayla fails to hide her laughter.

"You are—"

"Unbelievably gorgeous? Charming? Funny? The sexiest man in this house?"

She leans forward, slapping him on the knee as she stands. "None of the above."

"You slay me." He places a hand over his heart, then turns back to Rachel and points his thumb at Mick. "Do you know this woman?"

Rachel can't help a grin, and my stomach twists. Shit, Casey is a piece of work... although it's nice to see Rachel smile. She has a beautiful face, and it's even more enchanting—

*Enchanting? What the hell is wrong with me?*

She's gorgeous, okay? And her smile makes it even better.

"She's my best friend," Rachel murmurs.

"Which means you must be Ray-Ray." Casey leans back, wagging his finger at her. "You are a stunner."

"Um..." She glances at Mick, then softly replies, "Thank you?"

Mick lets out another groan, snatching Rachel's wrist and pulling her to her feet. "Please ignore this horndog. He should come with a warning label."

"I'm hot stuff, baby. I can't help it." He shrugs, his tongue poking out the side of his mouth as he winks and smiles at the girls.

"Keep it in your pants, Case," I growl.

He glances at me, raising his eyebrows in a "What the fuck's your problem?" kind of gesture.

I roll my eyes. Did he even notice how red and swollen her eyes are?

The guy's a walking penis. That's the only organ he thinks with.

"Welcome to Hockey House, Rachel." Asher extends his hand, flashing his straight white teeth and kissing her knuckles like he's Lord Bensen and not just plain ol' Asher from New York.

"Seriously?" Mick nudges him away. "You never kissed my hand."

"Well, you're not a lady." He shrugs. "But your friend here..." He gives her an appreciative smile that makes Rachel blush.

She dips her chin, tugging on the ends of her jacket sleeves to cover her hands.

"Here, let me take that," I offer, annoyed with myself that I hadn't even thought of it before. She's probably burning up. But I was kind of distracted by her sobbing. I'm so glad that's stopped now. She's definitely looking calmer now that Mick's here, but I can still sense her stress.

All these curious gazes and flirty guys are getting to be too much for her.

"I assume you're staying?" I speak over whatever drivel Asher is firing her way. "You can have my room if you like."

"Oh." Her beautiful green eyes round. "No, that's okay. I don't want to be a bother. I can just find a hotel or something."

"No way. You're totally staying. Liam can sleep on the couch." Mick crosses her arms, and I nod my approval.

"I really don't want to impose on—"

"It's no imposition." Ethan grins at her. "I'm pretty

sure Mick would maim us all if we let you walk out the door right now. Seriously. You're welcome to stay."

He raises his chin at Asher, who's nodding as well. "Yeah, of course. Let me get you some towels and show you around."

Asher takes the lead, grabbing Rachel's suitcase and guiding her upstairs. I chase after them, ducking around them to make sure my room isn't a total mess while Asher gets her towels and shows her where the bathroom is.

I scramble to gather clothes off the floor and dump them in the laundry basket before quickly making my bed.

She arrives just as I'm fluffing a pillow for her.

"And this is where you'll be." Asher smiles at her. "Liam, you can sleep in my office if you like."

Rachel's questioning look is adorable, and of course, Asher instantly becomes Mr. Bombastic and has to explain how this house belongs to his uncle, so that kind of makes it his, and he has the master bedroom downstairs with the en suite, and he turned the room next door into his office, which is basically a glorified man cave that he never studies in. I don't even know why he calls it an office.

"You're welcome to check it out anytime. I have a pretty impressive comic book collection."

Rachel's eyebrows rise along with her polite smile, and it's impossible not to snicker. She's trying so hard to hide how unimpressed she is.

Asher darts me a glare before leaving the room with a little huff.

I grab a pair of boxers to sleep in along with the rumpled T-shirt under my pillow. "Just made the bed for you. Sorry the sheets aren't clean, but I only put them on a couple days ago. I can change them if you want, though."

"No, that's okay." She brushes the air with her long fingers, and I'm pretty sure she's the kind of woman who will do anything not to be a pain.

"It's really no trouble, you being here. Mick's stoked."

"Yeah." Rachel's expression softens. "It's nice to see her too."

"And I'm... sorry... about your boyfriend."

Her face bunches and she nods, biting her bottom lip and running shaking fingers through her hair.

I wince. *Shit. I shouldn't have brought it up.*

"You look exhausted." I give her an empathetic smile. "I'll leave you to... get some sleep."

"Thanks," she mumbles, her eyes still cast to the floor.

I pause just as I reach the bedroom door and lightly rest my hand on her shoulder. She flinches, then goes still.

"You're safe here. But there is a lock on my door if that'll make you feel better."

She doesn't say anything, and I slip away to give her some privacy, my stomach churning as I descend the stairs.

Mick's making two hot chocolates in the kitchen, and I rest my hip against the counter. "Tell me about this Theo guy. Rachel seems pretty cut up."

"Yeah, I know." Mick pouts, pouring hot milk over the granules in one of the cups. "Poor thing. He was her first everything—serious boyfriend, roommate."

"They were living together?"

"Yeah. She only moved in a month or so ago. Things

must have gone downhill pretty fast. She's made the odd comment, but nothing serious. I wonder what the tipping point was."

"It's a hell of a long way for her to drive, and she was a wreck when she first got here."

Mikayla stops to eye me up, her expression thoughtful as she stirs the drink, then taps the teaspoon against the edge. "Don't worry. I'll get to the bottom of it. Not tonight, but eventually. Ray's like an onion when it comes to her feelings. You have to work slowly, gently peeling back one layer at a time. But eventually she tells me." She shrugs. "If I push too hard, she'll go into a corner, so I'll bide my time, give her plenty of TLC, and she'll open up like a flower." Her smile grows as she lifts the two mugs and starts walking for the stairs.

An onion.

Good to know.

"Hey." Mick catches my attention. "Get that worried look off your face. She's gonna be fine. I'll hit her up with an ice cream date in a few days and get the whole story. I know how my girl ticks."

She winks at me, and I can't help the sudden thought that I'd love to know how Rachel ticks too.

# CHAPTER 3
## RACHEL

Sleeping is impossible.

Even though Liam's bed is super comfy and my head sinks into his luscious pillow, I can't switch off. It's like I'm so exhausted, sleep can't even find me.

Every time I close my eyes, images of Theo's angry face flash through my brain, along with the rest of our ugly argument. I feel sick.

Sucking in a deep breath, I notice how this bed smells like the hockey player who held me tight, stroked my hair, and gave me a minute to fall apart. He was so gentle and kind... and he doesn't even know me.

*Theo was gentle and kind.*

My stomach clenches and I scrunch my eyes shut, turning over to get comfortable, but I can't.

My night is a mixture of light dozing, tossing, and turning, and by the time I officially greet the next day, I have a thumping headache.

Snatching one of the plush towels Asher gave me, I hug it to my chest and walk to the bathroom, avoiding my reflection in the mirror as I strip naked and soak under the hot spray. I use Mikayla's shampoo and body wash, needing to cleanse every inch of myself.

It feels good to wash away that ugly night, but when I finally get out and wipe the steam from the bathroom mirror, I'm confronted all over again by what went down.

My breakup with Theo was no ordinary argument.

It was vicious.

And I have the bruises to prove it.

They pepper my body like blobs of paint. Running my hand down my rib cage, I turn and wince, eyeing my mottled skin and the graze along my hip. My swallow is thick and painful in my aching throat as that awful night comes crashing back over me with a clarity that's brutal...

Before I even opened the door, I knew Theo had his friends over. Their voices carried all the way to the driveway, where I'd just parked my car after a double shift at the grocery store. The last thing I felt like facing was a room full of obnoxious, drunken men. He didn't even tell me they were coming.

But it was his house, right?

I helped pay rent and all the bills, but his name was the one on the lease.

So he could do whatever he liked.

I grabbed the bag of essentials I'd picked up at the store before leaving, and braced myself for a long night. My plan was to go hide in my room, try to watch a movie on my laptop or something. But their voices would carry.

Ugh. I'd get minimal sleep, and I had an early shift tomorrow.

Working two jobs and taking on these extra shifts was all for a good cause. I had to remind myself of that. Theo and I were saving for a trip to Hawaii, but I felt like I was working constantly, and coming home to a house full of Theo's friends was the last thing I needed.

With a heavy sigh, I opened the door and spotted the guys at the round kitchen table. Five of them, all with beers and cigars, playing a rowdy game of poker.

"Hey, Rach," Theo said around his cigar, which he knew I hated. The smell always turned my stomach.

But I forced a smile and went over to peck his lips. He grabbed my ass with his spare hand, and his friends all laughed.

Usually I wouldn't mind a little tap on the tush, but not when everybody was watching.

I eased away from him, unloading the groceries into the fridge and looking for the plate of leftovers I'd covered for my dinner. It was gone. I glanced over my shoulder and saw the remains by the sink. It couldn't have been Theo who ate it—he doesn't like my pad Thai, which meant one of his friends scarfed it down and nobody stopped him.

My belly rumbled with hunger, and it was hard not to slam the fridge shut. The bottles inside rattled, and a couple heads turned my way.

The brothers, Matt and Max, glanced at me. I forced a polite smile and felt my skin crawl when a smirk rose on Matt's face. I seriously didn't get why Theo considered that douche his best friend. He was a slimy creep, especially when he was wasted.

"Can you get us a drink, cutie?" he drawled, and I glared at him, hating the way he'd labeled me. It started a few weeks back when I was bending over to pick some-thing up, and he wolf-whistled and told me I had a cute booty.

From my boyfriend, I would have taken it as a compliment.

From his creepy buddy... it made my skin crawl.

Everything about the guy made my skin crawl.

"Actually, I'm just off to take a shower," I muttered, walking away from the fridge. "I *have* just worked a double shift." I couldn't help that last quip, throwing a pointed look at Theo, who wasn't even looking at me. *Dammit.*

I went to move past the table, but Matt shot out of his chair, blocking my path.

"It's just one drink. You're closer to the fridge than I am."

"I'm not your maid, Matt. You can get your own drink." Crossing my arms, I tried to stand up for myself, wishing Theo would do it for me. Couldn't he feel the change in energy around us? Couldn't he sense the dark vibe that washed through the room the second Matt stood from his seat?

Matt inched closer, his sour breath making my stomach pinch as he leaned forward and whispered against my cheek, "I want *you* to get it for me, woman."

He shoved me back with a force I wasn't expecting. Stumbling on my feet, I crashed against Max, then whipped my eyes at Theo.

His forehead creased, and he darted a look at Matt before tipping his head toward the fridge. "Just get him a drink. Don't turn this into some big thing."

My lips parted, anger sparking inside me. "I've just

worked a double shift and come home to find my dinner eaten by someone else. I'm exhausted. I want a shower, and I shouldn't have to get anyone a drink!"

Before I saw it coming, a hand clamped around my wrist and started dragging me toward the fridge.

"Let go," I grunted, trying to shake free of Matt's hold, but his hands were strong, and my pigeon arms and skinny legs were no match for him.

Propelling me across the room, he shoved me into the fridge. My shoulder smacked against it, and I couldn't help a small cry. Pain traveled down my arm, pins and needles spreading through my hand.

"Get me a drink!" he barked in my face, spittle hitting my cheek.

*This is insane.*

I looked to Theo for help, but he was staring down at his cards, shifting in his chair like he didn't want to piss off his friend.

*Just get him the drink, Ray.*

It would have been the easiest thing to do—just open the door and grab a beer. There. Done.

But my stubborn pride just wouldn't let me. So I stayed still against that fridge, refusing to open the door, taking one breath after another as I tried to pick my time to make a dash for the bathroom.

I got it wrong.

Before I could make a break for it through the kitchen archway, Matt's hand clamped around my arm, and his thunder fist barreled into my stomach.

I bent over, gasping for air, shock and pain radiating through me in equal measure.

*What the hell just happened?*

I crumpled to my knees, panic clawing at my throat while I tried to find my next breath. Cradling my stomach, I looked to Theo for help, but he just sat there in his chair, giving me this bug-eyed stare.

*Help me!* I wanted to scream at him, but I couldn't speak.

*I have to get out of here. Move, Ray. Move!*

I managed to inhale a breath and took off for the door, crawling across the floor in a bid to escape, but an iron hand snatched my ankle, and I was dragged back and made to stay.

Matt kept yelling at me, calling me every ugly insult his wasted brain could come up with while treating my body like a soccer ball. I curled in on myself, trying to protect what I could and wishing I could somehow fly out the window and get away from this nightmare.

I don't know how it stopped, but the room seemed to go still, Matt's voice disappearing, replaced with pants like he'd just done a workout.

I stayed on the floor, my heart thundering in my ears and pain radiating through my body. I kept my eyes shut until I heard the fridge wrench open and a bottle being snatched out of it.

Taking my chance, I scrambled to my feet and raced for the front door, but I didn't even get the handle turned before two strong arms were around me again.

"No you don't."

"Let me go!" I screamed and struggled against Theo's hold on me, but he lifted me off the ground, manhandling me down the hallway.

"Stop fighting," he barked in my ear. "I'm protecting you."

"What?" I screeched just as he let me go.

Opening our bedroom door, he pulled me inside.

"You didn't protect me," I whimpered, cradling my bruised side. "You just sat there and let it happen."

"Yeah, well, I brought you down here, now didn't I? We'll lock the door, and you'll be safe."

I gave him an incredulous look. "I'm not staying in this house."

"Yes, you are." His voice turned to steel. "You're not leaving me." Scrubbing a hand down his face, he huffed and cursed. "Fuck, Rach. Why couldn't you just get him a fuckin' beer? Was it really that hard?"

I narrowed my eyes at him, daring to show him just how pissed off and disgusted I was.

He turned away from my black look, barking over his shoulder, "Just stay in here, okay? We'll talk about this after the game."

He swung open the door, and I followed him, determined to walk down the hallway and out the front door. He couldn't keep me here like some prisoner.

Snatching my arm before I could pass him, he shoved me back. "I said stay in here!"

I stumbled, my feet tripping as the momentum took me backward, and whacked my hip against his chest of drawers before tumbling to the carpet.

The photos wobbled, and one toppled over.

Photos of us.

Romantic shots of a loved-up couple.

I stared at the one of him grinning at me while I laughed at whatever he'd just said. That man looked like he loved his woman. That woman looked like she couldn't have been happier.

And I didn't even recognize us anymore.

How could that image be Theo and me?

We looked so in love.

And now he was screaming at me and throwing me around like a piece of trash.

I looked up in time to watch his face pucker into a deep frown before he slammed the door shut. "Just do what's good for you and stay in there. I mean it, Rach! Stay put."

Pressing the back of my hand against my mouth, I smothered the sobs jerking through me.

I couldn't believe this was happening to me.

It was a living nightmare.

I thought I'd had my worst moment ever when my dad died, but this was next level.

Beaten and locked in a room?

I could try climbing out the window, but what if they saw me? What if they chased me down and pulled me back in here?

I could barely wrap my head around what had happened... what could *still* happen.

Fear had clutched me so hard and fast that I wasn't able to move.

And so I stayed.

Right there.

On the floor.

I cradled my aching body, curling into a ball and weeping into the carpet.

And I must have fallen asleep somehow, because the next thing I knew, there was movement in the room.

My eyes cracked open, and I squinted against the

hallway light as Theo's drunk ass stumbled around the bed.

"I won, cutie! Three thousand bucks!" He raised his hands in triumph, flopping onto the bed with a giggle. "I won!" Slapping the covers beside him, he beckoned me off the floor. "Come celebrate with me."

*Over my dead body.*

I clenched my jaw, refusing to speak a word to him.

We were through.

My heart let out a pitiful whine, a different kind of pain coursing through me.

I thought I loved this man. I thought he was my forever guy.

But he sat there and let his friend beat me. He shoved me into this room and ordered me to stay, like I was his dog or something.

I never wanted him near me again. The thought of him touching me, trying to "celebrate" with me, made my stomach convulse. Bile burned the back of my throat.

I wasn't joining him on the bed. I'd rather eat fly-infested horse shit.

"Cutie? You comin'?" His voice started to fade, and like the miracle I needed, he passed out, his snores reverberating across the room.

Forcing my stiff body up, I crawled to the edge of the bed, double-checking that he was asleep before wrenching out the first suitcase I could find. It caught for a second, and I let out a desperate whimper before pulling it free from under the bed.

Every movement hurt, but I ordered myself to grab what I could and shove it into the small suitcase. I grunted when the zipper fought me, then stilled, hoping the noise wouldn't wake Theo.

He slept on.

It was a small show of mercy, and I took it, carrying the suitcase down the hall and into the living room.

The guys had all gone, so I snatched my purse off the counter, glared at the fridge one last time, and headed for the back door.

Stopping by the table, I stared down at the pile of money Theo had won. The bills were clumped in the middle, a mound of fresh and crumpled. Everything from Washingtons to Jacksons.

A big pile of green that made Theo so fucking triumphant.

He was sitting there winning all that money while I lay terrified on our bedroom floor.

And in that moment, I hated him.

I didn't realize that love could turn to hate so quickly, but there it was.

A black vibration like I had never felt before coursed through me in waves so thick and strong, I could barely see straight.

And it made me act on impulse.

It made me become someone I never thought I could.

# CHAPTER 4
## LIAM

Sleeping on Asher's man cave couch was bearable. I mean, it's pretty comfy, I guess, but there are so many fucking lights in this room. From his big-screen TV to the gaming console and all the special pieces of tech in here, the buzz and flickering LEDs were enough to do my head in.

Thankfully, I managed to drift off and eventually sleep like the dead.

I felt kind of groggy when I woke up, but nothing an early-morning workout and breakfast smoothie can't fix.

Jumping up, I fold the blankets and make it neat, because Ashman is not the slob the rest of us are. Then I realize I need to grab some running shorts and a fresh pair of socks.

Hopefully Rachel will be sound asleep, and I can just sneak into my room and gather my stuff without disturbing her.

Unless she's locked the door.

Padding up the stairs, I avoid the creaks and tiptoe to my bedroom, only to find my door wide open.

*Huh.*

I check the bed and it's empty. She must be using the bathroom. I dart to my closet and hunt out the things I need, trying to be quick. But as I'm crouched down in front of my shoebox full of socks, I hear the door click shut behind me.

Crap. She's back.

And she mustn't have seen me behind the closet door.

I need to make myself known, but...

Glancing over my shoulder, I'm about to clear my throat when she drops the towel around her. My lips part, and taking my eyes off her is now an impossible task. There she is, standing naked in my room. I can't help checking her out. My eyes are glued to her smooth skin, trailing down her body from the edge of her shoulder, over her pert little tits, and down the planes of her stomach. The crop of dark hair between her legs makes my dick start to pulse, but my eyes keep going until I'm all the way to the bottom of her slender legs. Some would call her skinny—she seriously must be only 10 percent body fat. I know chicks who strive for that kind of thing, but I'm guessing Rachel probably complains about her protruding bones, calling herself gangly or—

She starts to turn toward me, and I brace myself for what is no doubt going to be an awkward conversation.

But then I see it.

Her perfectly smooth skin is mottled on the left side. Black-and-blue bruises speckle her torso and legs. There's a graze on her hip, but the worst of the damage is around her stomach and upper thigh.

"Holy shit." I can't help my whisper as I stand tall and gape at the damage.

She gasps and whips her head to look at me, her eyes wide and scared as I move toward her. There are more bruises on her arm, one up near her shoulder.

"Who did this to you?" I'm trying to keep my voice even, but it's an effort. Anger is circling my core, spiraling like a thick whirlpool as I drink in her injuries and imagine how they were inflicted.

She turns her back to me, but that just exposes a boot-shaped mark on the edge of her spine.

"Someone kicked you," I rasp, skimming my fingers, featherlight, over the nasty imprint.

She spins around, her green eyes glistening with a mix of pain and fear.

Someone fucking kicked her! Someone put that expression on her face.

Breaths spurt out of me as I work to control the rage firing through me. I have no time for assholes who hurt their women. I grew up experiencing that shit, and I can't believe Rachel is standing here shaking the same way my mom used to.

I reach for her hand, needing to touch her, comfort her, let her know this will all be okay.

But she shies away from me.

"I'm not gonna hurt you," I promise, my voice raw with emotion. "I would never hurt you."

Tears shimmer in her eyes.

"But I want to disembowel the guy who marked you like this. Was it Theo?"

She dips her chin, her body starting to tremble.

Shit, she's still standing there naked... almost like she

needs me to see it. Like deep down she wants someone to know.

And she's trusting me with this truth.

I guarantee Mikayla doesn't know yet. She was way too calm when she brought her empty cocoa mugs back to the kitchen last night. Ethan hugged her while she rinsed them out, and I heard her tell him that poor Ray was exhausted.

"She's such a soft, sweet soul, you know? Breakups suck anyway, but it's her first love. She's devastated."

I bet she is.

Devastated that the guy she's supposed to trust, the one she moved in with and gave her body to, turned on her. He showed his true, dark colors, and it probably shocked the hell out of her.

I remember the first time Dad lost it with my mama. She never saw it coming, and she was horrified and heartbroken.

But still she stayed.

Thank God Rachel didn't have the same compunction.

Brave girl.

Brave and strong.

Gently touching her elbow, I glide my fingers down her arm until her palm is resting within mine, and then I ever so softly tug her toward me.

It's a tender pressure that she can easily resist.

But she doesn't.

She inches closer until I can cradle her against my chest. Her arms slowly wrap around me, like she's not sure she wants this, but as soon as her head touches my shoulder, she fists the back of my T-shirt, clinging while she sucks in a rattling breath.

I cup the back of her head, ensuring that I'm not touching any of her bruises.

Her body starts to shudder the way it did last night, but her tears are silent.

"Do you want to tell me what happened?"

"No," she mumbles against my neck, and I have to accept that.

She's an onion. It's gonna be one layer at a time, and me being in here… her letting me see… that's a huge layer right there.

Shit, I want to know so fucking bad.

It was Theo.

That fucker.

I'm going to hunt him down and end him.

But right now, I've got this woman leaning against me, drawing comfort from whatever strength I can offer.

Shoving thoughts of murder out of my brain, I lightly rest my head against her cheek.

She's a tall willow that's been bashed about by a hurricane.

But she's going to endure.

And I'll make sure I do everything in my power to help her.

# CHAPTER 5
## RACHEL

Liam's chest is solid, and I lean into it, my nipples brushing against his T-shirt. But my slow brain takes a minute to register that I'm still naked.

I'm too busy soaking in his strength to be fully aware of my vulnerability until I feel a hard rod poking against my lower abs.

I frown, my head moving off his shoulder as I take a step back and gape down at his tented boxer shorts.

"Sorry," he mumbles with a helpless shrug. "You're beautiful. And you're naked. And you're beautiful."

All I can do is blink... and keep staring at his... well, it... That's a big tent right there.

*Stop staring at his penis!*

My head shoots up, and it's only then that I register what he just said.

*He thinks I'm beautiful?*

*That can't be right.*

I shake my head. "With bruises all over my body? I don't think so."

With a soft sigh—like he's disappointed I said that— he takes my hands, stretching my arms out wide so he can drink me in. It's squirm-worthy. His gaze is gliding down my naked body. Why am I not stopping this?

"You're beautiful," he says again, the look in his eyes so sincere that it's impossible not to believe him.

This is crazy.

I'm a mess, and he's standing here admiring me like I'm a piece of art. And he... he's still erect.

My eyes have tracked back down his body without my say-so, and I'm staring at his manhood again. Staring and struggling to swallow. And yep, I think my cheeks are on fire too.

"Here, just..." Liam spins, ducking into his closet and pulling something off a hanger. He throws it at me, and I catch it, pulling it wide to see it's his hockey jersey. "Put that on. It might make it easier. Encourage the little guy to calm down, you know?"

*Little guy?*

He's obviously not seeing what I'm seeing.

I keep the thought to myself as I pull the jersey on. It's hard not to wince. My body is feeling stiffer than it did yesterday, but as the fabric falls down just past my butt, I'm enveloped with this sense of calm I can't explain.

There's comfort in this jersey. I don't know what it is, but I kind of want to keep wearing it forever.

Glancing up, I check on Liam, about to ask him if that's better, but he's staring at me with parted lips, like he's struggling to form words.

Finally, he manages to croak, "Okay, that's really not helping." He turns around, resting his hands on his hips. "You in my jersey is way too sexy. Like, it's a problem."

My lips jump into a grin before I can stop them.

This is so bizarre.

I mean, I wouldn't call myself ugly. But I'm certainly not the stunner Liam is treating me as. I'm just your average girl, yet he's acting like I'm some cover model who's turning him on.

I tug on the bottom of the jersey, not really wanting to take it off but wondering if I should. My clothes are right there in my suitcase.

My clothes, which will never be good enough again.

Seriously, I want to throw on a pair of leggings and live in just those and this jersey for the rest of my life.

Liam glances over his shoulder, his eyes raking over my body before he winces and turns around again, shaking his head and muttering something under his breath.

Wow. He's really struggling.

And I'm in shock, to be honest.

Until Theo, I'd always been attracted to guys who were never interested in me. It was like my thing in high school. I fell for the guys who were out of my league all the time, and then the ones who did try to chase me... I wasn't interested.

I honestly thought I was cursed until Theo started flirting with me.

Then swept me off my feet.

Then knocked me off my feet and locked the door.

My stomach sinks, and I absentmindedly brush the bruise on my hip.

It's still so tender. My entire body feels like shattered glass that's been glued back together.

"Do I need to take you to the hospital?"

I glance up with a gasp, unaware that Liam had turned around.

Shaking my head, I take a seat on the end of the bed. "No, I don't want to do that."

"But what if he's broken your ribs or something? What if you have internal damage?"

"It doesn't feel like I do." I rub my hand over my stomach, Matt's thunder punch coursing through my brain as I lean forward and rest my elbows on my knees. Cradling my head, I stare at the carpet, curling my toes into it.

I don't want to have this conversation.

I want to go back to feeling all sexy and attractive.

Liam thinks I'm hot. Let's dwell on that for a while.

Liam.

A guy who I would have considered out of my league in high school got a hard-on because of me, and he told me I was sexy.

I want to soak in those awestruck feelings for a minute, not think about the fact that Theo and his asshole friend might have fractured one or two of my ribs.

Cradling my side, I run my fingers down my rib cage, convincing myself that they're only bruised.

I'm not going to a hospital over this. I'm fine.

"They're just bruises," I murmur. "They'll heal."

Liam grunts, sitting down beside me and resting his hand lightly on my back. "Look, it's your body, and if you don't want to go to the hospital, I won't force you there, but... please, just... If there's any lingering pain, or things aren't healing the way they should... promise me that I'm allowed to take you."

I sit up, soaking in his expression and wondering at

this feeling in my chest. He looks as though he knows what he's talking about. Does he have a doctor in the family or something?

I open my mouth to ask him, but he speaks before I can.

"You should report him."

I shake my head. "I just want to forget it happened."

With a little tut, he clenches his jaw but doesn't look like he's going to fight me on it.

Again, I get the sense that there's something lurking beneath the surface here.

"Liam, do you—"

"Does he know where you are?"

We start speaking at the same time, and my question is immediately abandoned by the thought that Theo might find me.

I mean, I had considered it, which is why I dumped my phone back in Vegas. I was still running on panic at that stage. But when I finally crossed into Colorado, I started to calm down.

But...

*Shit.* My brain starts to burn, questions firing through me faster than I can answer them.

*Does Theo know where Mikayla goes to school?*

*Did I ever tell him? I must have told him, but did he remember it?*

*Will he assume I came to see her?*

*What if he shows up?*

I jump off the bed, pacing to the closet and spinning around, fear clutching me so hard and fast, I can't breathe.

"Hey, it's okay." Liam stands, slowly moving toward me like I'm a cornered animal.

I brace my hands on my knees, my body starting to shake as I fight for air.

His soothing hand runs circles over my back. "I won't let him near you. If he comes here looking, the only thing he'll find is my fist in his face."

I wince and glance up at him.

"We'll keep you safe, okay? No one's gonna hurt you again. I won't let that happen. I promise."

Standing tall, I stare at his honest expression and shake my head. "You don't even know me. Why would you promise something like that?"

He shrugs. "It's what I do. I protect all my friends."

"But we've only just met."

His lips tip up at the sides, and he starts counting on his fingers. "You're Mikayla's best friend, which makes you one of mine, you cried on my knee last night, and now you're standing here in my hockey jersey."

My lips twitch with an unexpected grin, and now I'm trying to squash a giggle that's stirring in my belly. "And those are all reasons enough to put you in harm's way in order to protect me?"

His eyes drink me in, his fingers featherlight as they skim down my cheek. "I don't need to know someone to protect them. If an asshole tries to hurt an innocent person, I'm gonna do everything I can to stop it."

And there goes my heart. Melting into a puddle.

Who is this guy?

Seriously?

He's got the heart of a superhero.

And the body to match.

My eyes skim down to his feet. They're broad and big, looking mammoth next to my long, narrow toes.

"So please, trust that I won't let Theo touch you again. If that asshole is dumb enough to show up at Hockey House, he's gonna wish he was never born."

I glance up at Liam's steely expression, his jaw clenching tight as he steps back from me.

"I'll let you get dressed," he murmurs, moving to the door.

He pauses just before turning the handle and looks back with a sweet smile.

My lips lift in response, but I can't think of anything to say as he slips into the hallway.

His words are humming inside me, so strong and sure. Crossing my arms, I grip the edges of his jersey and force myself to take a full breath.

"You're safe here, Ray," I whisper. "It's gonna be okay."

# CHAPTER 6
## LIAM

I walk downstairs, my insides boiling as I picture those bruises on Rachel's delicate skin.

I can't believe that asshole kicked her in the back. What the fuck?

Thoughts of her whimpers make me shudder and send my mind straight back to my early teens when I had to hide in the closet with my sisters while Mom whimpered and cried between smacks and cracking knuckles. Dad would be drunk and yelling insults. Alcohol turned him into a crazed man, and Mom did her best to calm him, but it never worked.

Was that what Rachel went through?

Did she beg Theo to stop, but he just keep hurting her anyway?

My fingers curl into a fist, rage coursing through me as I try to reconcile with having to face this again. Storming into Asher's man cave, I yank on a pair of jeans and grab the long-sleeve tee I wore most of yesterday. It still smells okay. I can get away with it.

Shit, I forgot the stuff I was getting from my room. I can't go back up there again right now. Rachel needs a minute. Plus, seeing her in my hockey jersey is a sweet torture that I'm gonna have to psych myself up for. Holy shit, she is one smokin' hot chica, with my jersey just covering her perfect ass, plus those long legs.

*Yes, please!* my dick begs.

Fresh socks and my plan for a morning workout will have to wait.

Heading for the kitchen in bare feet, I try to dodge memories from my past, but they plague me anyway.

Watching my mom suffer was a living nightmare. When Dad came back from Afghanistan, he was never the same. At first, we bent over backward to help his body heal.

"Daddy lost his friends. He's very sad."

"Daddy's body needs to get better after the explosion."

"Daddy's brain is still healing."

We tried to be understanding and loving, but he wouldn't get help. He skipped out on the counseling sessions he was offered, refusing to talk through his trauma. Instead, his therapist became a bottle of Jack and our version of hell on earth.

Alcohol brought out the ugly in him. And if you didn't get out of the way fast enough, you'd find a fist in your face. I tried to protect Mama a couple times, but seeing her kids bruised was worse than taking them herself.

I begged her to leave him, but her love somehow endured. His weeping apologies the next morning always seemed to hit their mark, and she'd stay... or she'd let him stay.

Clenching my jaw, I rest against the kitchen counter, relief and admiration pulsing through me when I think about the fact that Rachel left.

I'm assuming this is the first time Theo got violent with her.

My expression crumples as I reach for a glass and fill it with water. I always feel bad when I judge my mom for sticking with Dad for so long. She loved him... probably loves him still.

I guess I just don't understand why. The guy lost all my faith and trust the first time he punched his wife in the face.

I snap my eyes shut, trying to stuff that awful memory back into the box I created for it.

All of my darkest ordeals are in there, locked tightly away so they can't haunt me anymore.

"Hey, bro. You okay?" Casey's voice makes me flinch.

I didn't even hear him come into the kitchen.

Now he's eyeing me with a curious frown, so I quickly iron out my expression and throw in a shrug. "Yep, all good."

"You look like you're trying to crush that glass with your fingers." He snickers and shakes his head. "Bad night on the Ashman's couch?"

Casey takes a seat, resting his tattooed arms on the counter. He's shirtless, and his ink is kinda impressive. Not that I'd ever get a tattoo—they're just not my thing—but they look great on Casey. It's like part of his personality, and I can't imagine him with plain skin like mine. He's a walking piece of art, and all of it's on display right now... unless he has something on his ass I don't know about.

He's still looking at me like he's trying to work out my secret, so I force a smile. If Rachel is anything like my mother, she won't want the world to know what she's been through. I had a lot of practice in high school and can easily fake breeziness when I need to.

"It was okay." I rub the back of my neck.

"You know the guy jerks off on that thing all the time, right?"

I go still, eyeing Casey with a skeptical frown until I realize he's not bullshitting me.

"No, I did not fucking know that," I grumble, plunking my glass down on the counter. Water splashes out the top of it, sprinkling the counter, while Casey's eyes start to twinkle. He's doing a shit job of hiding how much he's enjoying this.

I narrow my gaze and mutter, "I hate you."

He throws his head back with a barking laugh that's loud enough to wake the house. "The look on your face right now. Damn!" He slaps me on the arm. "Dude, what a great way to start my morning."

"By ruining mine?"

"You betcha." He wiggles his eyebrows and gets up, walking around me to the fridge.

"Still hate you, man."

"And I will love you forever." He wraps his arm around me from behind and lands a sloppy kiss on my cheek before grabbing a glass and filling it to the brim with orange juice.

I can't help a small grin as I wipe his kiss away, but my

smile disappears the second Rachel enters the room. There she is, looking all beautiful again.

She's changed into black leggings and a long sweater that reaches mid-thigh. Paired with a soft-pink scarf, she looks like a cover model about to do a winter shoot. Her long bangs hang down over her eyebrows, and she brushes them aside, her green eyes darting between me and Casey.

Shit, she's gorgeous.

Seriously, my insides are going nuts.

Even my dick is twitching.

There's just something about her...

And Casey sees it too.

"Hey, good-lookin'." He gives her a charming smile. "Can I offer you some breakfast?"

I frown at his back, quickly stepping around him. "Actually, I'm taking her out for breakfast."

Snatching Ethan's keys off the hook—I know he won't mind me borrowing his truck—I guide Rachel to the front door, ignoring Casey's "Can I come too?" and gently nudging her to the coatrack.

She pulls on her jacket and boots, then grabs her handbag as I usher her out the door. I'm barefoot in my boots, but I don't feel the cold, and I'm kinda in a hurry here. I wouldn't put it past Casey to chase us down in nothing but his boxers, so I hustle Rachel to the truck and get the heat cranking.

Rubbing her hands together, she gives me a small smile. "I was actually going to ask if I could have a word in private, so breakfast is good." Her seat belt clicks as she buckles up. "Where are we going?"

"Taffy's does a mean omelet. What kind of breakfast food do you like?"

"I could go for an omelet." She gives me a closed-mouth smile, her green eyes sparkling just a little before she turns to look out the window.

We drive to the diner in silence, and I find a parking spot near the front door. As soon as I stop the engine, I rush around to help Rachel out of the truck, but she lands easily, her long legs making the drop kind of small.

Without thinking, I take her hand and lead her to the front door.

She doesn't pull out of my grasp until we stop at the counter and I ask for a table.

Taffy's is one of those diners that caters to everyone from the early-morning retirees to the young moms and their babies over the lunch rush. The place is kinda old, but it's an institution in Nolan. I'm sure the owner is like a hundred by now, but she still shuffles around the place every now and again, saying hi to her regulars. When she goes, the place will probably get handed down through the generations and run just the same to honor a lady who has taken care of so many people in this small college town.

The chipper waitress has taken our order before Rachel finally pulls in a breath, like she's on the cusp of telling me what's on her mind.

But nothing comes out of her open mouth, so I give her a small nudge.

"What did you want to talk to me about?" I play with the sugar packets while she straightens the salt and pepper shakers.

"Don't tell Mick." She swallows, keeping her eyes on the shakers. "I don't want her to know what happened."

Words lodge in my throat, and it takes me a minute to find my voice. "But... she's your best friend. You should tell her."

"I can't." Her bangs swish as she shakes her head. "I don't want anyone to know. Please..." She looks up, hitting me with that green gaze of hers. It's bright with desperation. "If you hadn't seen me this morning, you wouldn't know either. So just... promise me you won't say a word to anyone." She closes her eyes, softly mumbling, "I'm so ashamed."

"Of what?" I lean forward, completely confused by the last thing she just said. "You haven't done anything wrong. You didn't deserve a boot in the back."

Her jaw trembles as she sniffs and starts drawing lines on the table.

"Rachel, look at me." Her eyes slowly track to mine. They're wide and vulnerable, looking almost too big for her narrow face. I soften my voice to a whisper. "Whatever you think you did, you don't deserve to be treated that way. Nobody does. I don't give a fuck if you burned his dinner or said the wrong thing. He has no right to punch and kick you, *ever*." My voice starts to rise without my say-so, but I have to get my point across.

Like hell she's taking any responsibility for this. There is never an excuse to beat on an innocent person. Never.

Rachel blinks at tears, biting her lips together and nodding.

I reach for her hand, brushing my fingers over the top of it. "You understand that, right?"

After a soft huff, she says, "Of course I do. That's why I

49

ran. I wasn't sticking around for some lame apology after what he did and what—"

Her voice cuts off, and fear pinches me in the chest.

There's something she's not saying, and it's making my stomach roil.

*Fuck.*

*Did he do more than just beat her?*

She sniffs. "But I... I fell for him. I fell hard and fast and believed everything he said to me. And it's... so humiliating. It makes me feel like I'm gullible and pathetic." She sucks in a ragged breath. "He just seemed so sweet and attentive. I thought he was the nicest guy. I went on and on about how amazing he was. I moved in with him after such a short time of dating. I gave him my virginity. I—"

"Hey," I interrupt in a bid to calm her down. Her voice is starting to pitch and rise, snot is now dribbling from her right nostril, and tears are trickling down both cheeks. I pass her a paper napkin. "You've got nothing to be ashamed of. *He's* the one at fault here. He led you on. He deceived you."

"And I was stupid enough to be deceived." She mops up her face, balling the napkin within her fist and frowning at me.

I reach for her hand, opening my palm on the table, but she doesn't take it.

"You're not stupid, you just have a gentle heart. And unfortunately, assholes like your ex can fool you. Don't lose who you are because of him."

She gives me a weak smile, her fingers finally resting on my skin.

I give them a light squeeze and smile at her. "I've only

known you one day and I can already tell I'm gonna like you a lot. I mean, I already like you, but you know..." I wink. "You're gonna burrow."

"Burrow?" Her head tips.

"You know... find a place in my heart."

Shit, I can't believe I'm saying this stuff to her. She's just escaped an ex who turned out to be a total fuckwit, and here's me telling her she has a place in my heart. What the hell is wrong with me?

I need to stop talking... like right now.

# CHAPTER 7
# RACHEL

I'm gonna burrow?

How cute is this guy?

My insides want to melt into a puddle of goo. That's the sweetest thing.

But Theo was sweet, too, and I let myself be fooled by his charm. I let myself believe he was the one. That he'd love me forever and keep me safe.

*Safe.* I scoff at the word, anger and heartache mingling together like a toxic poison in my chest.

He just sat there. Sat there and watched while Matt punched and kicked me.

Smashing my teeth together, I look down at Liam's hand. So strong and sure. Powerful enough to snap my fingers, probably. But he never would.

Even so... I can't go jumping on the love boat again.

I've learned my lesson about falling hard and fast... and I won't be doing it twice.

Sliding my fingers out of his grasp, I tuck them under the table and smile at him.

"You're sweet," I murmur, trying to soften the fact that I just pulled away.

He nods, his cheeks turning pink before he clears his throat and shuffles in his seat.

Thankfully, the omelets arrive, smelling fantastic and making me realize that I haven't eaten a decent meal since my lunch break two days ago.

My stomach cramps as I sprinkle salt on my eggs and add a little ketchup.

Liam pauses, watching me squirt a line of red sauce in a zigzag over my omelet and hash browns. The expression on his face is hilarious, and I can't help a small giggle.

"Ketchup on your eggs?"

"What can I say? I'm a saucy girl."

"You most definitely are." He winks at me, grinning at his double meaning, and I focus on my food, trying to ignore the tingles firing down my legs.

We eat in relative silence, glancing at each other every now and then before darting our eyes away to study the paraphernalia on the walls. This place is chaotic, like an old attic that needs a good tidying.

I kinda like it, though. It's homey.

And this food is delicious.

I clear the entire plate and even get a refill on my coffee.

Liam's eyebrows rise when I push the empty plate away from me.

"I hope you don't mind me saying this, but for a girl so slim, you can sure pack it away."

I smile into my cup, delaying my answer with a sip of

coffee. "I have a fast metabolism. I've always been like this. No meat on my bones, but not without considerable effort on my part."

He grins, and I keep babbling for some reason.

"Although, I'm sure it won't always be that way. My grandma used to eat like a horse, apparently, and was as skinny as a beanpole until she had kids. Then she got round and stayed that way." I let out a soft laugh, remembering the way Dad used to tease his mom. She'd always laugh it off, proud of her mom bod.

I miss her.

And I miss him even more.

An old ache that I've lived with since I was fourteen sears through me. It comes and goes. Some days the hurt is unbearable. Other days, I don't even notice it.

Right now... I would have done anything to have my dad bust through Theo's door and rescue me. He would have been livid. He would have put those assholes in their place and carried me away to safety.

"Hey." Liam's husky voice catches my attention. "Where are you right now?"

My face crumples in confusion.

"The look on your face." He points at me. "Are you remembering the other night?"

I dip my chin, not wanting to admit it. It feels like Theo wins if I do. Like what happened is going to haunt me forever and steal a piece of my soul.

"You know... talking about it can help."

I glance up at him. "Reliving it? Really? That's helpful?"

He winces. "Burying trauma doesn't always work."

Scraping his hands through his short hair, he squeezes the back of his neck, and I wonder if there's some bigger meaning behind his words.

Has *he* experienced trauma before?

Has he had to do some kind of counseling or—

"I'm not saying you need to see a therapist or anything... Unless, of course you want to, which is totally valid and probably really helpful. I just mean that sharing the burden can lighten it for you." He cringes, rubbing his forehead. "I feel like I'm saying this all wrong. I want to respect your privacy, I really do. But not to your detriment." He huffs, his hand landing on the table with a soft thud. "And my imagination has been torturing me." His expression buckles even further, as if he's in physical pain. "Wild scenarios that involve you being... more than... hit and kicked, which is hideous, but..." His gaze is agonized as he leans a little closer and whispers, "He didn't... he didn't force himself on you, did he?"

My eyes bulge. "No." I swallow, remembering my relief when Theo was too tired and drunk to demand I get into bed with him. I close my eyes. "Thank God."

"So, what happened, then?"

He's asking so softly. Part of me wants to tell him.

But when I open my mouth, I can't find the words.

I try a couple times but end up sagging my shoulders.

"I'm sorry," he murmurs. "I'm not trying to force you if you're not ready. This isn't about me." He rubs his forehead again, looking tortured but resigned.

And something about his words touches me. The fact that he's desperate to know yet won't demand it. Even if it pains him, he's going to put my needs above his own.

For some reason, it releases the block in my throat, and the words start flowing before I can stop them.

"I'd just come home from a double shift at work..."

# CHAPTER 8
## LIAM

It takes everything in me to control my expression while I listen to Rachel's quaking voice as she describes the way her asshole boyfriend just sat there and watched while that motherfucker, Matt, beat the shit out of her.

He just sat there.

Sat there and watched.

Sat there and let it happen.

I would never let someone talk to my woman that way. And if he touched her like that, I'd break the guy's foot off, then systematically snap every bone in his body.

My knee starts to bob beneath the table when she gets to the part about trying to leave and being dragged down to their bedroom, locked inside like she was his prisoner.

"And then he told me to do what's good for me and stay put." She sniffs, her glassy eyes finally releasing the tears she's been fighting. They spill down her cheeks, and she quickly brushes them away as the waitress walks past our booth.

The server can obviously sense something big is going down, because she quickly diverts with her coffeepot, and I can absorb what the fuck Theo said to Rachel.

*What's good for her.* I want to kill him.

"And I just kind of froze up, you know?" She pinches her bottom lip with trembling fingers. "My body was hurting, and I was so scared. I couldn't even find the guts to climb out the window."

I reach for her hand—the one that's gripping the salt shaker—and gently rub it with my thumb. "But you did leave. You had the courage to walk out the door that night. You drove miles to get away from him. That's courage, Ray. You were brave."

"I don't feel brave," she mumbles, her eyes fixated on something past my shoulder. I don't think she's really seeing anything. She has this glazed look about her, like she's picturing something in her mind. "I feel stupid for falling for him in the first place."

"Hey." I pat her hand. "He deceived you, remember? You're not stupid. He's a lying prick. An asshat. A cock-waffle. A shit biscuit. A turd pilot." Her lips start fighting a grin, so I keep going, coming up with ridiculous insults, like fart blaster and fuckcicle. "*Gilipollas,*" I say, switching to Spanish, and my voice rises as I rattle off a string of curses, each dirtier and more offensive than the last, until I thump back in my seat with a heaving chest.

Rachel's barely there smile starts to fade, her head tipping to the side as she studies me. I watch her long hair cascade over her shoulder and force my breathing to slow down.

"I don't speak Spanish," she finally murmurs. "I'd like to, though."

My lips twitch as I try to smile, to push this anger down deep so she doesn't have to deal with it.

"Can you teach me something?"

I can't fucking believe this. She's the one beaten and bruised, yet she's sitting here trying to make me feel better. I should be the one comforting *her*.

Scrubbing a hand down my face, I grip my mouth for a second, then smile across the table at her.

"*Eres asombrosa*," I say in a husky voice.

Her green eyes light, a smile forming on her lips. "What does that mean?"

I swallow, willing my voice to come out soft and even. But I end up kind of rasping, "You are amazing."

Her lips part.

"And I'm not saying that to make some kind of move or anything." I shuffle in my seat, resting my arms on the table between us. "I mean it, Rachel. You are amazing. You left. You limped out that door, and you left him. That makes you a strong, brave, incredible woman."

Her jaw quivers, and she bites her lips together.

I want to tell her that not all women are capable of doing that... but I don't want to make this about me and my story. Not right now. She can find out about that shit later. Right now, I just need her to know that she's not some gullible idiot.

Resting my fingers gently on the back of her hand, I'm about to tell her again when she sucks in a short breath and asks me, "Where'd you learn Spanish?"

I see what she's doing—trying to keep this light and

friendly. She's done with the heavy stuff now, so I run with it, forcing a smile. "My mama. She's from México."

"I like the way you say that." She grins. "Tell me something else. Say like a whole string of stuff in Spanish."

My lips curl at the corners, and because I know she won't be able to understand me, I waffle off a few sentences about how pretty she is and how her green eyes are mesmerizing. Then I tell her how grateful I am that she's trusting me with her secret. And just for good measure, I add, "*Deberías decibel a tu mejor amigo,*" which means *You should tell your best friend.*

Her smile stays in place, a soft laugh fluttering out of her. "I have no idea what you just said, but it sounded beautiful. I think you said *friend* there at the end, right? *Amigo?*"

I nod.

Her smile grows. "Can you teach me something before we have to go back? Even just one sentence."

"We don't have to go back. We can stay out all day."

Her eyebrows pull down in confusion. "Don't you have class?"

I shrug. "I'd skip class for you."

"No, you will not." She points her finger at me with a stern look.

My lips twitch as I resist the urge to tell her that I skipped my regular morning workout for her, which is almost a bigger deal than skipping a class or two.

"One thing, and then we're leaving. *Por favor.*" She bats her eyelashes while I give her an impressed grin.

"So you do speak a little Spanish."

She lets out a soft snort. "I can say 'please' and 'thank you.'"

"That's still something." I wink and then say, "*Me alegro de haberte conocido*."

She repeats the words, with pretty good pronunciation, then asks, "What does that mean?"

"It means... I'm so glad I met you."

Her cheeks turn an instant pink, but she looks me in the eye when she nods and whispers, "I'm glad I met you too. Thanks for being there for me last night. And this morning." She brushes the bangs out of her eyes. "And thank you for keeping my secret."

Her gaze dips to the table, and I reach forward and tip her chin up to look at me. "You can trust me. I won't say anything... although I do think you should tell Mick."

She lifts her chin away from my touch and gives me a smile that can only be described as stubborn. You know, a polite way of telling me that she's never gonna take my advice in a million years.

I concede with a soft sigh and follow her out of the booth. She insists on paying, since I apparently did her a favor by getting her out of the house this morning.

"And for not saying anything," she whispers before digging some cash out of her wallet. Her fingers are trembling as she holds out the money. "Keep the change." She smiles at the waitress who served us, then dips her chin and walks out the door.

I wave goodbye to the waitress, thanking her again for the great service, before walking out into a light sprinkling of snow. I grin up at the sky, sticking out my tongue and catching a few flakes before noticing Rachel standing next to the truck and looking like she's about to turn into a popsicle.

Rushing over to open her door, I'm about to cinch her waist and hoist her into the truck when I remember what's hiding under her layers of clothing. I stop myself just in time, relief pulsing through me. The last thing I want to do is cause her more pain.

Images of Theo's fuckwit of a friend punching her in the stomach, then pounding her as she lay on the ground make my insides vibrate with rage, but I manage to hide it by the time I've slipped behind the wheel.

At least I think I do.

The drive back to the house is kind of quiet because I'm stewing, and she obviously can't think of anything to say.

When we get back to the house, she gives me a small smile and whispers, "*Gracias,*" before disappearing up to my room.

I watch her long legs race up the stairs and lean back against the wall, grateful the house seems to be empty. Everyone's probably left for class already, and I probably should too. Reluctantly gathering my stuff, I check my phone and wince at the string of texts from Ethan.

*I don't mind you taking the truck, dude, but where the fuck are you?*

I missed three calls, too wrapped up in listening to Rachel's story to even notice my phone was vibrating. I always leave it on silent and usually rely on my watch to let me know when I get a notification, but of course I'm not wearing my watch because I forgot to charge it last night, and my charger is up with Rachel.

I get the sense that she needs some space right now, so I type an apology back to Ethan, then run upstairs to call out a goodbye to her before taking off to class.

As soon as I park Ethan's truck, I head toward the building I know he's due to come out of.

"Hey, Liam." A puck bunny whose name I'm struggling to remember waves at me.

I'm pretty sure her tongue spent most of the night in Asher's mouth last time we threw a party at Hockey House. They probably did it on the couch I slept on last night.

*Awesome.*

I try to hide my grimace, giving her a polite smile to counter the way her hungry gaze is devouring me.

Picking up my pace, I run down the concrete path and make it just as a swarm of students is exiting the building. Ethan towers above the clump of girls trailing him, but he's too busy texting to notice.

"Ethan!" I raise my hand to grab his attention.

The second he sees me, he flicks his fingers in the air, and I lob the keys at him.

"I'm really sorry, man. I lost track of time."

Ethan shoves the keys in his pocket and frowns at me. "What?"

"Where were you guys?"

"I took Rachel to Taffy's for breakfast."

"Why?"

I shrug, hoping I look casual enough. "We were hungry."

His frown deepens. "You're not making a move on her, are you?"

"No." The word comes out snappy and defensive.

*Shit. Pull it the fuck together.* I silently berate myself while Ethan's eyes narrow.

He crosses his arms, and it's moments like this when I hate being shorter than him. I might be broader across the chest, and I can beat him in an arm wrestle, but I'd love just two more inches so I could eyeball the guy more easily.

"She was a wreck last night," he warns me.

"I know. Which is why I wasn't making a move. I took her out to breakfast to get her away from Casey. He was standing shirtless in the kitchen, flirting his ass off, and she looked like she wanted the floor to swallow her. Gimme some credit, man."

Ethan's suspicious look slowly drops from his face, and he nods. "It's just... she's Mick's best friend, you know? And if you guys did hook up and it didn't work out... it'd be awkward as fuck. I don't want anything to come between you and me or Mick and me, so... just don't go after Rachel, all right?"

I work my jaw to the side, hating this conversation.

"And you need to let her heal first anyway. I always think it's sleazy to dive in on a girl's breakup pain, you know?"

I roll my eyes at him. "You cannot stand there and tell me you haven't done that before."

He goes instantly red and starts kicking the snow along the pathway with his boot. "I'm not proud of it."

With a snicker, I shake my head. "I would never do something like that, okay? Rachel just needed someone to talk to this morning, and Mick was still in bed, so I took her for coffee and an omelet. It was no big deal." The words get stuck in my throat for a second.

No big deal?

It was a fucking huge deal.

What Theo and his fucker of a friend did to her is...

I clench my jaw, my insides writhing.

There's no way I'm gonna be able to concentrate in class today. But somehow I have to keep this under wraps, because Rachel's not ready to share with anyone.

Anyone but me.

The privilege of that knowledge is huge. I let it ride through me, and it softens the tension in my stomach.

"I'll catch you later, man." Ethan slaps me on the arm.

"Yep. See you at practice."

I watch Ethan walk away before turning back in the direction of the building I'm supposed to be heading to. I have a criminal justice lecture happening in exactly eleven minutes... and I can't make myself walk into that room.

Instead, I spin on my heel and start jogging.

I run all the way off campus and head to a small boxing gym that employs me during hockey's offseason.

Walking through the door, I raise a hand in greeting to the owner, Hank, before dumping my stuff and hitting the bags in my jeans and T-shirt. I have to burn off some of this angst before I combust.

After five minutes of bruised knuckles, I grab a spare pair of gloves out of the storage room before hitting the bag with all the venom coursing through me. I don't know what Theo looks like, or that friend of his, but I pretend the bag is them. And I give it all I've got.

Jab, cross, hook, kick.

Hammer punch.

Spinning back kick.

Uppercut.

I give that bag everything until I turn into a sweating, panting mess.

"Dude, you got some steam to burn off today or what?" Hank laughs at me as he walks past the bag I'm hugging.

"Yeah." I somehow manage a raspy laugh, leaning my head against the bag and seeing Rachel's pretty face morph with fear and pain as Theo shoves her back into their bedroom and locks the door.

# CHAPTER 9
## RACHEL

Mick got home from school and her gym workout by five. It was actually a relief to see her. I'd been stuck in Hockey House all day, going slightly insane. I could have used my car, I guess, but the snow picked up after breakfast, and I'm not used to driving in it. I didn't trust myself not to skid out on ice or something. My little Honda Civic is hardly designed for Colorado winters. But then I never expected to be leaving Southern California and driving all the way out here.

To be honest, it was nice to have the place to myself, although Asher popped home during the middle of the day, and then Baxter arrived around three.

I kept to myself, started watching a romance movie, then quickly gave up and switched to an action, which made me shudder, so I ended up watching a law drama... which wasn't too bad. Although every courtroom scene made me think of Theo's uncle—the high-flying defense attorney—and my insides shriveled up all over again.

I couldn't stop glancing at my bag on the floor, my

stomach clenching every time I thought about escaping Theo and how I snuck out of the house... with all his poker winnings.

*Shit!*

Covering my eyes with my hand, I forget that Mick is standing in Liam's doorway watching me.

"Hey." She grabs my attention. "We need to get you out of this house. You've been moping all day, and it's time to go eat fatty, greasy food and make ourselves feel better."

"Fatty, greasy food is going to make us feel better?" I give her a skeptical frown.

She laughs, yanking me off the bed. "No, a little QT with your bestie is going to make you feel better."

"Well, that's true," I murmur, following her down the stairs with a grin.

But then my fingers start shaking as I pull on my jacket. Oh man, I hope she doesn't ask me about the Theo breakup. I'm so not up for that. Telling Liam this morning was frickin' hard... harrowing. I can't relive it again today.

Liam reacted pretty well. Sure, he looked mad, but he never raised his voice or shouted. He was sweet and comforting, reassuring me that the fault wasn't mine, that Theo tricked me and didn't let his true colors show until I was in too deep. How many women does that happen to?

I hate that I'm one of them.

I hate that I threw caution to the wind just because a guy I liked finally paid some attention to me.

Look where it got me.

I can't imagine Mick taking the news with the same calm as Liam. She'd freak out, get pissed, and it'd take everything in me to convince her not to fly to Fontana and scratch Theo's eyes out.

As satisfying as that would be... I don't want her going anywhere near Theo.

Or Matt.

My spine twitches as I imagine his reaction to the stolen money. He'd have my head. Theo's been his best friend since kindergarten, and they're freakishly loyal to each other.

I guess like Mikayla and me, although I doubt she'd just sit by if I tried to pound Ethan's flesh.

Not that I could. The guy's made of titanium.

And honor. And respect.

Just like Liam.

They're good men.

Shit. I can never tell them about the money.

Shame rides through me as I wonder why I even did it.

But I was pissed at Theo for not looking after me. And then treating me like property he could just throw around. In that moment, I felt I'd earned it. I didn't want to be some victim of abuse, so I took his damn money.

And I have no idea what to do with it now.

I spent a little of it on gas and breakfast this morning, but it feels like dirty money. I shouldn't use any more of it.

So why keep it, then?

But I don't want to send it back. Making contact with the guy repulses me... terrifies me.

Maybe I should burn the money.

But that feels wrong too. It's a lot of money. It could get me a ticket out of the country. I'd have to get a passport, but I could do it, right? Maybe I could fly down to Jamaica and visit my mom?

But then she'd want to know why I was there and—

"You coming?" Mikayla flicks her hand at me, hurrying me out of my thoughts and after her.

Jumping into the Uber she ordered, I try to hide my wince as I buckle up. Some movements hurt more than others, and I think I've done a pretty good job at keeping my expressions in check, but I'll have to be extra careful around Mick. She knows me better than anyone.

I shift in my seat, tentatively readjusting myself so I'm not putting any pressure on my bruised back.

Thankfully, Mick's not looking at me. She's in a super chipper mood and going on about... I don't even know what. Something to do with marketing that she learned about in class today. She's seriously getting into the idea of becoming a sports agent. She'd be great at it. If I was an athlete, I'd totally want to be represented by her. She's gutsy and feisty and knows how to get what she wants.

She might be pint-sized, but she's fierce... and I love that about her.

"Here you go, ladies." The driver pulls up in front of a pizzeria, and my stomach growls.

Mick glances at me, laughing as she thanks the woman, and we get out of the car.

"This place has the best pizza in town, and don't even get me started on their loaded fries." She threads her arm through the crook of my elbow and walks me inside. "But make sure you save room for dessert, okay, because they have these salted caramel choc pots that are to die for." Her eyes roll back in her head. "Like seriously."

I grin down at her, loving how expressive and fun she is.

I've missed her so much.

When she first told me she was moving to Colorado, I was petrified. I didn't think I could live without her just over the fence. But then Theo came along and made everything better.

Until he didn't.

And now I'm back with my bestie.

Taking a seat opposite her, I thank the waiter for the menu and peruse the options.

"I tend to go for the chicken and cranberry pizza with camembert. Because I'm fancy that way." She winks at me, and I can't help laughing. "But I know you're a spicy girl, so we could go for the tandoori chicken. That bitch will burn your tongue right off."

I giggle and take a sip of water. "Let's share your fave, and then we can get a dessert each. I know you said those salted caramel pot things were amazing, but you know I can't be passing up Mississippi Mud Cake."

Mick's head tips back with a laugh. "Too true!" Slapping the menu down, she gives me a meaningful smile that makes me nervous.

Are we about to get all serious about—

"I really miss your baking." She reaches for my hand and gives it a squeeze. "Like seriously. I miss your white chocolate brownies and your blueberry cheesecake and that lemon delicious soufflé thing you make." Her voice starts to quake. "And those cakes. Oh my gosh, those cakes!" She tips her head back with a groan that's basically orgasmic.

I look over my shoulder, cringing when I notice the

booth next to us is throwing curious glances at my friend. Lightly kicking her under the table, I quickly promise, "I'll make you a pumpkin pie this week, 'kay?"

"Yes!" She pumps her arms in the air. "Bring on the Thanksgiving goodness. I love this time of year!"

Great. Now she's shouting and *three* booths of people are turning to look at us.

I give them polite smiles, mouthing apologies for my loud friend.

"Mick, seriously." I make a face at her. "Chillax, little girl."

She leans forward and laughs at me. "I'm trying to get *you* to relax and lighten up. I know you've had the worst week, but let's just pretend that it's you and me and none of that shit matters."

Oh thank God. She's not after a serious chat.

I bob my head, a relieved smile blooming on my face.

"Okay. Tell me about your life in Hockey House. How's it going?"

She blows out a puff that makes the locks of hair around her face dance. "It's good." Her nose wrinkles. "I mean, it's just a temporary thing. I can't linger there forever, you know?"

"What does that mean?" I point at her. "You've got scrunchy face going on. Scrunchy face is never good."

"It means..." She purses her lips. "It means that sleeping every night with Ethan is epic. The sex is off the charts, and waking up in his arms every morning is my new favorite thing to do."

I smile, happy for her. The way her eyes are dancing is awesome. I want Ethan to be good and wonderful. I want him to be her forever guy, because I love her so damn much, and I never want her to hurt the way I am right now.

But then her happy grin starts to fade.

"But...," I prompt her.

She slumps. "But living in Hockey House can have its moments. I mean, I love the guys. I do. I fit... mostly. Baxter's not a huge fan, but I'm not sure he likes anyone, so..." Her shoulder hitches. "Hanging with the guys is fun, and I love gaming with Casey and teasing Asher for being a rich prick and shooting the breeze with Liam. He's the best to talk to, seriously. Ethan, Liam, and I will often sit on the back patio at the end of the day and talk about everything and nothing. It's one of my favorite things to do. And sometimes the house is filled with the whole team, and it's loud and fun and..." Her voice trails off into a sigh.

"But..." I raise my eyebrows.

And she slumps even farther down in the booth. "But guys can be gross, okay? Even I have my limits." She throws her hand up in the air. "Casey's dumps are smelly enough to drop an elephant from ten yards away, so sharing a bathroom with the guy can be fatal. And Baxter leaves his toenail clippings in the sink." She sticks out her tongue, pretending to gag. "And..." She holds up her finger. "This one tops it. I walked in on Asher jacking off the other day."

My mouth drops open. "Where?"

"In his man cave. Just sitting there on the couch with his pants around his knees. His bare ass on the cushions while he grunted and—" Mick shudders, like the memories are giving her hives. "He'd left the door wide open, and I was just popping in to return a comic book."

I slap a hand over my mouth, trying not to laugh at her, but it's impossible. The expression on her face right now is too funny.

"Are you talking about the couch that poor Liam had to sleep on last night?" I cringe.

Mikayla jerks up in her seat, her eyes popping wide as the realization dawns. Then her face cracks into a wide grin, and she starts to giggle. "Oh, poor Liam."

We laugh together, me trying to dodge my guilt at the fact that he was down there while I was taking over his big comfy bed upstairs.

Mick shakes her head, smiling at the waiter when he delivers our drinks. Pulling her soda toward her, she takes a big suck from the straw and sighs. "You know, I thought living in the sorority house with a bunch of girls was bad."

"That's just because you weren't living with the *right* girls."

Mick grabs my hand. "Move in with me?"

I let out a soft snicker and don't say anything.

What *can* I say?

Right now, I have zero idea what my future holds. My only thought had been to get away from Theo. Now what?

My stomach shudders as I think about the fact that I should probably be calling the restaurant and grocery store I worked for. I've gone radio silent on both of them, and I actually had a shift at both places today. Morning as a checkout girl, evening as a waitress.

Shit.

Will they call Theo asking where I am?

It's not like they can call my phone.

"So, I know I need to start apartment hunting at some stage, because as much as I complain about the guys, when they're gone for away games, I'm rambling around in that mammoth house all by myself, and I hate that too."

"So, what do you ultimately want then?"

"An apartment with like one or two really cool people who will let me be myself, aren't high maintenance, but also have some standards when it comes to cleanliness." She pauses, her expression openly pleading. "Seriously. Move to Nolan and live with me."

I let out this awkward-sounding laugh and focus on my own drink. Although my throat is swelling so fast, I'm not sure how I'll swallow any of it. Grabbing the straw, I poke it up and down through the ice while Mick sighs again.

"I've scored myself a part-time job at Champ's Sporting Goods. Ethan doesn't love it, because it puts extra stress on my workload, and sometimes we don't get to see each other, but he's playing hockey all the time, and it's only two shifts a week, so I'm totally managing. At least we get to share a bed any night he's not away."

"Yeah, but if you move out, you won't get to do that anymore."

A sad look flashes over her face before she pulls her lips back into a smile. "We can sleep over at each other's places. And if I have an apartment, it'll be somewhere else we can hang out when Hockey House gets too full. I just... can't afford it yet."

"What about your dad? He'd probably hook you up."

"He's already paying my tuition. I don't want to ask for even more. I have to find a roommate, but thanks to my

*Sig Be Sisters can go fuck themselves* scandal, I don't really have any friends." She's trying to say it as a joke, but I can see it's hit her kind of hard. The way her mother practically disowned her for embarrassing the stepfamily was brutal. "You sure you don't want to move to Nolan and rescue me?"

I laugh, yet again, wishing I could. But... is Nolan far enough away from Fontana?

Nerves twitter through me just as Mikayla's phone starts ringing.

She checks her screen, then glances at me. "It's your mom."

My stomach drops into my pelvic region while Mikayla answers with a bright smile. "Hey, Joey. How's Jamaica, mon?" She puts on a terrible accent, then starts laughing at herself.

I force a smile, swallowing hard when Mikayla's expression drops.

"Uh... in touch?... Ye-ah... Her phone?" She glances at me and mouths, "Where's your phone?"

I wince, closing my eyes before reaching out and flicking my fingers at her.

She passes her phone to me, and I force a little cheer into my voice. "Hey, Mom."

"Baby girl." She sounds surprised, which she has every right to be. "Where are you right now?"

Oh, her voice. An ache blooms in my chest. What I wouldn't give for one of her hugs right now. I just want to rest my head on her shoulder and cling. She'd rub my back and make those comforting noises while I sobbed and blubbered about what a jerk-face, asshole, dickweed I moved in with.

But I can't say any of that, can I?

Because she would freak out, and she's miles away and there's nothing she can do to help me.

So I keep it casual, like driving through the night to get away from Theo is seriously no big deal.

"I came to visit Mick."

"In Colorado?"

"Yeah." I cringe.

"Oh my gosh, why didn't you tell me?"

"Um... it was a spontaneous decision."

"I've been calling you for two days. Why haven't you answered?"

I press my fingers into my forehead, scrambling for a quick lie. "I... you know, it's embarrassing."

"Ray-Ray." A soft laugh masks the reprimand in her voice. "What'd you do?"

"I left my phone at a truck stop just outside Vegas." I bite my bottom lip. "By the time I realized, it was too far to go back."

"No wonder Theo was so grumpy when I talked to him."

My heart stops beating. "You talked to Theo?"

"Of course. I was worried. You never don't call me back, and I wanted to make sure you were okay."

"What... what'd he say?"

"That's weird, actually, because he said you were at work. So... what am I missing?"

My insides shrivel as Mom's cautionary warnings from weeks ago start to eat at me. "Um..." I bite my lip so hard it starts to hurt. "We, um... we broke up."

There's a pause while she obviously tries to figure out how to respond. I can just picture her face no doubt flooding with relief before crumpling with sympathy. "Aw, baby."

I close my eyes, grateful that she's skipping over the "I told you so. I knew moving in with a guy so fast was a bad idea."

With a little sniff, I try to rally my voice. "I just had to get away and give myself some room to breathe."

"What happened?"

"Um…" I bite my lips together, shaking my head as the truth tries to claw its way up my throat.

Never. I can never tell her what went down.

"It just… didn't work out, you know? We want different things."

It's such a cliché thing to say, but it's the truth. I want to be treated with respect. Theo wants his best friend to have free rein to do whatever the fuck he wants, which seems to include treating me like a piece of trash.

Mom lets out a sympathetic sigh and tells me how sorry she is.

"Is all your stuff still at his place?"

"Yeah, but I'll sort that out later. I can't even think about it now."

"What about work?"

I cringe, pinching the bridge of my nose and spitting out another lie so I don't have to deal with her reaction. "I've called them. They're letting me have a few days off."

"Well, that's good. I'm glad they're being nice about it."

"Yeah, they're awesome. They understand I'm kind of a mess right now."

"Oh, I know, baby. But this feeling won't last forever. Just give your heart a chance to heal."

"That's what I'm doing." I nod, annoyed by the burn in my eyeballs.

"And please get yourself a new phone. I hate you not being just a phone call away."

"I will, Mom. Promise. I'll send you the number as soon as I get one."

"Tomorrow?" Her voice pitches hopefully.

And I can't help a soft laugh. "Yes. Tomorrow."

"Okay. Love you, Ray-Ray."

"Love you, too, Mom." I pass the phone back to Mikayla. "Thanks."

"You seriously left your phone in a truck stop?" Her eyes bulge.

"Yes." I nod, avoiding her gaze. "I wasn't thinking clearly, okay?"

"Fair enough." She lets me off with a grin, and then the pizza arrives.

It's the perfect distraction, and I inhale three slices before Mick gives me a serious look.

"Hey, this thing with Theo…"

I swallow, wiping the grease off my lips with a napkin.

"Any chance of reconciliation? The whole wanting different things? Were there some deal-breakers in there?"

"Yeah," I rasp. "Some big ones."

She gives me a sad smile. "I'm really sorry."

I shrug.

"What are you gonna do now?"

I shrug again because… I seriously don't know.

# CHAPTER 10
## LIAM

It's been over a day since Rachel told me what those assholes did to her, and it's still eating me up, gnawing away on my stomach lining. Anger sizzles through me as my brain bounces from images of her on the floor getting kicked and then thrown into a bedroom to the sound of my mother's whimpers as she begged Dad to calm down.

It's doing my head in and turning me into a grumpy beast.

I'm aware enough to know how I'm behaving, but I can't seem to stop myself.

With a grunt, I fly forward on my skates, body-checking Jason with a hard smash into the boards and fighting for control of the puck. Clearing it, I shoot it toward Ethan while Jason shoves me in the back.

"It's practice, you fucking moron."

My gloved hand curls into a fist, and it takes everything in me not to spin and take a swing at our surly captain.

Shit. I have to pull myself together.

But seconds later, when I'm collecting the puck off Casey and get smashed into the boards as payback, I lose it.

"Fuck off, Jas!" I shove him hard, pulling off my gloves and making it clear that I have every intention of making him bleed.

Being the hotheaded jerk-off he is, he immediately loses his gloves, too, and we start tussling on the ice, shouts rising from the rink as the team heads our way to break it up.

Someone's arm curls around my chest, hauling me back, while Baxter grabs Jason's shoulder and stops him from lunging at me again.

"What the hell, you idiots!" Coach yells. "Get your asses over here right now!"

Glaring at Jason, I scoop my gloves off the ice and glide over to Coach, who is now fuming by the exit door.

His face is going so red that it's creeping into his balding scalp. His expression is a mix of impatience and total confusion as he shakes his head at me.

I know. I'm not the guy who loses his cool. I'm known for my calm, unflappable demeanor.

*Shit, am I fucking turning into my dad?*

The thought has bile surging up my throat. I clamp my teeth together while Coach has a go at me.

"I expect more from you, Carlisle. What the hell are you doing? Starting fights? Where's your self-control?"

"Sorry, Coach," I mutter, staring at the ice because he's right. I'm not the reckless jackass who does this shit.

Jason starts harping on about how he didn't do anything wrong and I'm obviously on my period or something.

Dammit, the guy is so fucking punchable. I will never understand how he made captain over Ethan. Even though his parents are loaded and donate huge amounts of money to the hockey program, it's not a good enough reason for this shitgibbon to be captaining our team.

"You're done for the day." Coach points at me. "Go shower up. And you better get your head on straight, you hear me? We have a game tomorrow night, and I need my best D-man. Do not let your team down."

With a heavy sigh, I flick the door open and head for the locker room.

It's fucking humiliating being kicked out of practice early, but Coach is probably right to get me off the ice.

Of course Jason got to stay.

My blood continues to simmer and boil as I smash my helmet down on the locker room floor and thump onto the bench seat. Burying my head in my hands, I let out a sharp breath, muttering expletives as I'm once again plagued with images I can never forget.

Dad's drunken face contorted with rage. His fist curled so tight that I thought his knuckles might pop out of his skin.

"Go!" Mama would shout at me. "Get your sisters." She'd start rattling off commands in Spanish because my stupid-ass Dad didn't speak it.

She'd force me to leave her alone in the kitchen to face the monster, and I hated myself every time I obeyed her.

But the few times I didn't, I was home from school for a week. Mama wouldn't let me leave the house with the bruises still showing.

"Fuck!" I smash my fist into the locker behind me,

then sit there puffing as the sting radiates across my knuckles.

I don't want to be a violent man.

I don't want to feel this kind of rage pulsing through me.

I work overtime to remain calm and cool and in control.

But Rachel's black-and-blue torso has brought all my nightmares straight back. And it's only made worse by the idea of the way she was treated. Violence against women and children is my kryptonite. I can't handle it. I wish I was a superhero and could bust into every abuse-ridden home and end it for good.

Slumping back with a heavy sigh, I stare into the empty locker room; the only sound past the heaving in my chest is the dripping shower to my right.

I need to calm the fuck down before I get back to Hockey House and see Rachel again. She doesn't need to carry my shit too.

I won't become my father.

I don't give a flying fuck if his DNA is part of who I am.

"So don't be him, you moron," I mutter. "Calm down and get over this. Be the guy Rachel needs right now. Let go of this shit."

Keeping up with the pep talk, I strip off my sweaty hockey gear and head for the showers, washing up as fast as I can and getting out of the locker room before the rest of the guys pile in.

I decide to jog home because it's as good a therapy as any.

By the time I reach the driveway, Ethan is pulling in

behind me. His worried face tells me he had a lightning-quick shower and probably left his gear in a mess trying to catch up with me.

I slow to a walk before reaching the front door, ignoring his concerned frown. As soon as we're inside, I shed my jacket and check the thermostat. It feels like an oven in here, but the temperature is set to what it always is.

My blood must still be boiling.

"Shit," I mumble, heading for the kitchen and an ice-cold drink.

Yanking a water bottle out of the fridge, I down half of it before finally glancing Ethan's way. His arms are crossed, and he's staring at me.

"What?" I raise my eyebrows while his dip into a sharp V.

"What? Fucking *what*? Really?" His arms flick out wide before slapping against his thighs. "You let Jason get under your skin. Of all the guys on the team, you are the last person to let that happen. He didn't even have to try that hard. What is up with you today?"

I clench my jaw, leaning back against the kitchen counter.

"And no, you're not allowed to say you don't want to talk about it, because I'm standing here watching you about to implode. So fucking spill, man."

Opening the fridge, he grabs a cold brewski and tips his head toward the back patio.

I follow because he'll probably chase me down if I flip him off and head for my room.

My face buckles with a frown. I can't head to my room because Rachel's up there. Because she got beaten and was so terrified, she had to drive for fifteen hours to get away from the guy who was supposed to protect her.

Anger spikes through me again, and I pull in a deep breath, begging myself not to lose it.

Scrubbing a hand over my face, I take a seat outside, staring at the snow-packed lawn.

"Need your jacket?" Ethan steps outside, pulling his on.

"Nah." I shake my head.

He sighs and bends down to start up the outdoor gas heater before taking the seat adjacent to me. "Spill."

My nose twitches and I look away from him, resting my hand on the patio table and tapping out a quick beat.

"Dude, you're in a foul mood, and it makes you impossible to be around. Whatever the hell is riling you up, just get it out. End the suffering, man. I beg of you."

He's trying to lighten the tension, but my muscles are still coiled tight.

Taking a sniff of the biting air, I blink a few times before eventually murmuring, "I can't tell you. Promised I wouldn't."

"O-kay. So I'm guessing it's not about you, then." He raises his eyebrows with a pointed look, and I shake my head, then shrug, because maybe I am making this about me and my shitty childhood.

I tip my head back with a long, slow sigh.

"Has your dad done something again?"

"Not that I know of." This makes me relax a little. I shift in my seat, threading my fingers together and resting them against my chest. "As far as I'm aware, he hasn't had any contact for months. It's been good."

Ethan nods. "I know you were worried when he first

got released, but that restraining order has kept him at bay, right?"

"Mostly, although my mother doesn't always make him stick to it." I roll my eyes. After everything we went through to get him out of our lives, she lets him back in without hesitation.

"Her love is everlasting, I guess." Ethan gives me a sad smile.

I scoff and shake my head. "I'll never understand it."

"People do crazy things when they're in love." He grins, and I can't help a soft snicker. I can't even remember what movie that's from, but Ethan loves his quotes. And he's been a hundred times worse since getting together with Mikayla. She's brought out the marshmallow in him, and the guy's in danger of turning into a romantic sap.

They all accuse me of being the Romeo in the house because I don't sleep around like it's my job to get laid. So I'm not into casual hookups. That doesn't make me a schmuck.

I don't know what the fuck I am right now... other than haunted.

And riled.

Fuck, I want to drive to Fontana and teach Theo a lesson. I want to turn back time and somehow be in that house when Matt demanded Rachel get him a beer. He wouldn't have gotten his dirty fists anywhere near her.

"Okay, your face is doing that thing again. Seriously, Padre, you're killing me. Would you please tell me what the fuck is going on with you?" Ethan's frown is sharp and irritated.

I've known him so long now that I can read his looks —he's not mad, he's worried.

I would be, too, if he was acting like this, so I have to tell him something.

Shifting again, I rest my forearms on the table, my thumbs tapping together. "Look, I can't tell you details. It's seriously not my story. I just..." Pinching the bridge of my nose, I let out another sigh. "I just want to help her."

"Ahhh, so it's a girl." Ethan wiggles his eyebrows at me. "Like a serious *I like this girl* or just a *she makes my balls tingle*?" My warning glare shuts him up... for all of two seconds. "So, this girl... why does she need your help?"

After a long silence on my part, Ethan's smile fades back into a frown, and he moves forward in his chair.

"Bro," he murmurs. "What am I missing here? Is this girl in some kind of trouble?"

It's impossible to hide anything from this guy, so I just look at him, letting him in without saying a word.

"Damn, man, what happened to her?"

I clench my jaw and softly grit out, "Her boyfriend let his friend beat her up, then locked her in his room so she couldn't get away."

Ethan's eyes flash with anger, his gaze going hard and dark, his lips pinching into a narrow line.

"Her *ex*-boyfriend," I clarify, more for my own benefit than his. I'm so fucking glad she left him.

"Do you know the guy?"

I shake my head. "No, but I want to track him down and beat the living shit out of him. And his friend."

Ethan nods, letting me know he'd like to be in on that mission. It's a relief to see how riled he is over this. It makes me feel like I'm not insane for feeling the way I have been.

What happened fucking sucks. We have a right to be mad about it.

The bruises on Rachel's body filter into my mind again. The boot print on her back.

I suck in a breath, my nostrils flaring as I snatch the water bottle and squeeze the shit out of it. The plastic crinkles and bends—a loud disruption to this suck-fest of a conversation.

Ethan glances at me. "Does he go to Nolan U?"

"No, the little fucker lives in California." I smack the squashed bottle onto the table, but it doesn't hide the noise of glass shattering behind me.

Ethan and I whip around together, our eyes bulging as we spot Mikayla standing in the open doorway. The glass she was holding is now scattered across the concrete tiles, liquid fizzing on the ground by her boots.

What is she doing there? I didn't even hear the door slide open.

*Oh shit. What did she hear?*

*It can't be good.*

Her cheeks are pale, her eyes the size of dinner plates. "Did you just say... California?"

I wince, my heart rate ratcheting up. "How long have you been standing there?"

She ignores my question. "Are you talking about Rachel right now?"

Ethan jerks forward in his seat. "What?"

I close my eyes, dipping my chin and giving it all away.

"Oh my—shit!" She spins and bolts back into the house.

"No, Mick, wait!" I chase after her, struggling to catch her as she darts up the stairs. "She doesn't want anyone to know." I lurch for her jacket, but she shakes me off.

"I'm her best friend!" Her eyes flash at me, and I swear, even though she's little, she can be hella scary when she wants to be.

I'm this close to shrinking away from her, but the thought of Rachel thinking I betrayed her stops me.

"Mick, I—"

She huffs and turns her back to me, sprinting up the last few steps and flying down the hallway. Bursting into my room, she scares the hell out of Rachel. I hear her gasp, just before Mikayla throws me a fiery look and slams the door shut in my face.

The lock clicks, and I have no choice but to curl my fingers into a fist and start pounding on the door.

"Mick! Let me in!"

# CHAPTER 11
## RACHEL

"Mick, open this door!" Liam is pounding on the wood while Mikayla stands at the end of the bed, hands on her hips, looking ready to cry. Her eyes are made bluer by the heightened emotions, and I wish I could be cluelessly curled up against Liam's pillows wondering, "What's wrong?"

But I know exactly what's wrong.

"He beat you?" Mikayla's voice cracks, her face crumpling with a mix of horror and disbelief.

I bite my bottom lip, tears clogging my throat and making it hard to speak.

"How did you find out?" My voice is so tiny, I'm surprised she can hear me.

"Liam." Mikayla's arms drop to her sides. "He told me."

"No I didn't!" he barks through the door. "She was eavesdropping. I never used your name; she just worked it out!"

I glance at the door, then back to my best friend. Now

her eyes are glassy, tears building on her lashes. "How could you not tell me?"

Looking away from her, I curl into a ball, pulling Liam's hockey jersey over my knees. It hurts my bruised body to crinkle up this way, but there's something comforting about being swallowed by Liam's jersey. "I didn't want to worry you."

Her shoulders slump with a huff.

Liam's still thumping on the door. He must have changed from the side of his fist to open-palm slaps. Both are noisy. And man, is he relentless.

Mick rolls her eyes, tipping her head to the ceiling before marching over to the door and unlocking it. Flinging it open, she growls up at the towering hockey player, "Would you stop with all the racket? I'm trying to talk to my friend here."

His nostrils flare, his glare scorching as he gently pushes her aside and walks to the bed. He jerks to a stop just before he reaches me, his eyes trailing over my body. I wrap my arms around my legs with a blush.

Yes, I'm wearing his jersey.

But it's comfy.

His lips twitch with the hint of a smile before he lowers himself to the edge of the bed like I'm a delicate petal he might crush if he moves too fast.

"Are you okay?" His voice is so tender, it makes me want to cry.

I sniff and nod, biting my lips together and glancing at Mick, who is huffing at the end of the bed and shooting daggers at Liam. She's pacing back and forth like a caged tiger, and I can tell she wants to unleash a little hell-fury on Liam for keeping my secret. She probably wants to go a little nuts at me too.

"I'm sorry." I say the words so quietly that only Liam can hear them.

"You don't have to say that," he murmurs, standing up and pointing at Mick. "Be nice."

"I'm always nice!" she snaps just as Ethan appears in the doorway.

He snickers and starts to laugh, but the sound is quickly cut off when she whips around to glare at him. Pinching his nose, he fails to smother his laughter but manages to bring it under control when Mick growls in her throat. Shoving his hands in his pockets, he gives her an "I'll be good" expression before casting his gaze to me.

Aw crap. Ethan knows too. I can tell by the look in his eyes, that pained sympathy, the way his lips are pulling into a frown.

*Shit. Shit, shit!*

Everyone in this rooms knows. I want this plush mattress to devour me so I don't have to face whatever they're going to say.

My stomach clenches as Mikayla pads around the bed to stand beside me. She perches on the edge, resting her hand on my knee while Liam's soft voice filters into the room. "Hey, it's okay. It's not your fault, remember?"

Mick glances at him, then back at me before letting out a little whimper and leaning in for a hug.

"Gently," Liam warns.

My best friend flinches, pulling back, her lips parting with horror. Whatever she's imagining is probably worse than what it is, so I close my eyes with a soft sigh and unfurl myself, lifting the edge of my shirt once my legs are straight.

Her gasp makes me wince, and I quickly lower it. "I'm fine," I try to reassure her, but she reaches for my shirt again, carefully lifting the fabric and getting another look.

I hear Ethan hiss, and I'm too afraid to look.

But then I can't help myself, and what I see is exactly what Liam showed me yesterday. He's hurting for me, but he's also furious.

*Not at you. At Theo. At Matt.*

I force myself to remember the facts. What happened to me was unfair. Unjust. Theo and Matt are asshole bastards who I never have to see again.

*You're safe here.*

*These men won't hurt you.*

I didn't think Theo would ever hurt me either. The same fear rises, but then Mick's tiny fingers are curling around my hands, gently nudging them apart so she can pull me off the bed.

"You have to tell me everything." Her tone is a soft coo... that leaves no room for argument.

I take her hand with a sigh and let her help me off the bed.

"I need to borrow your car." She glances at Ethan.

He stands tall, blocking the doorway for a second, his face the picture of concern. "Where are you going?"

"Ice cream. We're going to need large amounts of sugar to get through this."

I can't help a watery laugh. The matter-of-fact way Mikayla talks makes my heart squeeze and then expand. I love my best friend so freaking much.

Liam winks at me, and my smile grows a little before Mikayla is tugging me out the door.

"Take care." Ethan brushes his fingers lightly down her arm, then turns his kind smile to me.

I nod and move past him, my stomach jittery as I trail Mick down the stairs and put my jacket and boots on.

We find an ice cream parlor ten minutes down the road, and thankfully it's not too busy. The jukebox is playing "Blue Suede Shoes" as we walk across the check-ered floor. It's like stepping back in time, and I suddenly feel like I should be dressed in a poodle skirt and bobby socks with my hair up in a swinging ponytail.

Mikayla orders for both of us. "The largest caramel sundae you have on the menu with extra cherries on top and two spoons, please."

The guy behind the counter grins and punches in our order while I wander to the booth in the very back corner.

Sliding onto the shiny red seat, I wait by the window, my leg bobbing under the table.

Mikayla sits opposite me, her sigh heavy, her expres-sion sad.

I wince. "Please don't look at me like that. I don't want to be some victim."

"How do you want me to look at you?" she murmurs.

I shrug and nearly say, *"The way Liam did,"* but I don't want to rub in the fact that I told him before her. Or the fact that I had no intention of *ever* telling her.

"How did this happen?" She shakes her head. "I thought Theo was Mr. Sweet and Lovely."

"Me too." I purse my lips and hope the burning sting in my eyes doesn't turn to tears. I really don't want to be blubbering into our caramel sundae. "It wasn't just him. His friends were over and they were drunk, and Matt—" I shrug. "—was an asshole."

"So Matt did this to you?"

I nod.

"Who's Matt again?"

I sigh and dive into the story, rushing through it as quickly as I can. The ice cream arrives just as Theo's dragging me down to our bedroom. I clamp my lips together and force a smile at the waiter.

As soon as he's gone, Mikayla hands me my long-handled teaspoon and murmurs, "Eat. Just take three big mouthfuls of goodness, and then you can tell me about your douche nugget ex."

I do as she says and have to admit this is the best caramel sauce I've ever tasted. She nudges the extra two cherries toward me with the tip of her teaspoon, and I accept them with a smile.

She knows me so well.

Once the story's done (minus the fact that I stole Theo's money, because I can't admit that to anyone), she sits back with a heavy sigh. Licking the back of her spoon, she looks thoughtful for a moment.

"You need to report this. What those guys did was illegal. You can't beat up a woman for not getting you a fucking beer." She tuts and scoops up another mound of ice cream. "You can't beat up a woman ever, for fuck's sake!" Her voice starts to rise, and I quickly shush her.

She scowls into the bowl of slowly melting ice cream, swirling the caramel through the vanilla and making patterns while I lean closer so I can keep my voice down.

"It's not that simple."

"Why?"

*Because I stole three thousand dollars from the guy. Oh yeah, and...*

"His dad's a cop."

"So?"

"So... there's no way he'll let me press charges against his son, or his son's best friend. Besides, Theo's uncle is a top defense attorney. The most they'll get is a little slap on the wrist, and then I'd be living the rest of my life looking over my shoulder."

"You're already doing that," Mick mutters.

I glance at her, about to deny that claim, until she proves me wrong.

"I knew you were lying about your phone. You didn't leave it at a truck stop accidentally. You would never do something like that. But I couldn't figure out why you'd be so careless until tonight." Her expression pinches. "You threw it away because you were scared Theo would somehow track you down. Lemme guess, you haven't touched your credit card either, have you?"

I dig my spoon into the ice cream, a metal flag on top of the mound. It slowly tips to its side like a sad, tired soldier.

"You don't want to leave a trace or trail for him to follow. Because you're terrified he'll find you. Does he know where I am?"

"I don't think so. I've been trying to remember how much I told him about you and what you were doing. I'm pretty sure I mentioned the thing with your mom and how you'd have to leave school, and then..." I squeeze my eyes shut. "I can't remember if I gave him any new updates on you or if I ever said Nolan University." My voice gets thin and strained. "Things have been different since I moved in and picked up that second job. I've just been so tired working such long hours, and we weren't spending as much time together. You know, going on dates and stuff. I'd get home, cook dinner, and then we'd just schlump in front of the TV." I shrug, my insides going crazy at the thought that maybe I did mention Nolan and maybe he knows Mikayla's still here.

*Fuck. Fuck. Fuck!*

Crossing my arms, I slump down in my seat, refusing to look at her while I navigate the wild fears coursing through me. I focus on the caramel sauce. It's running down the mountain of ice cream like a spewing volcano. I feel like we've been eating forever and we're not even halfway through it.

"It's okay, Ray-Ray." Mick gently nudges my ankle with her foot. "I won't let him touch you again. He's not gonna find you here."

"What if I did tell him the name of your college? What if he remembers?" My nose prickles with the onset of tears.

Snatching the spoon, I tap it against my bottom lip, anxiety still ripping through me like a tornado.

"Hey, if he even comes near Hockey House, he's gonna regret it. None of the guys in there will let him near you." She ducks her head, trying to catch my eye, and I finally capitulate, no doubt looking like a nervous wreck. "You can stay. You'll be safe there."

"I can't stay." I shake my head. "I need to get out of the country. I have to—"

"No." Mick's voice is so strong and adamant. "That asshole is not driving you out of the country. You should be able to live wherever the fuck you want. And right now, you need your best friend and a bunch of tall, muscly hockey players who will squish Theo like a bug if he ever shows up on our doorstep."

The thought makes me grin for just a second, but then I wince.

Crap. It's like wincing has become my new favorite expression or something.

I hate this.

"Not to be bossy..." Mick stops when I start to snicker. Her comical look of warning only makes me laugh harder. She starts laughing, too, wagging her finger at me. "You're staying. No arguments, young lady. We need another vagina in that house anyway."

I gasp, my cheeks going instantly red when I spot the elderly woman in the booth next to us bulge her eyes in horror and start shaking her head with a disgusted frown.

"Shh, stop talking so loud," I tell Mick off.

But she just laughs and sings, "Vagina, vagina, vagina!"

I kick her leg under the table and she finally shuts up, giving the woman and her evil side-eye a bright smile.

I point my spoon at her, getting back on topic. "I'll only stay if they agree."

"Oh, they'll agree. If you don't get a rousing 'Puck yeah' by the time I'm done with my speech, I'll give you a million dollars."

Her wink and confident grin settle my nerves... until we pull back into the Hockey House driveway and I start to worry about what exactly Mikayla's gonna say to get us a 'Puck yeah!'

# CHAPTER 12
## LIAM

As soon as headlights illuminate the front of the house, I bolt out of my chair and run to the kitchen window.

"They're back," I call over my shoulder to Ethan.

"Would you calm down. They went for ice cream."

"Oooo! Did they bring us some?" Casey drops the remote on the couch, vaulting over the back to stand beside me in the kitchen.

He has no idea what's been going on, so I resist the urge to shout at him for being a jackass. Seriously, I need to find my chill.

And I will... if this ugly sensation would just stop eating at my insides.

The door clicks open, and the girls appear in the archway leading into the main living area to find four... no, six—Connor and Riley are here too—big guys staring down at them.

Rachel eases back while Mikayla's face lights with a grin. "Perfect, you're all here."

"What? No ice cream?" Casey crosses his arms.

I slap his shoulder with the back of my hand, and he gives me a little shove, which propels me into Asher, who ends up spilling his post-workout protein shake all down his front.

"Seriously?" He spins around with a growl while Casey starts laughing like a chimp and I mutter an apology, glancing at Rachel as I grab a dish towel from the kitchen and throw it at him.

Casey scores a slap on the back of the head from Ethan for being an idiot, and Connor and Riley look on with dopey grins.

"Would you guys stop messing around!" Mikayla walks to the coffee table and stands on it. "I have an important announcement to make."

That grabs our attention, and we all turn to look at her. It cracks me up that even standing on the coffee table only puts her at about eye level with Ethan. Her boyfriend winks at her, and she flashes him a quick grin before beckoning Rachel forward.

Riley's eyebrow arches with approval as she shuffles into view, and Connor gives her a double take.

"Hey." He smiles at her, and something sharp spikes inside my chest.

I frown at the back of his head before noticing Rachel's shy smile and little wave.

"Don't worry about those two. They're harmless." Mikayla gives Rachel's shoulder a light squeeze as she clears her throat. "Everyone, this is my best friend, Rachel, and she's just discovered that the guy she was living with is a first-class meathead. He's an eleven out of ten on the asshole scale, and because she's a smart, beautiful woman who knows her worth, she's left him."

"All right!"

"Clever girl!"

"Whooo!"

I grin at the cheers she's getting and wish with every fiber in my body that she'd glance my way. But she's too busy blushing at the floor.

"So... she's currently without a home, and I was just wondering if you guys would be okay with her crashing here for a little bit until she figures out what she wants to do. And before you give me a rousing 'Puck yeah'—" She raises her hands, glancing at Rachel with a quick wink. "—you also need to be aware that if Theo the Thundercunt or any of his friends come within a mile of my girl here, I'm expecting you to run some interference for us. You're welcome to hit them with your car, shove your hockey sticks up their butts or squish their balls flatter than a crepe. Whatever takes your fancy. We all cool with that?"

"Puck yeah!" We don't even hesitate before shouting it in unison.

We're so loud, Rachel actually flinches, her eyes popping wide for a minute before a stunning smile takes over her face.

My mouth goes dry as I soak her in.

She's so fucking gorgeous.

And sweet.

And she's staying.

Her gaze finds mine across the room, and she gives me a doubtful frown. "I can move to the couch if you want."

"Don't you dare," Mikayla answers for me. "You're not sleeping on Asher's wanking couch."

"It's not my—" Asher shuts up fast because he's got no argument.

Mikayla's look says it all, and I can't help wrinkling my nose in disgust. "I'm getting the disinfectant." Casey and Connor crack up laughing while I gather the cleaning supplies. "Ray, you can stay in my room for as long as you need it."

"Thank you." She mouths the words at me when I turn with an armload of rags and disinfectant.

We share a smile that somehow feels secret.

Oh man, this girl's gonna burrow. She's gonna burrow deep, and I'm helpless to stop it.

Warning bells start clanging inside me as I take the Lysol spray and head for Asher's man cave. He chases after me, wanting to check the bottle to make sure it's safe to use on leather.

"Is semen good for leather? Have you googled that?" Casey yells after him.

Asher gives him the finger while Ethan starts to laugh, snatching Mikayla against his side and kissing her.

Rachel retreats up the stairs, and I watch her go for a minute.

"Nice of you to give up your room," Asher murmurs, squinting at the small text on the back of the bottle.

"Nice of you to let me use your man cave," I mutter. "Although I'm wondering if the couch in the living room is a safer bet."

"Shut up. It was like one time, and I didn't even know Mick was home."

"Ugh. She walked in on you?"

Asher grins. "Whether a door is open or shut, you should always knock."

"Or... just close the door if you want to spank your monkey. It's not rocket science."

"Hey, it's my house. I can jerk off with the door open if I want to."

I give him a droll look. "It's your uncle's house, and we've got chicas living with us now."

"Yeah, yeah." He brushes his hand through the air while I drop to my knees and start cleaning the couch.

It's probably fine, but I'm making a point here.

Asher stands there with his arms crossed, watching me and rolling his eyes when I use way too much spray. My mind wanders off to Rachel, who's probably shedding her jacket and standing there in leggings and my hockey jersey.

Fire burns low and deep in my belly, making my dick twitch.

Her in my hockey jersey is one sexy vision.

But I can't go there.

For way too many reasons...

Like the fact that she's healing after a traumatic night with the guy she thought she loved.

Like the fact that she's Mick best friend and things could get messy.

Or the fact that I'm an ace at falling hard and fast, then getting left feeling like total shit.

Kylie—my girl from last summer—is case in point. I was ready to drop to one knee after just two months of flirting in the sunshine while she was getting ready to end our summer fling with a goodbye kiss.

Talk about misreading the signals.

You'd think after living with an unpredictable parent I'd be an expert, but when it comes to romance, I'm a clueless sap. And I can already tell that Rachel has the power to crush me... even if she doesn't mean to.

# CHAPTER 13
## RACHEL

Living at Hockey House is noisy.

Not bad noisy, just constant noisy. Unless the team is playing an away game, and then the only sounds to keep Mick and me company are the buzz of electronics and appliances. So, of course we cranked our music to ward off the sense of missing them.

I don't even know why I missed them when they were away last weekend, I just did. Hockey House isn't the same without big men lumbering around, throwing out F-bombs and hassling the crap out of each other.

I grin down at my half-eaten plate of lasagna while Casey gives Asher grief over the fact that he totally bombed with the chick he was trying to hit on at the bar in North Dakota on Friday.

"She just waited too long to tell me she had a boyfriend," Asher grumbles. "I never would have hit on her if she hadn't been staring at me with her fuck-me eyes."

Ethan snickers, shaking his head. "She so didn't have a boyfriend."

Casey makes the whistle of a falling missile, his cheeks puffing out as an explosive noise rumbles in his mouth.

This gets Liam laughing, and I can't help pitying Asher just a touch as his cheeks turn red. He scowls down at his plate, stabbing at the side salad with a little growl, then loading his fork with a mammoth mouthful of lasagna.

I'm glad he's enjoying it.

I'm pretty sure I couldn't take another bite if I wanted to. It's delicious, but I filled up on béchamel sauce taste tests. It was one of my better ones, and I can never pass up a creamy, cheesy sauce. The meat was yummy, too, and I had so many spoonfuls of it as I tried to perfect the flavor. By the time the lasagna was actually cooked and ready to eat, I felt like I'd already had my dinner.

For a girl who can put away her fair share of food, it's kind of surprising. But I have my period right now, and I'm never very hungry when I'm battling cramps and a headache.

The guys are loving it, though, and that was my main reason for going to all this effort. They eat lunch at the athletes' dining hall most days and will often have dinner there, too, but when I mentioned to Liam this morning that I was thinking of making a "thanks for letting me live here" lasagna tonight, he told me the table would be full.

"It's a guarantee." His wink sent happy sparks flying through my body.

"So good," Casey groans, mopping up the red sauce with the last chunk of garlic bread.

I grin as some of it drips down his chin. He brushes it off with his finger and sucks the sauce away with the etiquette of a pig. Meanwhile, Asher is straightening his knife and fork neatly on his plate and giving away the fact that he was raised in a boarding school where manners were close to godliness.

He told me that the other night but didn't need to. It's so obvious that I nearly giggled at him.

Baxter ate with us for once but finished in record time. After a mumbled "Thanks. It was good," he left the table to go study. Ethan's eyebrows shot up as he walked away from the table.

"Wow. He gave you a compliment. Damn, he must think the food is freaking ambrosia." He grinned at me. "Seriously, take that as a big win, Ray."

"Big, big win," Asher agreed.

It's hard not to feel like a master chef when I hear stuff like that. When I watch these happy people around the table, I feel like I've found my calling. I've always loved food, especially cakes and desserts. What I wouldn't give to be able to spend my days designing sweet treats for people to enjoy.

Liam leans back in his seat and gives me a proud smile. I'm pretty sure I could take a hot soak in those eyes of his. Every time he looks at me, he makes me feel like I'm something special. It's hard not be affected by it.

We haven't spent that much time together this week. Between hockey practices, workouts, studying, and games, the guys are stupidly busy. I don't know how they fit it all in. I've been doing what I can to support them— cleaning, baking, washing dishes. They seriously love me for it.

Not that my goal in life is to be a domestic goddess, but I actually really enjoy helping them out, and their appreciation is so over the top, yet genuine, that it just makes me want to do it even more.

Theo never even noticed when I did stuff around the house. It was like he expected it. These guys don't. Although, Mikayla forbid me to start doing their laundry.

"Don't you dare," she practically growled at me. "I don't want them starting to think you're their personal Cinderella. Cooking and baking is fine because you seriously love that stuff. Cleaning is understandable because you like things neat and hygienic, but you are *not* touching their smelly laundry. They're big boys. They can wash their own shit."

I nodded and complied like the good girl I am.

I also decided that Casey could clean the bathroom upstairs because he seriously does the smelliest dumps, and I don't have a gas mask worthy of such a mission. Not that I own any kind of gas mask, but seriously, it'd have to be military grade to cope with the stink that comes out of that man.

When I told him that, he laughed so loud that I actually jumped, and then he took the cleaning supplies off me and scrubbed the toilet until it sparkled.

Ethan and Liam are still in shock. I don't know if they've ever seen Casey clean anything.

"You're good for this place," Liam murmured in my ear, and that was the last thing he said to me yesterday.

I kind of wish he'd take me out for breakfast again, but he's kind of been holding back... or am I just reading into it too much? He is a really busy, studious guy. I'm probably being overly sensitive. Or maybe just needy.

Because in spite of the fact that our first breakfast was covering the most hideous topic ever—Theo and Matt—I still want to go out with Liam again.

He's sweet.

And handsome.

*Stop crushing on him. Look away, Rachel. Look away.*

I force my eyes to scan the table, enjoying the satisfied smiles the guys are giving me.

"Seriously, can you move in here permanently?" Asher asks.

Casey lets out a loud burp, which makes my nose wrinkle. Then he winks at me with a grin. "That's just me telling you how much I loved the meal."

"Sure." I nod, sticking out my tongue while Mikayla laughs and nudges me with her elbow.

"Okay, guys. We're on cleanup." Liam lightly taps the table and starts gathering plates.

I go to rise, but he turns to me with an adamant eyebrow raise. "You stay put. You've worked hard enough for today. You get to relax now."

"You've worked hard too," I argue with a smile but remain in my seat, checking out his butt as he walks away from me.

Yeah, he really is cut. Buns of steel, I'd say. My fingers tingle as I imagine touching him, and a flush runs through my body. Biting my lips together, I beg my face not to catch fire. My cheeks feel so hot right now, I must be neon.

Mikayla's phone starts to ring, and she grabs it off the coffee table, frowning at the screen. "Who's that?"

"If you don't recognize the number, don't answer it!" Asher calls from the kitchen.

She plunks down in the seat beside me, and I glance past her arm, my blood running cold as a gasp fires out of me.

"What?" Mikayla's head jerks in my direction.

"That's Theo's number." I can barely get the words out, my body starting to shake uncontrollably as I jump up from the table and crash right into Ethan's solid chest.

He gives my arm a light rub before holding out his hand. "Give it to me."

"No. Wait," I beg him, but he answers the phone before I can pull it out of his hand.

"Hello?" His forehead puckers with a deep frown, and I'm dying on the inside, just waiting for him to unleash a little hell, but instead his voice remains calm. "Sorry, dude. I don't know a Mikayla. I think you must have the wrong number..." His head jerks back as he plays the part of Mr. Confused. "Nope. Don't know Nolan U either. Whoever gave you this number has got it wrong. Never heard of her or it... Can't help you, man... Yep."

He hangs up and I deflate, not realizing there's no chair behind me.

Two strong arms catch me, and I hit a wall of muscle.

"It's okay," Liam whispers, guiding me to a chair.

I sink into it, my fingers shaking as I cover my mouth and try not to cry.

I don't want to give Theo any more of my tears, but... shit, shit, shit! He's looking for me.

He probably wants to punish me for taking all his money. Or maybe for leaving him.

How did he get Mick's number?

"Hey." My best friend grabs my attention with her soft voice. "It's okay. Crisis averted."

"He's looking for me," I whimper.

Liam's hand crests my shoulders, giving them a comforting rub while the rest of the guys gather around the table.

"What did that fucker do to you?" Casey growls. His angry face is kind of scary and intense.

I lean away from it, dipping my chin and not wanting to say.

I'm still so ashamed by how it all went down. By what I did when I left. By falling for Theo in the first place. For trusting him so blindly and ignoring the odd pinch in my gut whenever he did something that made me unsure. I kept bashing away those red flags because I didn't want to admit that my first serious relationship was failing.

I wanted a boyfriend.

I needed someone to love me because I was lonely and desperate.

Casey's still waiting for an answer. I can feel his stare and eventually glance at him, mumbling, "Just turned out to be kind of mean."

Is that a good enough response?

Casey's pained expression tells me he's probably doing what Liam did and jumping to the worst conclusion possible.

So I huff and quickly say, "He let his friend hit me, then locked me in his room. I ended up running away in the middle of the night after he was asleep."

"He let his friend—" Casey balks. "What the shit?" He's obviously horrified, while Asher gapes at me, his skin paling.

"He's probably super pissed with me," I mumble.

"He's not getting near you." Asher's voice is pure steel,

color coming back to his cheeks as he crosses his arms and shares looks around the table.

The guys are all standing, and I feel like I'm tucked up within their fortress.

I've gotta admit, there's some comfort to that.

But can I honestly sit here and expect them to become my personal bodyguards?

That's not fair to anyone in this house.

If Theo's as stubborn as I think he is, he's not just going to drop this. His dad might even help him hunt me down.

Cold fear pools in my belly, and I cross my arms over my body, hunching forward.

I should use Theo's money to get out of here. If he's as pissed off as I think he'll be, he's no doubt gathering a posse to track me down and make me pay.

Shit. If that happens and I don't have the money, it'll be so much worse.

I can't touch any more of it. I should send it back, but how do I do that without giving away my location?

This is all such a mess.

I need to get myself a job and start saving. If I can work hard enough and fast enough, I'll be able to split before Theo finds me.

And then I can unburden these amazing men who would probably risk life and limb to keep me safe. I can't expect that of them. I can't put Mikayla in harm's way either.

I need to sort out my shit and move along. Quietly.

Just disappear without a trace.

That way Theo can't find me, and these guys will have full deniability if his father tries to hunt me down as well.

# CHAPTER 14
## LIAM

The day after Theo's phone call, Rachel went on a job-hunting mission. I'm not even sure why, but she seemed obsessed with finding work and paying her way.

It only took her three days, but she managed to score a waitressing gig at a local family diner. They'd just lost a woman to maternity leave, and Rachel stepped right in, working long shifts five days a week and even doing extra shifts when asked.

Man, that girl knows how to work. I don't think she's said no once to any overtime, and she ended up working sixteen days in a row once. She was exhausted, but I didn't hear her complain.

Mikayla got a bit pissy about it, telling her off for not looking after herself. She forced Rachel to take Thanksgiving off and go to Denver with us. She spent the day with Ethan's dad, Jack, while I hung out with my mama, sisters, and abuela. We had a nice time together, but I couldn't help wishing I was with Rachel... and Ethan and Mick.

We ended up getting together on that Sunday, when Ethan and I got back from our away games in Nebraska. We took the girls out for lunch, then to the movies. We had some good laughs, and it's safe to say Rachel is shooting to the top of my "favorite people" list. She's awesome. I love her smile and her sense of humor. I love that she cried at the end of the rom-com we took them to. I love that when Mick teased her about it, she turned bright red. And I love that she couldn't stop talking about how great Jack is. The girls stayed with him while we were traveling. They were gonna come watch us play, but the cost added up too fast, and they decided a weekend in Denver would be fun. Jack was happy to play tour guide, and they had a blast together.

Because he seriously is the best dad in the world.

Ethan's a lucky guy.

We drove back to Nolan on Sunday night, four happy clams, until our early alarms started ringing the next morning and back to reality we went.

But you know, maybe I like this new reality. Sure, school is still crazy busy between classes and extra tutoring sessions to catch up what I missed during away games, and then there are the hours of training and work-outs, plus the odd physio appointment to keep my body on track. If I get an hour or two of my own time a day, I'm a lucky SOB.

But that hour or two... and what I do with it... well, that's the part I like.

Fighting a grin, I shake my head and crunch through the snow, pounding my boots on the entry mat before walking into Eat Your Faves diner. It's my new favorite place to hang.

The food's okay, not that expensive, and it's got a really great atmosphere. Filled with college students during the breakfast and lunch rushes, then families between 6:00 p.m. to 8:00 p.m. After that, the students filter back in and get noisy until closing or they're booted out by Boss Lady. I don't even know her name, but the evening-shift manager is one scary-ass woman.

I often show up at nine. You know, to study. And sure, maybe I'm keeping an eye on the handsy guys who get rowdy.

I guess I'm grateful the manager is tough as nails and won't tolerate any shit.

I slide into a booth, grabbing a menu and scanning it, even though I'm not that hungry.

Dinner was about an hour ago, and my body doesn't need any more food, but I need a reason to be here, so I'm eyeing up the desserts when a sexy waitress stops at my booth with a smile that could melt a guy's brain in a heartbeat.

"Hey, Hockey Man." Rachel laughs and rests her fist on her hip. "What are you doing here? Again." She tips her head, trying to look like she wants to tell me off, but she's fighting a smile the whole time. "You know, if you have a slice of late-night pie every day, you might just get yourself a little pooch." She pats her stomach, and I can't help lifting my shirt.

Sure, it's cocky, but I work hard for these washboard abs, and I love the way Rachel's lips part and her gaze skims over me like she wants me.

I shouldn't do it.

I'm basically running at a fire and asking it to burn me.

Lowering my shirt, I dip my chin so she can't see me fighting a laugh when she mutters, "Or maybe not."

"I'm just here for a coffee and some studying." Grabbing my bag off the floor, I unzip it and pull out my laptop as if to make a point, but she sees right through me.

Shaking her head, she goes behind the counter and grabs the coffeepot and a mug.

As she's pouring the black brew into my cup, she gives me a sideways glance and murmurs, "You're here to walk me home."

"Maybe."

Okay, fine. I have to admit it. Mikayla told me Ray's car is in the shop and won't be available until the end of the week, so she walked to work and was planning on walking or calling one of us for a ride home.

The streets are well lit, and it's only a mile from our house, but I don't care. Knowing Ray, she wouldn't want to bother anybody and would walk home alone, in spite of the fact that it would probably terrify her.

Creeps are everywhere, and she can deny it all she likes, but I bet she's been stressing about what she's gonna do when her shift ends. She never says anything, but I know she still worries that Theo might pop out of the shadows at any moment.

It's been three weeks since his phone call, and I still catch her flinching every time a phone starts ringing or vibrating within earshot.

She's scared he's gonna find her.

So, if I have to be here every night to walk her home, then that's what I'm gonna do.

Resting her long fingers on the table, she bends down

to look me in the eye. Those green orbs of hers sparkle with amusement. "You're like my personal bodyguard. You're gonna protect me from the bad guys, huh?"

"Yes." I look her right in the eye, making sure she knows I'm 100 percent serious.

Her lips part ever so slightly, her expression turning soft and mushy. I can't take my eyes off her green gaze, and when she touches my face, something in my chest hitches, like my heart's just had an electric bolt fire through it.

Her soft breath kisses my mouth just before her lips do. They're sweet and supple, tasting like orange lip gloss and something I can't identify until she pulls back with a surprised blink.

She looks about ready to apologize, but before the words can even leave her mouth, I reach forward and take her face in my hands. Rubbing my thumb over her bottom lip, I figure out what *that something* is.

It's pure addiction.

Gently pulling her toward me, I lean forward, stopping just before I reach her lips. It's my silent way of asking permission, and thank God she doesn't make me wait.

Her lips hit mine for a second tasting, and this one is intense, a fiery hit charging through my body as she kisses me like I'm her new brand of oxygen.

Parting her lips with my tongue, I enjoy the barely audible groan that vibrates in her throat as her tongue licks the length of mine. My fingers lightly dig into the back of her head, threading between those silky strands as I fight the urge to sweep everything off the table and perch her fine little ass on top of it.

This kiss is blinding me to the fact that this is a public place.

I want her.

My entire body is straining with desire, her hot tongue sucking the cells right out of my brain.

"Oi! Rachel!"

She jerks away from me like her boss just stuck her with a cattle prod. Slapping a hand over her mouth, she spins with wide eyes as the lady behind the counter crosses her arms and narrows her eyes at me.

"She's got work to do."

"Sorry," I murmur, smearing Rachel's gloss into my lips and licking the taste off.

Rachel won't even look at me as she darts away from my booth, forgetting the coffeepot.

She has to return moments later to collect it, and I swear her cheeks are neon.

I lightly run the back of my finger down her arm and whisper, "To be continued?"

Her lips twitch, and she gives me the slightest nod before blushing her way across the room and serving two patrons who are fighting laughter as she tries to clear their plates and ask if they'd like any dessert.

# CHAPTER 15
## RACHEL

Well, the rest of my shift was super awkward, but Liam was waiting for me outside at exactly ten thirty. And the sweet smile on his face helped me forget the fact that I tried to devour him in front of a bunch of people I then had to serve.

The icy air makes me shiver, and I pull my jacket a little tighter around myself as we head home.

It's kind of becoming our routine any night I'm working the late shift. If Liam can't make it earlier to study, he still somehow miraculously arrives at closing to walk me to my car. I was so relieved when he showed up tonight. I wasn't too keen on walking home. Even though the streetlights illuminate the snowy sidewalks and I probably have nothing to fear, it's a huge reassurance to have this wall of muscle strolling along beside me.

He doesn't seem to be afraid of anything.

I wish I could be more like that. Mikayla wouldn't be scared to walk a mile on her own.

Glancing at Liam, I tuck my hands into my pockets,

wondering what kind of trip we'll have tonight. Sometimes we chatter away, talking nonstop as we catch up on each other's days. Other times he has a hockey buddy with him, and I'll listen in about aching muscles and misfired pucks. The conversation always continues into the house, drawing the rest of the team until they're all talking over each other, lamenting or celebrating whatever went down. They're all so close and supportive. Even when they're getting in digs, they're doing it with grins on their faces.

Every now and again, we'll drive home with barely a whisper between us.

Kind of like now.

We clump through the snow, our breaths creating white puffs in the air as I wonder what he's thinking.

Did he mind that I kissed him?

*Of course he didn't! He kissed you back.*

Nerves fire through me as I relive the way his tongue melted against mine. I swear my lady parts started dancing, a hot salsa working its way up to my nipples, making them pucker.

Seriously. It was so freaking hot.

Hot enough to make me forget about the fact that we were in a public place and I could get caught by a very unimpressed boss.

"He can't keep coming in here if he's going to distract you. I need you focused."

"Yes, Marianne." I bobbed my head and promised I'd never let it happen again.

She eventually huffed and waddled back to her post in the kitchen so she could bark at the chef. Despite her growly behavior, she's actually a pretty decent manager.

Really fair. And she's giving me so much extra work. Plus, she agreed to pay me in cash.

The money pile at the bottom of my suitcase is steadily growing... just as fast as my urge to leave Nolan is diminishing.

I know I can't stay, but when I'm hanging out with Liam like this, the idea of leaving is a killer.

Another shiver runs through me, and I curl against the icy breeze.

"C'mere." Liam wraps his arm around my waist, tugging me to his side.

I burrow into his jacket, which makes it awkward to walk, but it's so worth it. We shuffle home at a slower pace, and by the time we reach Hockey House, my nose is frozen and my lips are numb.

Pulling the beanie farther down on my head, I step away from Liam so we can ascend the stairs more easily, but his hand captures my elbow and tugs me away from the door.

"What?" I giggle at the look on his face.

He's wearing this mischievous smile that melts my heart to goop as he guides me around the side of the house and stops within the shadows.

"What are you doing?" I grin as he nudges me against the house and leans in.

"To be continued?" His wolfish smile elicits another giggle out of me, but the sound is smothered by his warm, delicious lips.

I sink into the kiss, the darkness of our hiding spot ridding me of any inhibitions.

Wrapping my arms around his neck, I pull him so close his body is falling against mine. He's squishing me against the house, but I can barely feel it. All I can taste is his tongue. All I can hear is the way our jackets are rustling together as his hands glide around my waist.

He squeezes me to him, and my breasts flatten against his chest. He'll barely be able to feel them, what with the jackets in the way and the fact that... well, they're not very big. I'm skinny from head to toe, which means small boobs and minimal ass curvature.

Liam switches the angle of our kiss, groaning into my mouth and sounding as though he's enjoying himself.

I grip the collar of his jacket, feeding off his warmth, the fire inside me building to an inferno as my body wants to do way more than just kiss this guy.

The urges pulsing through me are strong enough to derail any sensibility. Like seriously, I'm ready to strip naked right here and run my tongue over those very fine abs of his. We could fall into the snow and I probably wouldn't even feel its icy sting if Liam was sliding into me.

My chest hitches as my imagination takes flight and this searing-hot kiss ratchets up a few more degrees.

This is crazy.

I'm seriously lusting after this guy with a power I've never felt before.

Liam, with his sweet smile and kind eyes.

Liam, who makes sure I get home safely from work.

Liam, who I want to do unspeakably dirty things to.

The phone in his pocket starts buzzing, and it takes us both a second to register what the noise even is.

Pulling away from me with a reluctant moan, Liam grabs it out of his pocket and winces.

"It's my little sister. I better get it."

"Okay." I let him go, brushing my fingers over swollen lips that are still tingling.

*Holy hotcakes.*

My heart is thundering, a wet sensation buzzing between my legs as Liam slides his thumb across his phone screen.

"Hey, sis. What's up?" He starts laughing within seconds, grabbing my hand and pulling me toward the house.

Is he as affected by that make-out session as I am?

I can barely walk straight, and he's chatting with his sister like we've just been out for a Sunday afternoon stroll at the park.

"I just got home," he says, leading me through to the kitchen after we've shed our jackets and boots. The tops of his ears turn pink, and he smiles. "Not a date, just... walking a friend home from work." He winks at me, and now my cheeks are getting hot.

I brush my hand over one of them and reach for the kettle, needing something to do.

"Anyone want a drink?" I call into the living room.

"Yep!" Ethan replies. "Hey, lil' mouse? You want a hot chocolate or something?"

"Ha!" She keeps her eyes on the big TV screen as she negotiates some maze with the gaming controller. "Baby, do you even need to ask?"

"I'm just being polite."

"Since when are you ever polite?" Her nose wrinkles as her tongue sticks out the side of her mouth and her thumbs start going crazy.

I shake my head at the screen and grab mugs out of the cupboard.

Waving to get Liam's attention, I hold up a mug and raise my eyebrows at him. He shakes his head, and then his eyes take on this dreamy kind of quality.

"You can meet her if you want. Here..." He puts the phone on speaker, and my body goes stiff as a board. All except my eyes, which are bulging at him. "Sofia, say hi to my friend, Rachel. She's staying at Hockey House for a little while."

"Your girlfriend?" The young girl's voice perks up.

"Friend," Liam qualifies, but he can't seem to look at me as he says it.

"Hi, Sofia," I call into the phone.

"Is that Sofia?" Casey appears in the kitchen. "Hey, kitten!"

"Hi, Casey." Sofia's voice goes drippy sweet while Liam casts a glare at his roommate.

"What?" Casey mouths, lifting both hands with a knowing grin that makes Liam softly growl.

I giggle at the exchange between them.

"So, Rachel. How do you fit into Hockey House?" Sofia asks while Casey wanders into the living room and starts trying to distract Mikayla.

"If you make me miss out on my new high score, I'm gonna put scorpions in your bed."

Casey hoots with laughter. "Where the hell are you gonna find scorpions, mouse girl?"

"Oh, I will find a way! Now back off. I'm serious, Casey."

I snicker. "She's so intense sometimes."

"Is that Mikayla?" Sofia asks.

"Yep. My best friend." I smile at the phone. "That's

how I fit into Hockey House. I'm just staying for a little while to..." I glance at Liam, unsure what to say.

He smiles at me, about to tell her something, and for once, my stomach doesn't clench with worry.

*Huh. Looks like I trust him.*

I trust that he's going to say the right thing.

It's a nice feeling, and I'm just about to give him a grateful smile when Sofia gasps.

Liam goes instantly tense, his playful expression dropping away, replaced with a hard alertness that makes him look like a Marine. "What is it?"

"Dad just pulled up." Sofia's voice is peppered with panic.

Liam's eyebrows dip together. "Is Mom home?"

"No."

"Call the police."

"No," Sofia whines. "She hates it when I do that."

Liam huffs, scrubbing a hand over his head. "Fine. Just go to your room, then. Lock the door. I'm coming." He hangs up and is rushing out of the kitchen before I can even say anything.

My heart is thundering because I instinctively know things aren't good.

Ethan's running into the entryway after Liam. "I'll drive."

They've done this before. I can tell by the tension in the air, by the knowing glances between people.

Liam has silently told Casey to stay put. The house clown gives him a serious nod, and Mikayla's forgotten all about her high score to share a worried frown with Ethan.

He blows her a kiss before bolting out the door after Liam.

I rush back into the kitchen so I can look out the window, watching their headlights disappear down the driveway.

"It'll be okay," Mikayla murmurs behind me.

"How often does this kind of thing happen?"

"Not very. But it always sucks when it does." Casey sounds frustrated, and I spin to watch his usually goofy face harden into a scowl. "I don't know what the hell is up with that family. Liam doesn't say shit. He hates talking about it. But..." He sighs, running a hand through his hair. "It must be bad. It's about the only thing that gets him really riled up."

Mikayla's small arm curves around my waist, and I wrap her in a hug.

She rests her head against my shoulder, and we squeeze tight. I know we won't be heading to bed any time soon. I don't care how long it takes, I'm waiting up to check on Liam as soon as he walks in the door.

# CHAPTER 16
## LIAM

Mom's house is just over an hour southeast of Nolan. We used to live near Ethan, but Mama moved my sophomore year of college, in spite of Sofia's protests. Thankfully, she's settled into her new high school, and things have been going pretty well.

But of course Dad found out where they were. We had nearly a year of nothing, but then Mama let it slip, and he, of course, had to come visit.

*Why the fuck does she still pick up when he calls?*

There's a restraining order out against him, but it's not one my mother put in place, so she lets him break it all the time. When he's having a soft, tearful day, she always capitulates, and it kills me every time.

Ethan drives like a NASCAR driver, and we make it there in under an hour. We're lucky we didn't get busted by any cops. I was so busy worrying about what Dad might be doing that my only concern was the delay if we did get pulled over.

Screeching to a stop in front of Dad's badly parked

sedan, I scan for Mama's car, grateful that she listened for once. I called Sofia on the way down and told her to make Mama promise not to go home. She listens to her youngest daughter. She used to listen to me, too, but that was before I got her husband thrown in jail.

Sofia is safely locked inside the house. If Dad did smash a window, her bedroom is secure, plus she has the closet to hide in.

I just hate the fear he's probably putting her through by just being here.

I was hoping he'd give up and assume nobody was home, but he's slumped on the front steps, saliva dripping from his bottom lip as he sits there sobbing and yelling.

"Can't even see my own kids! I just want to see my family!" His voice crescendos as I shut Ethan's truck door and wander across the lawn.

My teeth are smashed together, rage curling through me, but the emotion is pushed aside by something else that's just as heavy.

Dad is pathetic.

My dad. The guy who used to be my hero. The one I was supposed to look up to as I navigated life is a total loser.

I hate having to face that reality.

Shoving my hands in my pockets, I stop a few feet from him, Ethan taking up post just behind me.

"Dad." I catch his attention.

He jerks, looking up at me with glassy, wild eyes. For a second, I'm not sure he recognizes me. He's so fucking drunk. And he looks like shit—his cheeks sunken in, making his eyes look too big for his pasty face.

*Fuck. Has he started using as well?*

Clenching my jaw, I look away from the pitiful sight, battling the urge to fist his collar and scream in his face. *"Why couldn't you just get help? Why do you let the drink own you this way? You've ruined our lives!"*

Somehow, I find a calm I don't feel and manage to say, "You shouldn't be here. I have every right to call the cops. This isn't your home."

"My family's here," he whimpers. "Why are you keeping me from my family? You destroyed us!"

His roar is like a thunderclap as he lurches from his spot on the concrete steps and lunges at me.

I raise my arm to block his weak fist, quickly grabbing his wrist and spinning him around. A knock to the back of his knee has him crumpling, and he lands in the snow. I push him forward, his chest easily hitting the cold front lawn, then rest my hand on his shoulder.

"Calm down."

"You don't get it!" He wrestles and rages, but his struggle is in vain. I'm stronger than him now. I know how to fight and subdue an attacker. He forced me to learn.

Plus, Ethan's right beside us. Dad's got no chance.

"Calm down, Dad. Just take a breath."

"You don't get it!" His shouts are decreasing in volume, his writhing starting to slow as his murky brain registers that this is a fight he can't win.

"You're drunk. You need to go back to your apartment and sleep it off."

"I hate my apartment," he whimpers.

"Then sleep in your car."

"I hate my car." The words come out as a sob, and I

feel like I'm talking to a five-year-old who's still learning how to regulate his emotions.

Isn't he supposed to be the parent?

I close my eyes with a huff, then glance over my shoulder at Ethan.

"What do you want to do?" he asks.

With a heavy sigh, I stand and shake the snow off my jeans. "I'll go check on Sofia, call Mama, then... I guess we'll drive this asshole home. He can't spend the night in his car." Even though I was the one to suggest it, I wasn't serious. I may not like the guy, but I don't want him freezing to death.

Dad's still sobbing into the snow and can't hear what I'm saying.

"I'll keep him here," Ethan murmurs.

I nod, avoiding his gaze and walking for the house. Letting myself in, I head down to Sofia's room and tap on the door.

"It's me," I call.

The lock clicks, and she eases the door open. Her face is blotchy from her tears, but her eyes are dry when I give her a sad smile.

"Is he gone?" she whispers.

"I'm gonna take him home in just a minute. I wanted to check on you first."

She sniffs, crossing her arms and making herself seem young and vulnerable. I guess she still is. Shit, she's only sixteen. She shouldn't have to deal with this from her own father.

"Hey." I grip her shoulder and pull her into a hug. She tucks herself against my chest, and I rub circles on her back. I'm trying to think of something soothing to say, but it's always the same shit, right?

"*It's gonna be okay.*"

"*It's over.*"

But it's not over, because my dad is a relentless bastard, and he'll come back again. It's like his radar is honed to Mama. He can't live without her, but he couldn't live with her either.

Or at least, she finally got to the point where she couldn't live with him.

Or more accurately, I couldn't see her get hurt again, and I forced her hand.

I'm not sure she's ever fully forgiven me for that, although she has admitted that it was probably for the best.

She's never looked at me the same since that night, though. I'm not sure she ever will.

"I hate that he's our dad," Sofia whimpers, fisting the back of my jacket. "It's so humiliating."

"I know." I kiss the top of her head. "Have you spoken to Mama?"

"Yeah. I called her as soon as I hung up with you. She was gonna come back, but I managed to talk her out of it. She would have been too exposed trying to get from the car to the house, and she didn't want the neighbors seeing if Dad did get her." Sofia sniffles, her body shuddering against my chest. "After we hung up, she probably called every neighbor on our street, begging them not to call the police. Telling them you were coming to deal with it."

I sigh and rub Sofia's back with a little more fervor.

She's shaking so much, it's like she's cold.

"How bad was it?"

"Just yelling and pounding on the door for a bit. Then he went quiet and I thought he'd left. I opened my door and was about to call Mama when I heard him starting to cry."

"And the neighbors obviously didn't intervene."

"They know the drill. As long as he doesn't touch us, they won't do anything," she mumbles. "I still can't believe they put up with all the racket, though. I'd be so pissed if I was them." She whines in her throat and pulls away from me, slashing tears off her cheeks. "I hate having to face them in the morning."

"They understand. It's not your fault, Sof." I kiss her cheek. "He only makes *himself* look bad."

"And us look like victims."

"You're only a victim if you act that way. Don't let him take your dignity." I've said this to her before.

"I know. I know." She tuts, then lets out a heavy sigh.

"You need to get some rest. You've got school in the morning."

She rolls her eyes. "I'm fine."

I snicker and kiss her forehead. "You know Mama will get all stressed if she comes home to find you still up and about. She wants her baby girl tucked up safe in bed."

Making a face, she wrinkles her nose at me and sticks out her tongue.

"You gonna be okay if I go? Or do you want me to stick around until Mama's home?"

"You go." Her shoulder hitches. "As long as you take him with you, I'm all good."

"Okay." I smile at her, resting my hand on her cheek. "You're brave and strong."

"Yeah, yeah." She lightly pushes me out of her doorway, but she's fighting a smile as she does it.

"*Te amo, hermana.*"

"Love you, too, bro." She blows me a kiss, and I head down the hallway, pulling out my phone as I go.

My mom answers after one ring. "*Estás bien?*"

"*Sí.* Everything's fine. I'm gonna take Dad back to his place. Sofia's getting ready for bed. It's safe for you to come home now."

Her soft sniff tells me she's fighting tears, and I wait her out. Finally, she lets out a sigh and softly murmurs, "He's not a bad man."

"He is when he's drunk. Thanks for not trying to come back tonight. It makes things easier for everyone."

She sniffs again, and I feel the chill all the way down my spine. A sick sensation clutches my stomach until she finally whispers, "Thanks for taking him home. Don't be too hard—"

"Yep." I cut her off before she can start telling me to go easy on my old man because he's really a good guy and he doesn't mean it.

I can't deal with that tonight.

"Love you, Mama." I force myself to say it, not wanting to end this awkward call on a bad note.

"*Te amo mucho, mi hijo.*" Her voice quavers, giving away her tears before she hangs up.

I grip the phone in my hand, squeezing hard before managing to call out a goodbye to my sister and walk out the door.

Locking it behind me, I shuffle toward my dad, who is now leaning against Ethan's truck.

"Keys." I hold out my palm to him.

It takes him a second to register what I'm saying before he clumsily digs them out of his jacket pocket.

Unable to look at his pitiful expression, I turn to Ethan. "You know where to go?"

"I'll follow you."

I nod and walk to Dad's sedan, grateful for my best friend.

Grateful that he doesn't expect me to apologize for this shit.

He never even makes me feel bad.

As I slam the car door closed and crank the engine, my thoughts make their way to Rachel. What she's going to think about all this?

What do I even tell her?

Ethan's the only person outside my family who knows what went down that horrible night. Except for the cops. I had to tell them everything—multiple times.

What the hell will Rachel think of me if I tell her the truth?

Or should I just gloss the surface and paint a picture that's not as bad as it feels?

Rubbing my forehead, I pull away from the curb, trying to decide whether this tightness in my chest is an eagerness to get back to Hockey House or a dread that makes me want to drive like an old man who can't see straight anymore.

# CHAPTER 17
## RACHEL

It's nearly three thirty in the morning when the guys return home. I've been sitting on the couch, dozing on and off. Mikayla gave up about an hour ago. We'd finished watching an unmemorable rom-com, and she was romanced out.

"You sure you don't want to go to bed? Who knows how long the guys will be."

"I'm staying up." Nothing she could say would sway me, so she kissed my cheek and padded upstairs.

And I kept waiting.

And worrying.

Wrapping my arms around my knees, I sat in a ball, squished into the corner of the couch and staring at a blank TV screen. I couldn't bring myself to pick another movie, so I soaked in the sounds of the humming electronics and stared at the couch cushions until my vision blurred.

But then the door clicked, yanking me out of my stupor.

Instantly alert, I got off the couch and shuffled to the entryway.

"Are you guys okay?" My whisper scares the crap out of Ethan.

He jolts with a soft "Ah!" and nearly drops his jacket. "Holy shit, Ray." Slapping a hand over his heart, he takes a deep breath while I blush up a storm and mumble an apology. "You're like a ninja."

I snicker. "Promise I won't attack you."

His lips twitch, and he gives me a little wink before asking where Mikayla is.

"In bed already."

"'Kay." He turns to check on Liam. "You good?"

"Yeah, man. Thanks for everything. I'll catch you tomorrow." Liam's voice is low and sad. There's a huskiness to it that I've never heard before, and it makes my heart hurt.

Tonight has been rough for him, and as soon as Ethan starts walking up the stairs, I do the only thing I can.

I step into Liam's space and wrap my arms around him.

He goes still for a second, then lets out a soft sigh before his arms ease around my body and he hugs me back.

For a really long time.

We just stand there in the entryway, him holding me like he's drawing strength from my soul while I lightly brush my fingers through the back of his short hair.

Eventually, the sound of a door opening upstairs pulls us apart. Liam glances up the stairwell, then guides me out of the entryway and into the living area. The dim lighting I've spent the last hour or so sitting in highlights the contours of his face, and I can see how tired he is.

"I guess I should let you get to bed," I whisper.

He shrugs, letting out another long sigh. "Not sure I can sleep yet anyway. I'm so tired, but..." He rubs his eyes.

The toilet upstairs flushes, and I look to the ceiling before leading him to the couch.

"I should probably let you go to sleep, though. I can't believe you waited up."

"Of course I did." My voice rises with surprise. "You looked so stressed when you left. I had to make sure you were okay."

Sinking onto the couch cushions, I take his hand and pull him down to sit beside me.

His large body plunks down, and I curl up beside him in my usual catlike ball. Tucking my cold toes under his leg, I rest my head against the back of the couch and give him a sad smile. "Do you want to talk about it?"

"Not really." His laughter is short and hollow.

"Okay." I brush my teeth over my bottom lip. "But do you *need* to talk about it?"

Squeezing the bridge of his nose, he finally croaks, "Probably."

"Is your sister okay?"

"Yeah, she's fine. She, uh... When I left, she was doing okay, and Mama's home now, so they'll be tucked up in bed. We drove Dad back to his place, and we basically had to carry him inside. We dumped him on the couch, and I just have to hope he'll wake up with a hangover and a bucketload of regret like he always does."

Liam's voice has taken on a bitter edge, his jaw clenching when he's done.

141

I rub my hand down his arm, curling my fingers around his fist until it loosens. I thread our fingers together—an intimate gesture, but I want to comfort him any way I can right now.

This man beside me is good and kind. I've been living in the same house as him. I've seen what a gentle soul he is, and I hate the idea that he's hurting.

"How long's it been like this?"

"Since I was eleven. It was worse back then because he lived with us." His voice goes raspy, and he's staring at the wall like he's in a trance. "He was a soldier and came back from his tour wounded and suffering major PTSD. We helped him as much as we could, but he wouldn't go for therapy. I don't even know why, he just..." Liam's shoulder hitches. "He turned to the bottle, and it brought out the ugly in him."

My stomach tenses as I think about what that might mean.

Liam's gone quiet, his face a mask of pain, and I'm not sure if I should ask him to keep going. I'm trying to make him feel better, not relive what was an obvious nightmare.

But then he sighs and keeps talking. "He used to go off. You could feel it building, you know? And then he'd just explode. My mom would always stand in the way. She ended up black and blue, but she didn't want her babies getting hurt." He sniffs, his voice turning thick and gummy. "I tried to help her out a few times, but he was so much stronger than me, and she couldn't handle me getting hurt. He broke a few of my ribs once, and she begged me to keep my sisters safe. I could see how much it was killing her, so I did what she told me. Whenever

Dad started to lose it, I'd take my sisters upstairs, and we'd hide until it was over."

Tears build on my lashes, and when I close my eyes, a few trickle free. I don't bother brushing them away. All I can picture is little Liam, probably terrified, trying to keep his sisters calm while they listened to the carnage downstairs.

"She'd be bruised and hobbling around the house for a few days afterward. And Dad would cry and apologize and buy her flowers and promise to never do it again."

"But...," I whisper.

"Yeah." Liam nods, then glances at me, his expression crumpling when he notices my tears. Frantically brushing them away with his thumb, he shakes his head. "I don't have to tell you this shit. I don't want it being some kind of trigger for you. Shit, I'm sorry."

Before he can turn away from me, I rest my hand on his cheek and guide him back so I can look into his eyes. His beautiful, tortured eyes.

"I'm okay. I'm not crying because I'm thinking about what happened to me. I'm hurting for you. For what you and your mom... your sisters... what you had to go through. How long did you all suffer like this?"

With a soft sigh, he nestles his cheek into the palm of my hand. "Years. Mama wouldn't let us say anything, because... she loved him. Despite the fact that he hurt her, she could see his mental suffering, and she was desperate to help him. But he's a stubborn asshole, and one night... I just couldn't stay in that closet anymore." His voice began to shake, his gaze going distant like he was walking back in time and reliving it all over again.

"You don't have to," I whisper.

143

But he doesn't seem to hear me.

"I was sixteen. Bigger. Stronger. I... He was whaling on Mama, and... I couldn't do it. I couldn't sit in that fucking closet anymore listening to her cries of pain. She was begging him to stop, but he wouldn't." Liam's forehead bunches, his nostrils flaring as he grits out the rest of the story. "So I stormed down those stairs and I grabbed him. And I threw him across the room. He crashed into the TV, and I swear, when he stood up, I thought he was going to kill me." His lips quiver when he squeezes his eyes shut. "This was a trained soldier, and he came at me like I was some terrorist rebel or something. His fists were like cannonballs, and I fought him as best I could. I got in a few good shots before the police showed up. Cut his chin bad enough to leave a scar. But... it was a bloodbath." He shakes his head. "He broke my nose and busted open my cheek. Mama couldn't even look at me. She was sobbing and Sofia was screaming while the police dragged Dad away. He was cursing, and... it was like he was possessed."

I brush my thumb across his cheekbone, feeling his raw pain as if it were my own.

"She couldn't look at me for days. I don't know if it's because she couldn't face what he did to me or because I broke her rules and got involved. If I hadn't, Maria—my older sister—she never would have called the police." He tips his head back, resting it against the couch and looking like this story has aged him by a decade.

"Did your dad go to jail?"

"Yeah. Mama didn't want to press charges and tried to explain that it wasn't Dad's fault. She went on about the IED and how he'd lost his entire unit and was suffering from PTSD. But it wasn't enough. Not with Maria's testimony. And mine. The old guy was put away for twelve months. And when he got out... he didn't want to come back home." Liam nodded. "It was a good thing. Mama was sad, but life was peaceful, you know? We got on with living, and it enabled me to leave and go away to college without worrying about her. Well..." He lets out a harsh laugh and shakes his head. "Mostly not worry about her. My old man is one stubborn bastard, and he still shows up every now and again. Even though I made sure there's a restraining order out against him... he just can't seem to stay away."

"Is that why you went to a college relatively close to home, so you can still be there when they need you?"

"Maybe," he murmurs. "But Nolan was always in the cards for me. They have a great hockey program."

I smile, loving the way his voice lightens at the mere mention of hockey.

"You gonna go pro?" I grin at him.

"Nah." He shakes his head. "That's Ethan's dream. And Casey's."

"What about you?"

He works his jaw to the side. "Actually... I'm wondering about becoming a cop." His face bunches. "I know there are some really shitty ones out there, but there are also guys like Martin and Darius, who showed up to a domestic call and saved a terrified family from a drunken man." He sniffs. "They checked in, you know? They'd drive by on their shifts to make sure we were getting on okay. Darius even wrote me a letter of recommendation when I was applying to Nolan U. They're good people, and I want to be a cop like that. I want to help keep innocent people from getting hurt."

"Wow," I whisper, my voice filled with admiration.

He glances at my face, his lips rising with a soft smile. Curling his fingers around my wrist, he caresses the soft skin below my watch strap.

Can he feel my pulse? A thick, steady beat that's drumming for him... and only him.

"You know, I've never told anyone but Ethan that story."

I smile, my eyes glassing with even more tears. "I'm honored that you told me."

Gently brushing the tears away, he leans in and kisses my forehead. "Thanks for listening."

"Always." Snuggling against his side, I curl into his solid body, and his arm drapes over my back.

When he tugs me a little closer, I'm overwhelmed with such a sense of comfort and warmth that I'm pretty sure I never want to move again.

Which is why Mikayla finds me still snuggled against Liam's side when she runs downstairs a few hours later to tell me her exciting news.

It's daylight, but my body feels like it should still be pitch-black outside. The owls should be hooting, and I should still be in dreamland while lying against a wall of muscle that fits against my body perfectly.

I think I'm running on two hours' sleep—if that—and my brain feels like sludge as Mikayla shakes me awake.

"What time is it?" I croak.

"Nearly seven thirty."

"Are you insane?" I frown at her. "Who are you, and what have you done with my best friend?"

She laughs. Miss I Hate Mornings is standing there laughing and grinning and—

"Seriously, Mick," Liam groans. "We're running on fumes here. You better have a damn good reason for waking us up so early."

"What are you talking about?" She sits on the coffee table in front of us. "You're usually up an hour ago and heading to the gym."

He jolts, then has to catch me when the sudden movement practically catapults me off the cushions.

Pulling me back to his side, he squints at his watch and groans.

"The guys didn't want to wake you," Mikayla murmurs. "Ethan figured it's only one workout and Coach will understand." Her grin grows a little wider. "When he came up to kiss me goodbye, he said you two looked so adorable that everyone was tiptoeing around you. They were a bunch of mimes down here because no one wanted to wake you."

"Except you," I grumble.

She laughs. "Yes, well, I just got a text from my dad that warrants a wake-up call."

The joy on her face makes me smile. Having gone years with no contact from her father, Mikayla has been rebuilding what was lost, and it makes my heart warm to see it. Her bitch of a mother lied to them both, saying neither wanted to see the other, hiding correspondence and everything. But the truth is out there now, and all those years she stole from her ex-husband and daughter are being won back.

"You know how he invited Ethan and me to his resort for Christmas?" She grins, and I nod. "Well, he's just extended the invitation to you as well!"

"Really?" I run a hand through my hair, fisting the

back of it and trying to not sound as scared as I feel. "But doesn't he live in California?"

"Yes." Mikayla's excitement fades as she picks up my mood, and then she suddenly realizes why I'm asking. "You don't have to worry about that." She squeezes my arm. "It's miles away from Fuckwit. He won't even know you're in the same state. California's huge."

"Yeah." I let out a nervous laugh, feeling like an idiot. Of course it's huge. Of course Theo won't know I'm there. Why would he? The chances of bumping into him are slim to none.

"And I really want you to see Dad again. He's dying to give you a big ol' hug and see how little Ray-Ray's doing." Mikayla's voice has softened, and I glance at her pleading expression.

Great. Now I'll never be able to say no.

Sensing Liam's gaze on me, I glance his way and try to find my smile. My tired face feels stiff.

He studies me for a moment, then turns to Mick. "Can I come too?"

For reasons I can't even explain, relief blossoms inside me, lifting my tight lips into a genuine grin.

*Did he seriously just say that?*

*For me?*

"I'm sure that'll be fine." Mick grabs her phone and starts texting. "Will your mom be pissed that you're missing Christmas?"

And the relief burns away as I realize he shouldn't be offering this. His family needs him. I can't expect him to come just because I'm nervous over something that has a very slim chance of even happening. Just because knowing he'll be there helps me breathe easier.

Why is that?

Have I come to rely on this man without even real-izing it?

Do I even *want* to rely on a man again?

A knot forms in my belly, and I nearly miss the fact that Liam is talking again.

"I mean, sure, she'll be disappointed, but she'll survive." He glances at me with a smile. "Cali sounds like fun."

"Yay! Ethan's gonna be stoked." Mick jumps up, holding the phone to her ear and racing out of the room. She's either calling her dad or her boyfriend, making Christmas plans that I should seriously be more excited about.

A winter getaway at a luxury resort with my best friend and two guys who are quickly becoming some of my favorite people?

It sounds amazing.

But...

"What about your dad?" *I have to ask, right?*

Liam clenches his jaw. "I'll give Ethan's dad a call, see if he'll be willing to keep an eye on him for me. Or at least make sure he's on standby if he goes and does something stupid again."

"Are you sure?"

Swiveling to face me, he runs his fingers lightly over my ear before resting them in my hair. "I'm sure I want to be there with you."

Then he leans forward and kisses the tip of my nose.

And that knot in my stomach starts to unravel, making way for a blooming sensation that feels so good, it just might be addictive.

# CHAPTER 18
## LIAM

To say the resort is lush is an understatement.

Not only did Mikayla's dad arrange his father-in-law's private jet to come and collect us, but we then drove to the five-star oasis in a stretch limo, clinking glasses of bubbling cider together as we celebrated how freaking awesome this all is.

Of course, Mama was sad I wouldn't make it home for Christmas, but when I told her why, she was genuinely happy for me. Sofia hit the roof, hissing and whining about how it wasn't fair that she couldn't go. Yes, she's a junior in high school who still knows how to act like a six-year-old. Thankfully, Jack came to the rescue and invited my mother, sisters, and Maria's boyfriend around for Christmas dinner, so I can relax knowing that someone's going to treat them right and look after them.

Meanwhile, I can soak up some California sunshine with my best friend and these gorgeous ladies.

Staring out the window, I drink in the sun-soaked

scenery, already missing the snow. I'm used to white Christmases. This is going to be a new experience.

Rachel lets out a happy sigh beside me. She's been great this week. More smiley and relaxed. I've kept making sure she gets home safe each night, and we've made out a couple more times around the side of the house, or in her car, before the icy cold has forced us inside.

I like kissing her.

Her lips are soft and sweet. I like the little moans of approval she gives me, and I love the way her body fits against mine. I can wrap my arms all the way around her.

I want to fall asleep beside her again, but she hasn't invited me up to my room yet. I don't want to be the creep who pushes that on her, so I'm trying to be patient, but man, I want her. I want her so badly.

Let's just say Asher's not the only one to fulfill a certain need on that couch in his man cave. And every time I do, I'm picturing Rachel's soft lips, feeling them brush over every inch of my skin. I'm hearing her breathy pants as I bury myself inside her and make her come.

"Oh my gosh, look!" Rachel's hand lands on my thigh, and I get a quick glimpse of her excited face before following the direction of her finger to look at the looming gates ahead of us.

"That's the resort!" Mick clambers out of her seat to push her face next to Rachel's so they can drink it in together.

It looks amazing. That's a rich man's paradise right there.

Luna Luxury Resort is embossed in gold letters above the grand entrance. As soon as the mammoth wooden gates open, we drive through the stone archway and start drinking in the lush golf course. I've never seen such vibrant green grass in my life.

The driveway must be at least a couple miles long as we wind our way through palm trees and fountains until a stone mansion appears as if formed from the earth's crust. It juts out from the side of a large hill—a masterpiece of apricot and creamy white stones.

The main building is four or five stories of impressive architecture, and shooting off from that in various directions are pathways that lead to individual villas.

"I feel like a celebrity," Rachel murmurs, her laughter a little giddy when she shares a cute smile with Mick. They let out this squeal together, which I'm sure is not human, and I bulge my eyes at Ethan, who's cringing behind his girlfriend's back.

The limo pulls to a stop outside the grand entrance, and a man in a tailored suit hurries down the wide steps to greet us. His smile is broad, and I can tell before he even opens the door that this must be Mikayla's father.

"Dad!" She jumps into his arms, sharing a tight hug.

Rachel watches on with misty eyes, then shares a meaningful look with Ethan. "You did that," she whispers, reaching out to squeeze his forearm. "Thank you."

He looks about ready to cry for a second but manages to just blink and nod. And I watch Rachel slip out of the car with a look of awe. Because that's what I'm in.

She has the most amazing way of making people feel seen and heard and cared for.

And my heart is tumbling over itself as I watch her give Mr. Hyde a kind smile.

"Ray-Ray." He holds her hands wide and takes her in. "You are stunning."

She blushes and dips her chin.

"I know, right?" Mick points her thumb at her. "She's become quite the hottie."

Mr. Hyde laughs and kisses her cheek before stepping forward with an outstretched hand to greet Ethan, then introduce himself to me.

He's a nice man—confident and friendly. I instantly like him, which makes it easy to follow him through the entrance and listen to his instructions on where we can go and what we can use and do while we're here.

"Everything's on the house." He hands us four cards. "Those will give you access to your suite. I've put you all in together. I hope that's okay."

"Totally fine." Mick waves a hand through the air. "Just being here is amazing."

He grins and pulls her into a sideways hug. "Whatever activities you want to do, just mention your suite number. Same for any food and drinks. The resort has three restaurants. The breakfast buffet opens at seven and runs until ten thirty. If it's okay with you guys, Emilia and I would love to have dinner together tonight, and then we have a special lunch celebration planned for Christmas Day tomorrow. Does that sound okay?"

"Uh... yeah!" Mick's enthusiasm is infectious, and we're soon all nodding and getting excited.

"Before I take you to your suite, I'd love for you to meet Emilia and the kids."

He gives Mikayla a cautious look, but she's grinning and bobbing her head. "Great!"

We walk across the polished white tiles while a porter

takes our bags and heads off in the opposite direction. A shiny grand piano is filling the space with peaceful tunes, and I nod my appreciation at the pianist, who smiles back at me, then turn right and head down a plush corridor that leads outside.

"The kids are in the indoor pool right now. They've got so much energy to burn, we try to tire them out as much as possible." He winks at his daughter. "Remind you of anyone?"

"She's still like that," Ethan teases her, and Mr. Hyde tips his head back with a laugh. "I bet she is." He chuckles. "And I don't even want to know how you tire her out, so just keep that tidbit to yourself." He winks at Ethan while Mikayla turns tomato red and Rachel has to cover her mouth to hide her laughter.

My eyes travel down her body as she walks ahead of me, and I can feel that fire burning bright as I imagine how I'd tire her out.

*Shut up! Now is not the time!*

I force my wayward brain to behave in the nick of time, because as soon as we walk into the indoor gym and pool area, we're bombarded by three dripping children. They are all so excited to meet their big stepsister, talking over each other to try and get her attention.

Rachel crouches down to introduce herself as Emilia gives Mikayla a laughing hug, then smiles up at Ethan, obviously impressed by how handsome her stepdaughter's boyfriend is.

I swear, it's like a Hallmark moment. A snapshot of what a happy family should look like. I shake hands and smile politely. I laugh when I should, but my insides are ringing by the time we finally get out of there.

I love my sisters and my mom, but we will never have what just happened in there. It was all noise and laughter and smiles. The love was so fucking bright, it was blinding. And it felt completely foreign to me.

For all my plans for the future, my hopes of becoming a cop and protecting the universe from evil, my ideals of growing old with some woman who looks at me like I'm the only guy on the planet... I'd never considered kids.

I don't want to analyze the why, because it's probably some deep psychological shit about not wanting to become like my father. Kids are so vulnerable, and I'd never want them having to face what I did.

But could I be a dad like Michael Hyde or Jack Galloway?

Could I be happily married and have this Hallmark life?

I honestly don't know.

Following Mr. Hyde through to our suite, I try to push the uncertainty from my mind. I don't want to live in the future. I want to live in the here and now and experience this Christmas break without bogging it down with serious shit.

But I can't shake this yearning inside me.

Even though I've never had it, I think I want that noisy, happy chaos. I want that blinding love. I just don't know how to get it.

"And here we are..." The door beeps and Mr. Hyde pushes it open, revealing so much more than a suite.

"Holy shit," Mikayla whispers, her mouth dropping open as we step into a luscious apartment that looks like it's been made for Hollywood royalty.

There's a large living area in the middle, looking out

over a stunning view of palm trees and the golf course beyond.

"You've got a great view of the sunset from here." Mr. Hyde spreads his arms wide in front of the massive window, then picks up a small tablet. "Here are your controls for everything—the fire, the lighting, music, entertainment system. I'm sure you can figure it all out." He hands the tablet to his daughter, then tips his head at me. "Liam, I've popped you in this room." He opens a heavy door to reveal a massive bed with about a hundred pillows on it. "And Ray, you're just in here, sweetie. I've given the master bedroom to Mikayla and Ethan." He points over his shoulder, indicating a set of double doors that must lead into another slice of luxury.

I can already hear Mikayla cheering. "This thing is huge!"

"You better be talking about the bed, Mickey Blue!" Mr. Hyde walks away to go check on his daughter while Rachel and I share a grin.

"Need a hand with your bag?" I look around, trying to figure out where our luggage ended up.

"I think it's already in here." Rachel walks into her room, and I stop in her doorway, spotting her bag nestled against the wall.

She walks into the en suite bathroom and starts making noises about things smelling nice. "This must be so expensive!"

"I know, right?" I call from the doorway.

Her head pops out of the bathroom. "Come look at this."

I do as I'm told, spotting myself in the floor-to-ceiling mirror as I step into the en suite. I'm so big beside her, my broad chest seeming to fill up the room as her delicate hands lift different bottles for me to smell.

"I like this one the best." She sprays a little perfume into the air, then steps into its mist.

Unable to stop myself, I rest my hand on her hip and guide her back toward me, sniffing her neck and checking her expression in the mirror.

Her eyes are closed and she's tipping her head back, giving me easier access to her soft skin. I brush my lips against the base of her neck, enjoying the whispering sigh that comes out of her.

"I think you smell the best," I murmur against her skin.

She shivers and pushes back into me, her eyes popping open and connecting with mine in the mirror. The heat and hunger she's flashing me is so strong, I feel a spark travel through me.

I curl my fingers into her shirt and tug until her body is flush with mine, so she can feel the effect she's having.

Just one look and I'm standing at attention already.

Her eyes bulge, her lips parting enough for her tongue to swipe across her bottom lip.

Holy shit, I'm undone.

"I want you," I whisper, sucking her earlobe before lightly scraping my teeth down the side of her neck.

I'm desperate for her to tell me she wants the same thing, but Mikayla's voice cuts between us.

"Where are you guys?"

Rachel jerks away from me, knocking over the sweet-smelling bottles on the counter. "Oh, I was just showing Liam all the goodies in here."

Her voice is trembling, but that doesn't stop me from smiling at her and brushing my hand over her butt.

"So many goodies," I whisper.

She turns beet red, and I force myself to step back so she can move into her room and talk to Mikayla.

Her voice is going a mile a minute as she gushes about how luxurious this place is, and I give myself a moment to calm the hell down so I can follow her without showing Mikayla the tent in my pants.

Staring at my reflection, I shake my head but can't help a small chuckle as I think about the fact that I've finally figured out what I want for Christmas.

Will Santa make my wish come true?

Will I get to unwrap that gorgeous woman on Christmas morning?

Fuck, I hope so.

# CHAPTER 19
## RACHEL

Christmas Eve dinner is exquisite. I've never tasted food like it and end up having a lengthy discussion with Emilia about how great everything tastes. Her father's been in the restaurant business for decades. He started out as a young teen working for his family's pizzeria, then shifted to a fine dining restaurant before branching into hotels and resorts.

"He just slowly built it up over the years, but he always knew food was key. His first hotel was a tiny thing near Sacramento, and everyone told him no one would bother coming, but he made it the classiest place he could, hired a top chef, and sure enough... people came. At first it was just a dinner reservation, but then they started staying the night. Before we knew it, our Hotel Lujoso was a hit. Dad branched out from there, and we've gone from strength to strength. Since Michael's come along with all his ideas, the business has been booming. But it always comes back to the food." She winks at me.

"I'm a big fan. I love cooking and... especially baking. Designing desserts."

"Oh really?" She touches my arm, her big eyes sparkling. "Well, I must introduce you to our pâtissier. He's from Toulouse, and his desserts are divine."

"That would be amazing. Thank you."

"He's back the day after Christmas. I'll be sure to introduce you before you leave."

It makes me wish we were staying longer. I love it here. After hanging out with Mikayla's family and watching Liam and Ethan play with the kids in the pool, we spent the day exploring the resort, racing around in golf carts and feeling like full-blown billionaires. It's seriously like entering a whole new world. We're in this bubble that feels somehow magical. The four of us have had a blast together, and I think this just might be my best Christmas yet.

Mom called this afternoon and met Liam and Ethan. After a chat, they left me to have a moment with her, and all she could do was gush about how gorgeous they are.

"I know, right?" I giggled. "Hockey players."

"And you're living with them? How do you control yourself?" She gave me a mischievous wink, and I gave her my best impression of a red traffic light. "Rachel Josephine Beauford, what are you not telling me? Is there something going on between you and Liam?"

I bit my lip, totally giving myself away.

Mom's lips parted.

"I don't know," I rushed out. "We've kissed a few times and he's really nice, and I like him a lot."

"But..."

"But we haven't taken things further."

"Do you want to?"

"Um…" I bit my lips together and seriously must have been neon because Mom started laughing at me.

"Oh, you want to. What's holding you back?"

I wrinkled my nose. "I'm not sure. I guess I rushed things with Theo, and it's making me… cautious."

Mom nodded, and it suddenly occurred to me that I still hadn't told her what he did to me. My stomach clenched and I fisted the duvet, hoping my face looked serene enough on the video call.

"Baby, I know you didn't expect that to fall apart. And I know it really hurt. And yes, maybe moving in with him the way you did was too fast and too soon. But that doesn't mean you can't fall in love again. Listen to your gut."

"I thought I did that with Theo." I blinked, my lips pursing as I gazed at my mother's face on my screen. She was giving me that *think hard about this, Ray-Ray* look, so I did and finally gave in with a sigh. "You know, I did have my doubts," I muttered. "I just didn't want to listen to them. I was sad you were leaving and scared to live alone."

"Aw, baby." Mom's smile was tender. "And how do you feel about this new phase of your life? Are you happy? What does your gut say about Liam?"

I took my time to respond, really forcing myself to think it through, to try and listen to my body.

"You know you're smiling, right?"

I glanced at my screen, saw the grin on my face, then looked at Mom.

"I think you've got your answer, kiddo. So you go have some fun this Christmas, you hear me?"

"Yeah. You, too, Mom."

"Oh, I will. I'm having myself a Jamaican celebration. I'm in heaven, baby. Don't you worry about me."

Her joyful laugh rings in my head again as I walk the pathway back to our suite. Ethan's a touch buzzed, and he's singing an out-of-tune love song to Mikayla, who laughs and jumps on his back.

Liam walks beside me, his hands tucked in his pockets, while I resist the urge to reach for him. We haven't told anyone about our kissing yet. All Hockey House knows is that Liam meets me at the diner each night after work.

I'm not sure any of them know how much I like him or how much he wants me.

He's pretty good at keeping his expression in check when others are around.

I don't even know why we're playing this so quietly. It's just been instinct to keep it all a secret. I mean, it's not like we're a couple or anything.

He just hangs out at the diner whenever he can, and we kiss.

I just think about him all the time and have formed a crush that is so uber, it's practically all-consuming. A crush I've been trying to deny myself because I don't want to make another mistake.

But it's Liam.

How could he possibly be a mistake?

I know he wants me—he told me so this morning when we were checking out my en suite bathroom. His teeth lightly scraping my neck still sends a shiver through me. My body took ages to stop tingling.

I want more.

I want him.

Bubbles of anticipation pop in my stomach as we walk into the suite. With Mikayla still on his back, Ethan spins to face us. "Merry Christmas Eve, bitches."

Liam laughs. "You, too, man."

"I'm gonna go do dirty things to my woman."

"You have fun with that."

Mikayla giggles, sucking Ethan's neck and shouting, "Oh, we will," just before he swings the door shut.

Liam and I stand there in awkward silence for a moment, looking at everything but each other. I so desperately want to make a move, but I'm terrified. What if I lunge at him the way I want to and he gives me a polite rejection?

*He wants you! He made that abundantly clear this morning.*

*But he's not making a move right now, is he?*

A squeal followed by raucous laughter floats out of the master bedroom.

I glance at Liam, letting out a nervous chuckle when our eyes connect... and then everything goes still between us. He's staring at me, his swallow thick and audible. My lips part like I want to say something to entice him, but I've got nothing.

Two thick beats seem to pulse through the air... and then a switch suddenly flips.

We're rushing at each other, our bodies colliding just before our tongues meet in a deep, heady kiss.

Liam's hands weave around my body, pressing me flush against him while my gut screams, "Yes! Yes! Yes!"

"I want you," I manage to whisper between kisses. "I want you now."

"Yeah?" His eyes search my face like he needs to be sure I'm not just saying this for his sake.

My head bobs repeatedly, and a wolfish grin skitters across his lips as he sweeps me off the floor and hurries into my room, flicking the door shut with his foot before placing me on the bed.

# CHAPTER 20
## LIAM

Rachel fists my jacket and pulls me down on top of her. I only manage to catch myself on my elbows before squashing her. She's hungry for it. Her fervent kisses are a dead giveaway, and oh do I want to sink into her hot oasis.

But when she starts tugging at her dress and pulling it up over her hips, acting like we're gonna hit a homer fully clothed, I have to pull back.

We're both out of breath, our desperate kisses making it impossible not to be, so it takes me a second to find my voice.

"We don't have to go so fast." I run my finger across her hairline.

She frowns. "What do you mean? Do you not want to...?"

"Of course I do." I grin. "But I don't want it to be this rushed thing that's over like an explosion." I brush my nose against her cheek. "I want to take my time with you." Nibbling along her jawline, I lightly suck the spot just below her ear and enjoy the sweet exhale that kisses the side of my head. "I want to pleasure you, sweet Ray. I want to make you come and come some more."

Her swallow is thick, and I pause to look at her.

There's a nervous edge to her expression, and something cautions me to do this right. To make her the center of every decision right now.

Running my knuckle across the curve of her chin, I softly ask, "What do you like?"

She blinks, her large green eyes brighter than I've ever seen them. "What do you mean?"

"Well," I whisper, running the tip of my tongue up the length of her throat before nibbling her earlobe, "what gives you pleasure?"

"I... I don't know." Her voice is featherlight as she grips the back of my jacket.

I sit up, perching on my knees to stare down at her as I loosen my tie and slip off my jacket. She bites her lip, reaching up and pulling my tie all the way down until it comes undone. Her fingers are trembling as she unbuttons my shirt, and I gently stop her when she's half done, slipping it over my head and throwing it toward the end of the bed.

I'm now in nothing but black dress pants, socks, and shiny shoes.

I kick those off, and they clunk to the floor just before I reach for Rachel's heels. Her long, narrow feet rest against my thighs once she's shoeless, and I run my hands up her legs, wriggling them beneath the silky material of her dress.

"You've had sex before," I murmur, enjoying the twitch of her muscles when I reach the soft skin near her pussy. It's gonna be a fine pussy. I can already tell. Everything about this woman is exquisite.

She nods. "Yeah, I've had sex."

"So... what turns you on?" The pads of my fingers brush along her skin as I shift again, hovering over her while she turns bright red. "You can tell me, Ray."

"No one's ever asked me that before."

I jerk back, failing to hide my frown. "What? Really?"

She nods, looking away from me. And now I'm hating Theo just a little more than I did before. What kind of asshole doesn't find out what his woman likes? Isn't that the whole point of sex? To please her, making her scream your name because you're that fucking good?

"Have you ever had an orgasm before?"

Her eyes bulge like she can't believe I'm talking about this so freely.

Resting my hands on the side of her face, I force her to look at me. Her lips purse, and she gives me a pitiful frown. "I don't know. Maybe?"

My lips twitch at her sweet expression, and I plant my mouth over hers. Her soft tongue grazes mine, and I deepen the kiss until she's moaning in her throat. Pulling away, I brush the tip of my nose against hers and promise, "When I'm done, you'll know."

Her eyes start to glow with a look of excited anticipation. There's still a little tension there; I can see it in the twitch of her lips before she tells me, "I don't know what I like, though. I don't even know how to tell you."

"Okay." I skim my tongue across her mouth before nibbling my way to her neck. I inch down her shoulder, pushing the strap of her dress aside.

And she's not wearing a bra.

My dick twitches like it's doing a celebratory dance as I murmur against her skin. "Let's try this. I'm going to get you naked." I glance at her face, enjoying the heat in her gaze while I push her other strap down and start inching the fabric down her body. "And I'm gonna touch you."

I can feel the pulse pounding in her wrist when I move her arms to unhook the dress from her. I nudge the fabric down to her waist, and now I'm staring at two boobs that are so perfect, they should be cast in stone for posterity.

Brushing my knuckle over her puckered nipple, I enjoy her sharp intake of breath before rolling it between my thumb and forefinger.

She closes her eyes, her body heaving like it's taking everything in her just to breathe. I lean over her, brushing my tongue up her side before kissing a trail around the curve of her perfect tits and whispering, "If you don't like what I'm doing, you tell me to stop and I will."

"Mm-hmm." Her gasp is soft and sweet when I reach her nipple and suck it between my lips.

"But if you like it..." I lick the tip. "Then you let me know and I'll do more. Okay?"

"Okay." She nods, resting her hand on the back of my head while I give some much-needed attention to these pieces of art in front of me. I take my sweet time—sucking, nipping, licking until she's groaning and gripping the back of my head.

She doesn't tell me to stop, so I keep going, trailing my nose down the valley of her body until it dips inside her belly button.

"Lift your hips," I tell her, pulling her dress away and grabbing her panties at the same time.

I sit back to strip them off her smooth legs, then drink in the view. Her eyes slide open, and she watches me watching her. There she goes, biting her lip again. I try to ease her uncertainty with a look that tells her how much I love the view.

"You're so hot." My voice is a husky mess. "You're so fucking beautiful."

Her emerald eyes sparkle at me as I rest my hands on her knees and inch her legs apart. My lips caress her inner thigh, and her muscles quiver. Working my way toward her oasis, I feel her flinch, and then she's trying to scramble away from me.

"What are you doing?"

I take in her gobsmacked expression. She's risen up to her elbows and is staring at me like I've lost my mind.

Curling my hands around her legs, I lightly pull her back, caressing her with my thumbs while stating the obvious. "I'm kissing you."

"Down there?" She cringes.

I glance at the glistening folds that are practically begging me to suck them before having to check. "Do you not want me to?"

"I've just... I've never... I mean, are you sure you want to?"

Holy shit. She's never had a guy go down on her before.

How is that possible?

What the fuck is wrong with that Theo shithead?

I'm guessing his idea of sex is very different to mine,

and I cannot fucking wait to show Rachel how it's meant to be. You know, according to the Book of Liam.

With a wolfish grin, I lick my lips, then dip my head and lightly suck her clit into my mouth.

She lets out a surprised gasp, and I pull back to check on her. "I can stop if you don't like it."

"I like it." She can barely get the words out. "I like it!"

So I do it some more. I lick and tease and nibble until her sweet symphony of gasps crescendos to loud cries of ecstasy.

"Liam," she screams, her legs trembling as I slide two digits into her hot, wet core and curl them.

She releases another loud cry, and I take her over the edge, licking circles on her clit until the vibrations in her body start to splinter.

Her groan is magnificent, her long fingers digging into my scalp as she bucks her hips and rides this wave of pleasure.

I sit back to enjoy the view, keeping my fingers inside her and rubbing her clit with my thumb while she arches her back and buries her face in the pillows.

Her body is gorgeous, her boobs jiggling as she pants and tries to catch her breath. I slip my fingers out of her, running her sticky sweetness up between her breasts before placing my glistening lips on hers.

She sucks my tongue, licking her flavor right off me while my cock twitches in desperation.

Her arms curve around me and she buries her fingers in my shoulders, hooking her leg around my butt and rubbing against the hard shaft in my pants.

"I want more," she whispers between kisses. "I need all of you, Liam."

# CHAPTER 21
## RACHEL

I can't undo his zipper fast enough. Shoving his pants down, I fight the fabric, an urgency firing through me as I come off the end of whatever that just was.

I've never experienced anything like it before. His hot tongue and sweet lips must hold magical properties. My entire body was buzzing with this new kind of energy. The heat firing through my limbs was otherworldly. And then when he slipped his fingers inside me and curled them, hitting some kind of spot I didn't even know existed, I took off like a rocket.

My body is still quivering, and now all I want is that special kind of friction only lovers can make. I need him inside me with a desire that's overwhelming.

Hence the clumsy fingers and urgent pants dropping.

I need to get him naked.

I need—

*Oh wow.*

My hands freeze mid-debriefing, my eyes transfixed by a dick that's... beautiful. Can dicks be beautiful? I don't know. But hockey is wasted on Liam Carlisle. He should go into penis modeling immediately.

I gape at his stiff rod, long and thick, protruding from a mound of black curls. His strong thigh muscles support him as he kneels before me, his perfect cock pointing directly at me like it's found its target.

*Oh yes, baby. I am happily your target.*

I run my fingers down the smooth surface of his shaft, my heart pounding with anticipation.

Liam nudges his underwear the rest of the way off before digging around in his pocket for a condom.

He gives me an impish smile as he unwraps it, murmuring, "I was hopeful," before throwing the packet off the side of the bed and rolling the condom on.

It seems such a shame to dress it that way, but I know these things are necessary. Maybe one day that smooth skin will touch my inner walls, and holy shit, will that feel fantastic.

But right now, I'll settle for whatever he's about to give me.

*Settle for?*

*What they hell am I thinking?*

There's no settling for a guy like Liam. He's first prize, and as he leans over me and checks my eyes for permission, I know I'm the clear winner in this scenario.

"Yes," I mouth, my lips rising into a smile as he parts my folds with his fingers and inches his tip into my opening.

A soft gasp fires out of me before I can stop it.

He's bigger than I was expecting, and I can feel myself tensing up in surprise.

"What do you want, Ray?" His soft whisper tickles the

skin of my neck. His body is vibrating as he holds steady, not pushing any farther until I give him permission.

So much control.

So much honor.

This man is better than anything I could have expected.

Opening my legs a little wider, I run my hands down his back, cup his marble ass cheeks, and give them a firm push.

He slides into me, a shock of painful pleasure coursing through me as I make room for this man. He fills me... all the way to my freaking soul.

Tipping my head back with a gasping sigh, I squeeze his ass again and rock my hips, silently encouraging him to get moving.

And he does. Pulling back, he thrusts again, and I feel that kick of pleasure once more. His large body covers me, his back muscles moving beneath my fingertips as I run my hands over his skin.

His pecs slide against my sensitive nipples, heightening my pleasure as we create a steady rhythm that starts to build.

He groans into my ear, "So fucking good. So beautiful, Ray."

His hands dip beneath my butt, his fingers massaging me as he goes even deeper, his thick shaft hitting a new angle that's setting off rockets again. They're bursting inside me like fireworks, a display that's just as heady and mind-blowing as the last.

"Oh." I let out another gasp that's high and breathy, the scream starting to build in my throat again. "Yes. Liam." I cry his name. "Yes!"

Tipping my head back, I run my nails down his spine as he plows into me, picking up the pace until his breaths are as out of control as mine.

My chest is bursting as another orgasm starts to rock my body.

I'm being so frickin' loud right now, and I don't even care. I can't think past the sensations that are lighting my body up like a Christmas tree, splitting me down the middle as Liam plunges into me over and over.

"Ah." He starts to cry out, too, grabbing my knee and hooking it over his hips until his piston pumps falter and he's drawing back and plunging forward with three long thrusts that hit. The. Spot.

As he spills himself inside me, I'm torn apart by a sensation that's so fucking good, I can't keep silent.

I probably deafen the poor guy, but holy mother of all things tasty, Liam "Perfect Penis" Carlisle is rocking my world.

# CHAPTER 22
## LIAM

After Rachel milked me like a queen, I couldn't move. All I could manage was fumbling the condom off with a tissue and flopping down beside her. My jelly muscles pulled her against me, her perfect ass nestling into my crotch as I covered us with a blanket, then spooned her. I'm pretty sure I was smiling as we drifted off to sleep.

Around 3:00 a.m., I stirred, woken by gentle kisses on my neck. Light fingers drifted down my body, curling around my dick and quickly bringing him to attention. With a lazy smile, I wrestled a condom out of my pants pocket, then found a home between her legs. We made sleepy love. It was slow and dreamy, like we were floating on a cloud or drifting in a pool of crystal-clear water. The room was pitch-black, and I couldn't even see her face, but I could hear her sweet moans in my ear.

When my body felt like it was close to coming, I sought out her clit and caressed it until she came with a lusty cry that made me feel like a king. Her inner walls clutched me tight, and I came right after her, burying my face in the crook of her neck and inhaling her sweet scent.

Now it's Christmas morning, and I'm waking up with the only present I've ever really wanted. I didn't even know it until I opened my eyes and felt her weight against my chest. Her long leg is slung over my thighs, her arm draped across my stomach. If I wasn't busting to pee, I would stay here for the rest of my life.

Sliding out from under her as gently as I can, I tiptoe to the bathroom and wince when the flush sounds like a rocket engine taking off. It's so damn loud, and I don't want to wake her. But when I walk back into the room, she's sitting up in bed, tucking the sheet around her naked torso.

"Morning." She curls her mussed-up hair behind her ear with a shy smile. I love her bed hair. I love her rosy cheeks and those big green eyes peeking up at me beneath her bangs.

"Merry Christmas." I smile.

She grins, her face lighting with excitement. "I got you something."

"No way." I grab my boxer briefs off the floor and slip them on while she rummages over the other side of the bed and gives me a shot of her very fine ass. I love that curve, her smooth skin. She's so fucking beautiful.

I've thought that a million times already, but I can't imagine ever not thinking it.

She sits up, sucks in a breath, and holds it while passing me a wrapped box.

"I'm gonna love it," I assure her.

"You don't know what it is yet."

"Doesn't even matter what it is." I pause my unwrapping to smile at her. "You gave it to me, so I'm gonna love it."

The look on her face is too kissable not to lean forward and press my mouth to hers. She runs her long fingers down my face, and we share this gooey look. The kind you see in rom-coms the morning after their first night together.

Shit. We're a fucking rom-com!

And I love it.

Tearing off the rest of the paper, I lift the lid of the box and let out a soft laugh, pulling an Avalanche hockey jersey out and holding it wide.

"Because I keep stealing yours," she murmurs, then guides me to turn it around so I can see the name on the back—SAKIC 19. "Ethan said he's your favorite player."

"Forever and always." I grin, pulling the jersey on and modeling it for her.

"You look so great." She laughs. "You should seriously wear that all the time. Just that jersey and boxers... or no boxers. That's optional."

She winks at me, and I grin, bending down to brush my nose across her cheek. "I'm up for that, as long as you wear the same. Although, the only name I want on your back is mine." I growl and she lets out this adorable squeal before giggling against my mouth.

I deepen the kiss, lightly pushing her back against the covers so I can feel her legs wrap around my hips.

Her heel digs into my ass as my tongue swipes against hers.

I could take her all over again, right now, but I bought her a gift, too, and I'm dying to give it to her.

"Stay here," I whisper, jumping back from the bed. "I won't be a sec."

She gives me a mystified smile as I sneak out of the room... and of course bump into Ethan, who's in the living area wearing a bright red pair of Christmas boxers. There's a huge gold bow covering his bulge, and I stutter to a stop and point.

"Christmas present?"

"You know it." He crosses his big arms across his chest and narrows his eyes at me. "Have a good night?"

I can do nothing but give him my best smile.

He snickers and shakes his head before pointing at me. "Christmas present?"

Holding out the bottom of the jersey, I nod. "Sakic. Thanks for that."

"She was determined to get you the perfect gift." He lifts his chin toward Rachel's bedroom door.

"Hence the reason you're not that shocked to find me sneaking out of her room this morning?"

"Something like that." The smile on Ethan's face has a hint of mystery that I'll have to find out later, because right now, Rachel's waiting for me.

I turn to grab her gift from my room, then pause and swivel back to check in with my best friend. "Hey, uh... you're cool with us hooking up, right? I know you told me not to because if everything fell apart, it'd get awkward, but—"

"There was no way you could ever resist her. Yeah, I get it." He brushes a hand through the air. "I've been watching you too. Or at least seeing how much happier you've been lately. I'm not gonna stand in your way, bro." His shoulder hitches. "Just don't break her heart."

"Not planning on it." I grin at him, and he ends up snickering because he knows I'm not the type to ever treat a woman badly.

"Merry Christmas, man."

"Merry Christmas." I practically laugh the words, this giddy sensation bouncing through me as I pick up Rachel's gift and carry it back to her room. Nerves clatter through me when I face the same predicament she just did—have I gotten the perfect gift?

Her eyes light when she sees the neatly wrapped parcel. It's so obviously a book, but she doesn't seem disappointed by it as she holds out her hands and wiggles her fingers in the air.

"I can't believe you got me something."

"Why?" I plunk down beside her.

"I don't know." She shrugs, then laughs at herself.

Tucking her hair behind her ear, I smile at her. "You bought me something."

"That's because I have a massive crush on you."

"Ditto." I nudge my nose into her cheek, enjoying her soft giggle.

She turns to smile at me, holding my chin and wrinkling her nose. "Last night made that abundantly clear."

"And all the kissing leading up to last night didn't?"

She laughs and shakes her head. "Well, yeah, kinda. But I know you hockey boys have a rep, and for all I know, you kiss girls all the time."

"Casey and Ash sleep with girls all the time, but that's not my style. I save it up for someone really special."

Brushing those long locks over her shoulder, I kiss the skin I've just exposed. "A girl like you."

Her skin is warm against my lips, and I trail my fingers down her naked back. She shivers and grins at me before finally opening my gift.

"Oh my g—Liam! How did you know!" Her voice pitches with excitement as she hugs the fat recipe book to her chest. "This is the exact one I wanted!"

"Mick gave me a heads-up when she found me stressing at my laptop in the library. I wanted to get you something I knew you'd love."

"I do! I do!" She holds the book out so she can run her hand over the cover. It's a book filled with fancy sweet treat recipes. "I'm gonna make every single thing in here!"

"And maybe even redesign some stuff so you can add it to your list for that bakery you want to own one day."

Her cheeks turn a pretty pink as she bites her bottom lip and wrinkles her nose. "Mick told you?"

"Yeah. I think it's amazing. You'd be awesome at something like that."

"I've wanted to do it since I was a kid. I'm not sure how it will happen, but one day. Maybe. For now, I will have so much fun with this!" She hugs the book again, like it's her new favorite teddy bear.

Her excitement is gorgeous, and I drink her in, my heart squeezing so hard that I'm starting to realize this ain't no simple crush.

What I felt that first night she arrived at Hockey House... that was a crush.

What I'm feeling right now is strong and over-powering.

*Here you go again.*

Thoughts of Kylie whistle through my brain. I fell so hard and fast, and then she ripped the rug right out from under me.

But that's not gonna happen with Rachel, right?

She's way too sweet to lead a guy on.

I sit there watching her flick through the pages, oohing and ahhing over various recipes. Showing me the colorful images, she talks a mile a minute about how she can't wait to make this or that.

She's gorgeous. I love the shape of her face and the smile that's dominating it right now. I love—

"Thank you." Her eyes sparkle as she grabs my chin and pulls me in for a deep kiss.

It doesn't take long for the book to be pushed aside so we can celebrate Christmas in a whole other way.

She makes me leave the jersey on and rides me like a rodeo queen. I massage her perfect breasts as she pumps my cock, then pull her against me when I'm close, lightly scraping my teeth across her shoulder, then digging my fingers into her hips when I explode inside her.

I cup the back of her head, drawing her in so I can swallow her cries of pleasure, lashing my tongue against hers and rubbing her clit until she comes while I'm still inside her.

It's one hell of a way to start a Christmas morning.

We shower separately so I'm not tempted to ravage her in the bathroom as well, and I'm soon happily walking down to breakfast in my new Sakic jersey. She's already at the buffet when I walk in, filling her plate with bacon and eggs. I love how much she puts on her plate. The girl loves to eat.

I grab some food and join her at the table with

Ethan and Mick. They're already nibbling on pancakes when we take a seat. Mick looks between us, smiling sweetly before wishing us a Merry Christmas.

It's all quite polite and civil. Mick shows off the bracelet Ethan bought her. It's a thick leather band with these cool bone carvings woven into it. Very Mick. He also bought her a keychain with Mickey Mouse on it, but she's refusing to acknowledge that gift. Ethan can't stop laughing as he describes her reaction when she opened it.

"Because, you know, she's my little Mickey Mouse." He hugs her to him, kissing her forehead with a loud smooch.

"And now I officially hate you," she grumbles.

He lets out another loud laugh, his eyes dancing as he looks at us. "And now she's refusing to give me my present until I apologize, so..." He shrugs. "Looks like I might be going gift free this year."

"You got those boxers." I point at him, wondering if he's wearing them now.

He grins, telling me he is, and Mikayla snips, "That's not his real gift, and he won't be getting it at this rate."

Rachel snickers. "You guys are so stubborn."

"How was your night?" Mick ignores the barb and tips her head with an innocent look.

Although it can't be that innocent, because my stomach is clenching.

"Oh, uh... fine." Rachel's cheeks flood with color, and she refuses to look my way.

"You sleep okay?" Mick's fork taps the plate as she stuffs it full of pancake pieces.

"Yeah. Good. It was a good night." Now Ray's head is bobbing too fast.

Mick's fork stops midair, her lips quirking into a dangerous grin. "Sounded better than good."

"Excuse me?" Rachel squeaks.

"You're noisy when you come." Mick starts to laugh, sharing a delighted grin with Ethan before shoving the pancakes into her mouth.

Rachel eyes bulge, and I swear she's about to crawl under the table and die of embarrassment.

Ethan snorts, dipping his head and doing the worst job ever at hiding his laugh, while I run my hand down Rachel's back and lean in to whisper, "Looks like we don't need to keep this under wraps anymore."

"Oh my gosh." Rachel covers her face.

I give in to a soft chuckle, pressing my lips against her cheek and saying so softly that only she can hear, "You can be as loud as you want with me. It's sexy as hell."

She swallows, fighting a smile as I pull back and wink at her.

It takes a good five minutes for Mick and Ethan to stop laughing and for Rachel to finally go back to her normal color. I've never seen her so red before.

Finally brushing her bangs out of her eyes, she lifts her chin and gives them an imperious look. "You know what? You're right. I didn't just have a good night... I had a fucking fantastic one."

Mikayla gasps, her expression lifting with pride as she raises her hand for a high five.

Rachel slaps her palm.

"My girl!" Mick grins. "Using her naughty words and everything. I've never been so proud."

"Shut up." Rachel laughs, then dives into her breakfast, taking Mick's teasing about the reasons for her ravenous hunger like a true pro.

Now *I've* never been so proud.

And holy shit... the way I'm feeling right now... I might never have been this in love either.

# CHAPTER 23
## RACHEL

Christmas Day was perfect. Mikayla's dad and family are seriously cool. The food was divine, and the Christmas games they'd organized for the kids were a blast. We all got into them. Watching Ethan and Liam chasing the children and making them squeal with excited laughter made my lady parts dance. Even Mick was affected by it, not that she wanted to admit how sexy two gorgeous men giving pony rides to children is.

Yesterday, Emilia introduced me to the pastry chef at their classiest restaurant, and he let me help him make a batch of crème brûlées. It was the most fun I'd ever had in a kitchen. The guy treated me like I was a valuable asset. He even gave me some tips on how to perfect my chocolate lava cake recipe.

I never want to leave this place. Seriously. It's the best.

But I'm aware it's just a bubble, and as a way to ease out of it, Mikayla and I decide to go shopping at the mall in the nearby town.

The boys drive us over there and are planning on

heading to the local rink to see if they can score some ice time. They haven't booked or anything, so it's a long shot, but worth a try.

As I'm getting out of the car, Liam captures my wrist and tugs me back to his side. His kiss is sweet, his smile enough to make me float.

"Have fun shopping."

"I will." It's hard not to giggle the words.

Seriously. This is ridiculous. I'm acting like a lovesick fool, but it's impossible not to.

Three nights with Liam and I'm a goner.

I'm kind of surprised by how *not* freaked out I am by it all.

Maybe it's the bubble thing.

"Come on, lovebird." Mick drags me away from the car.

"Like you can talk," I tease her. "I've never seen you so happy."

She grins at me, doing a giddy little skip. "It's true. I'm in love with Ethan Galloway."

I smile at her, my heart blooming. She deserves this. I hope she and Ethan last forever.

Yes, I'm still a romantic. Even after everything I've been through with Theo, I want to believe in love.

Glancing over my shoulder, I watch the car Ethan's driving pull out of the mall parking lot and wonder if I'll ever love Liam. Wondering if I already kind of do.

These feelings are similar to what I went through with Theo but more intense. The sex—not that I should compare, but what the hell—is off the charts. Theo never tried to make me come. He got in, he came, he got out. Not that it didn't feel good for me, too, but Liam's main purpose of sleeping with me seems to be "give Rachel multiple orgasms."

And oh boy, does he pass with flying colors every time.

He keeps asking me what *I want.* It's like he's trying to study my body, figure out every one of my pleasure points. He wants to master me... in all the right ways.

And I want to let him.

But is this all too good to be true?

I've rushed headlong into a relationship before and gotten severely burned. And now I'm doing it all over again. I thought Theo was amazing and perfect. And sure, I think Liam is way better than him... but he can't be perfect. No one is. So what are his flaws? What's going to show up? And will it be something we can survive? Or am I going to give my heart to this guy only to be shocked by an ugly surprise I didn't see coming?

"Ray-Ray!" Mick waves her hand in front of my face. "Focus up, sweet thing. We've got two hours, and you know I'm not the world's best shopper. I need a new pair of jeans, and I want that to take like five minutes so we can then go hit up the mini golf course. It's at the north end of the mall."

Snatching my wrist, she pulls me into the heart of the mall, and it's like competing in *The Amazing Race* trying to find her a pair of jeans she likes. The longer it takes, the shittier she gets. I've been through this before, so I end up leaving her in the changing room and scouring the store myself, stacking options over my arm and delivering them until I finally hear a "Yes!"

"Let me see." I force her to model them, because she's not always the best judge when it comes to clothing. But she passes the test this time around. The jeans hug her butt perfectly, highlighting her gorgeous legs before tapering in just above the ankle.

"Hot." I nod.

"Perfect." She grins, unzipping the fly and stepping back into the changing room.

Once those are purchased, she's instantly in a better mood, and we head to the mini golf area, already hassling each other over who will win. Mikayla is stupidly competitive, but I've improved over the years, and now she really has to work hard to beat me. I love it when her face gets all scrunched up if I'm ahead of her.

"Should we stop for a quick sugar fix?" Mikayla veers left toward Shake Shack.

"Did all the shopping tire you out?" I tease her.

"You know it did." She winks at me, then laughs... and I'm about to join her. But the air in my lungs freezes.

Like ice-cold, *I can't imagine ever breathing again* freezes.

Because... no, this cannot be happening.

I can only see his profile right now, but I know it's him. I can tell by his height, his build, the arrogant smirk I can see on half his face.

*Shit. Shit. Shit!*

"Ray?" Mick spins when she notices I'm not right behind her. "What's up?"

"We have to go," I manage to rasp.

"What?" She looks over her shoulder, obviously hunting for what I'm gaping at.

"Don't turn, don't turn, don't turn." The words rattle out of me, and Mikayla thinks I must be talking about her, but I'm not.

I'm quietly begging Matt not to swivel this way.

What the hell is he even doing here?

We're hours away from Fontana.

Why is he here? Does he have family up here? I should have known that. I should have researched every aspect of his life before I stepped into that private jet.

How could I be so careless?

How could this be happening? Of all the freaking malls in California, he had to be in this one? It's like the universe is laughing at me, pointing its finger at my face and mocking me. *"You stupid girl. This will never be over for you."*

Oh fuck, he's turning.

"We have to go," I squeak, grabbing Mikayla's wrist, but not fast enough.

He spins, his face blank until his gaze hits mine.

Watching his eyes light with recognition is terrifying.

My breath hitches and I spin, yanking Mikayla through the mall.

"What is happening right now?" She picks up her pace when I break into a sprint. "Rachel!"

She's yelling at me, but I can't respond. We have to get out of here. We have to—

I steal a glance over my shoulder and a half gasp, half sob punches out of me.

"He's following us." My voice pitches, my arms flailing as I bolt down the stairs.

"What are we running from?"

"Him." I point over my shoulder but don't stop.

"Who is that?"

Spotting an exit sign, I surge toward it, slapping down the bar and bolting into a parking garage. We run past the rows of cars until I hear the door smashing open behind us.

"Get down." I pull my best friend between two cars and force her down beside me, trying to catch my breath.

"Rachel." She pinches my chin, making me look at her. "Who is that?"

"His name's Matt." My expression buckles. "And he's Theo's best friend."

Her lips part the way I knew they would, her expression murderous. "Is he the one who—"

I dip my chin, unwilling to look at her. I'm squeezing the life out of her hand, but thankfully she puts up with it, curling her fingers around mine as we crouch behind a blue SUV.

Probably dragging us into an isolated parking garage was a really dumb idea. I should have stayed in the mall where people were milling around. He wouldn't attack us in public, would he?

"Rachel!" His roar bounces off the concrete walls.

I flinch and whimper, resting my head against the car door and closing my eyes.

"You fucking thief! Where the hell are you?"

My swallow is thick, and I freak out that he can hear it.

"You better give that money back, you little bitch! Don't think for a second that we've forgotten about you!"

"What is he talking about?" Mikayla whispers, but it's too loud.

I press my finger to my lips, trying to shut her up, then lift my chin when I think I hear him coming.

He's searching between cars.

*Shit!*

"We have to go," I mouth.

Mikayla frowns but can obviously taste my fear. With a short nod, she turns, about to peek around the back of the SUV, when he suddenly appears.

I scream, lurching back as he makes a grab for me.

Mikayla pounces to her feet, shoving him back.

It's like watching a raccoon take on a bear. She pushes him with a grunt but barely moves him an inch. He goes to shove her out of the way while I scramble back on my ass, too terrified to do more than scream at him again.

Matt's massive hand wraps around Mikayla's short arm as he tries to throw her aside, but she lashes out with her fist, clipping him in the chin.

He grunts, then turns on her with wild eyes, his upper lip curling before he pulls her forward and slaps her across the face with the back of his hand. Her whimper is soft as she takes the blow, but it only seems to ignite her. With a feral yell, she goes after him again, trying to wrench her arm free of his grasp while kicking at his shins and lashing out at his face.

She's tiny but fierce, and I wish I had even an ounce of her courage.

Matt wrestles to push her away, finally gaining a bit of control and smashing her back against the car before raising his fist and landing a clean shot right across her cheek.

"No!" I scream as she crumples like a limp noodle.

Matt's head swings back toward me, and I feel like I'm facing the Terminator.

"Shit," I cry, jumping to my feet and running around the back of the car.

I can't leave Mick behind, but I can't let Matt touch me again. He's gonna kill me!

Scrambling into my purse, I dig out my phone, nearly fumbling it as I make a call I should have made the second I spotted Theo's asshole friend in the mall.

# CHAPTER 24
## LIAM

As soon as we dropped the girls off and programmed the rink's address into the car's nav system, Ethan started peppering me with questions.

"So, you and Ray, huh? How long's that been going on?"

I look out the window, not really wanting to answer him, but he won't let up.

So I give in with a soft sigh. "We kind of started making out a couple weeks ago, but we hadn't taken it further."

"No dates or anything?"

I wince and shake my head, feeling bad that I haven't done that yet. She deserves a nice date. I wonder what she's into. Fine dining with candlelight or burgers at a picnic table? I can imagine her enjoying both.

"Well, you guys sounded pretty happy to be together on Christmas Eve... and Christmas night... and come to think of it, last night—"

"Okay, okay, she's a screamer."

Ethan chuckles. "You know Casey will have a field day if she's that loud in Hockey House."

I cringe, hating the thought already, but the idea of not having her when we return is even worse, and I never want to inhibit her noisy behavior. I love that she lets me know what she likes. Not only is it affirming, but it's hot as hell. I never want her to stop crying my name or filling the room with her sexy-ass moans.

Shit, I'm getting hard just thinking about it.

"We'll find a workaround," I murmur. "We'll just have to take advantage of those times nobody's home."

Ethan sighs. "You know, Mick's been making noise about wanting to move out."

"What?" I bolt up in my seat. "Why?"

"Not 'cuz of us," he assures me. "We're good. She's just aware that this thing was supposed to be temporary."

"But we love having her."

"I know. Well..." He tips his head. "Not sure about Bax."

"He's leaving after graduation."

"That's still six months away, and... I think Mick kind of wants her own space a little, too, you know? She loves us, she does, but Hockey House can get busy, and as much as she will never admit this to me, she is a girl, and she misses her kind sometimes." He grins, but there's a sad edge to his smile.

"You're gonna miss her."

He huffs and shakes his head. "It's not like she's leaving me. She just wants to find a small apartment close by. A space to call her own. Find a female roommate to live with."

"Rachel." I sit up.

"That's what I was thinking." He nods. "Maybe we can help find them a good place, you know? Make it some-where close so we can still hang out easily. They can come for dinner all the time, and then it gives us a place to hang as well. You can have all the noisy sex you want, and no one's gonna hassle you about it." His grin grows wide and wolfish.

I shake my head, unable to help my laughter.

We reach the rink and try for a slot, but it's booked full. We hang on the sidelines for a while, watching a group of tweens do their best to act like hockey pros. We analyze their moves and point out the guys who look like they could go all the way. A few girls are skating, too, and I think the one with the long black hair has the most potential out of all of them.

"Look how fast she is." I point with a grin.

Ethan's nodding, his eyes glued to the rink like he's reliving a memory of years ago when we used to skate just like this.

"Good times," I murmur, and he nods, obviously pleased that I read his mind so accurately. We watch for a few more minutes before I glance at my watch. We've got over an hour to kill. "So, what do you want to do now?"

Ethan shrugs, and I'm about to throw out some suggestions when the phone in my pocket starts vibrating.

I spot Rachel's number and instantly smile. "Hey, pretty lady."

"Help. Help. Help!" she sobs.

My heart spasms for a second, and I jerk to a stop. I don't know what my face is doing, but Ethan quickly grabs the phone, putting it on speaker just as Rachel's yelling, "He hurt Mick and now he's after me."

"Who hurt her?" he barks.

I blink, trying to regulate the chaos in my chest. "Where are you?"

"P-Parking garage. We—" She screams, and I swear to God, that's the worst fucking sound in the world.

Her phone clatters, and I start sprinting. Ethan's right on my heels. He's still holding my phone and trying to call Rachel back.

"It's going straight to voicemail. Fuck!"

Shoving through the door, we haul ass into the sunlight and wrench the car doors open. The tires squeal as Ethan punches out of the parking space and spins the car back toward the mall.

The trip is a tense one. We can't talk. All Ethan can manage is a string of incomprehensible cursing while I sit there wondering who attacked them. My mind is an asshole, planting images in my head that are vile. I'm about ready to puke as I grip the dashboard, my body moving with the sway of the car as we take corners too fast and end up bolting into the parking garage.

"What level?" Ethan yells at me.

"I don't fucking know!" I bark back. "Just drive them all and keep your eyes open."

We find the girls on the third level.

Mikayla's sitting on the ground, leaning against a car tire and cradling her face while Rachel crouches beside her.

The second the car stops, she whips around, the fear so stark on her face, she looks like she's about to faint.

"Where is he?" Ethan slams out of the car. "Where the fuck is he?"

Rachel jumps up, running straight into my arms. I wrap her in a secure hug, cradling her head against my shoulder. Ethan crouches down beside Mick, obviously torn up when he eases her hands away and spots the egg on her cheekbone and blood coating her lips.

His expression is murderous, his chest heaving. He's obviously trying to rein it all in, but I'm worried he won't be able to.

"I'm fine," she mumbles.

"You're not fine! You're bleeding!"

"That asshole made me bite the inside of my cheek."

His expression buckles like the pain is his. "Look at your face." He brushes his thumb lightly over the egg.

She flinches and moves away from him.

"I'm gonna fucking kill him." He spins to glare at Rachel. "Who was that asshole?"

Rachel lets out a shuddering sob as she curls against me. I tighten my hold on her, firing Ethan a warning look, but Mikayla speaks for me.

"Stop yelling at her," she grumbles. "You're not helping."

He whips back to no doubt yell at his girl, but the wince of pain scrunching her expression shuts him up. Instead, he lets out an agonized sigh, his voice dropping to a feather-soft whisper. "I'm gonna pick you up, okay? Get you back to the resort."

She nods. The fact that she doesn't put up any kind of fight speaks volumes. No sarcastic quips. No biting remarks or calling him Captain Hero.

I can see how much this worries Ethan as he scoops

her into his arms and carries her to the car. "I've got you, lil' mouse." He brushes his lips across her forehead as she slumps against his chest.

"Come on," I whisper, guiding Rachel toward the car. I can sense I need to play this gently. She's a shaking mess, her body trembling against mine as I help her into the back seat and wrap my arm around her.

She snuggles up to me, whimpering softly as tears flow from her eyes.

"Did he hurt you?" I run my thumb across her cheek.

"He just pulled my hair." She sniffs, wiping her cheek against my new hockey jersey. "Mick stopped him, though. She stopped him."

I'm desperate to hear the rest of that story, but I can sense it's time to just let Ray and Mick feel the safety of this car. They can unpack the ordeal once we're back at the resort.

For now, Ethan and I share a dark look in the rearview mirror while we listen to our women recover after a fuckwit I am ready to end ruined our day.

# CHAPTER 25
## RACHEL

My tears have dried by the time we get back to the resort, but I'm still shaking. Matt's fingers fisting my hair runs through me on repeat, this torturous reel I can't shake from my mind. My scalp is burning, but I don't want to make a big deal of it because Mikayla's the one with an egg on her cheek and dried blood on the edges of her mouth.

She fought so hard for me.

And I just sat there like a fish out of water, squirming on the ground, useless.

I was useless.

She fought like a wildcat, and I froze up.

"Here we go." Liam takes my hand, helping me out of the car and treating me like cracked porcelain.

Pulling me to his side, he rubs my arm as if he's trying to warm me up. But I'm not cold. I'm just...

Shit. I don't know what I am.

"Mikayla?" Michael's voice pitches when we walk into the reception area. She's still in Ethan's arms, and the fact that she's not fighting this is making me feel sick. She hates coming across as weak or needy... and the only time she doesn't is when she's legit weak and in serious need of help.

Shit! I did that to her.

"What happened?" Her father rushes around the front desk, bolting to his daughter's side while I struggle to look at him.

Is he going to blame me for this?

He should.

Ethan mutters something that I don't hear, but it makes Michael's face go pale.

"Come with me." He orders us down a side corridor and into a private lounge, pulling out a first aid kit from the top cupboard and crouching in front of his daughter when she wilts onto the couch. "Do we need to take you to the hospital?"

"No." Mick shakes her head but winces.

"You might be concussed. How's your head? Is it pounding? What's your vision like?"

"Can you stop asking me so many questions, please?" Her words are kind of muffled as she obviously tries to talk around the cut inside her mouth.

"You think this is too many questions?" Michael's face bunches as he pulls out gauze and antiseptic cream. "Believe me, Mickey Blue. I have a ton more."

"What happened?" Emilia bursts into the room. "I just got a call from the front desk."

"We don't know the details yet." Michael pauses to look around the room, frowning at the guys before taking a look at me. His expression softens briefly, but then his forehead is wrinkling again and he's throwing all the attention back to his daughter. Softly dabbing her cheek, he hisses at the same time she does, sharing her pain like it's his own.

"Let me get an ice pack." Emilia winces when she takes a look at Mikayla's face. "Did someone punch you, honey?"

"Yes. Someone did." Ethan's voice is steely as he rests his hands on his hips and starts pacing.

Liam nudges me out of his path, leading me to a chair and pulling me onto his lap when my legs start to buckle.

A cold tension descends into the room while Michael dabs the blood off Mikayla's lips and Emilia fusses with the ice pack. I stay quiet, tucking my head into the crook of Liam's neck so I don't have to look at anyone.

I can hear Ethan's agitated footsteps as he prowls the room, huffing and radiating an angst so thick, it's hard not to be coated in it.

"Would you stop pacing?" Mikayla finally snaps.

I lift my head, happy to hear her getting her spark back.

Ethan jerks still, spinning around to glare at her. "I can't!" He throws his arms up. "Look at your face." His voice cracks. "I want to kill that fucker!"

"Get in line." She tips her head back, blinking up at the ceiling.

Emilia gently rests the ice pack on Mick's cheek, then steps back.

"Baby, c'mere." Mikayla flicks her fingers at Ethan. "Just... I need you to sit beside me. Please."

He slumps onto the couch with a huff, but his movements are tender as he lifts Mikayla into his lap and cradles her against him. Taking the ice pack off her, he holds it in place, looking miserable but at least calm.

I know she didn't say that for her benefit. Mick's not a super affectionate person. I mean, she sits on Ethan's knee and stuff, but she doesn't need cuddles the same way I do. What happened just now was Mick's way of trying to make her boyfriend feel better.

"I look like shit." She sighs. "But I'm gonna heal. It's seriously not as bad as it looks. I promise." Sitting up, she holds his face in her small hands and manages to get a minuscule smile out of him.

It's short-lived, but it's something.

The tension in the room starts to ease until Michael huffs, "Would someone please tell me what the hell is going on! Why is my daughter sitting on the couch looking like she's just competed in an MMA fight?"

I let out a shuddering sigh and cover my mouth.

Mikayla catches my eye, her sad frown telling me I can't say nothing.

Closing my eyes, I suck in a ragged breath and confess, "It was Matt."

"Who's Matt?" Michael barks while Liam goes instantly tense beneath me.

"He's friends with my ex," I murmur. "He..." My nostrils start to tingle as tears build in the back of my throat. "He beat me up once. And my ex let him." Talking is becoming hard work, but I push on, knowing I have to get this out. Mick's dad deserves an explanation. "I, um... I ran away. And..." My breath catches, and I stare across the room at Mick.

Her eyebrows buckle. My face must be showing just

how terrified I am to admit this, but doesn't she have a right to know?

"And I stole all their poker winnings." I can't look at anyone, so I dip my chin, staring at the carpet while the shame rides through me. "Three grand...ish. I just took it all. Grabbed it off the table and bolted out the door. That's why he's still so angry with me." I cover my eyes with shaking fingers. "I never wanted to see either of them again. I thought it'd be safe enough here. They live in Fontana, for fuck's sake." My arm flicks into the air. "But there he was. The second he saw me, I knew he was still so pissed. I had to run." A dry sob comes out of me, shaking my entire body. "I didn't mean for any of this to happen. I tried to hide her, I swear. I never wanted Mick to get hurt. I'm so sorry." The sobs are turning wet and real. "This is all my fault, and I'm sorry, Mick. I'm sorry."

"Oh shut up, Ray." Mick's crying now too. Jumping off Ethan's knee, she walks across the room and pulls me into a hug. "This is not your fault. I couldn't let him get you. I'll always fight for my girl. You know that." Pulling away from me, she brushes the tears off my face. "You don't have to apologize for anything."

"But you got hurt."

"I'll heal. Seriously, bodies heal. That's what they do." Her voice pitches as she turns to look around the room. "Everyone just needs to stop fussing and focus on the real issue here. Making sure that asswipe doesn't come anywhere near Ray again."

"You need to report him." Michael says the words quietly, but they're still heavy and awkward.

Especially when I have to follow it up with "I can't. Theo's dad is the chief of police in Fontana. His uncle's a defense attorney. All reporting them will do is stir up a hornet's nest. Plus, I... I stole that money. I'm a thief. I..."

"You're not a thief." Liam massages the back of my neck.

I spin to face him. "I am. That money wasn't mine, but I took it because I was pissed at the way they treated me. I wanted to punish them."

"And they deserved it."

"It still doesn't make it right," I mumble.

The room falls silent, and I don't know what to say.

Emilia clears her throat, and I glance at her as she shares a silent conversation with Michael. My parents used to do that. Before Dad died.

Dad.

My stomach shrinks just thinking about how he'd react to all of this. He'd be livid at Theo and Matt, but he'd also be disappointed in me. Sad that I took that money.

If he'd been alive, I wouldn't have.

I would have run straight to his house, knowing he'd protect me.

But he wasn't there, and I miss him so much right now. My body is aching, yearning for just another moment of his time and attention. Another Ty Beauford hug. They were always so perfect, full of comfort and warmth and security.

I cover my face with my hands, my legs buckling under the weight of my sorrow. Liam catches me against him, pulling me into a hug.

"So, where did that asshole go?" Ethan asks, his voice gruff. "How'd you scare him off?"

"Oh, well, that was easier than I thought it'd be."

Mick's voice perks up, and I peek between my fingers to watch her grin. "The second he grabbed Rachel's hair and tried to punch her, I rushed up behind him and kicked him right in the balls." She lifts her chin in pride. "That bag of ass didn't even see me coming. Crumpled like a rag doll and started whimpering. Had to cradle his junk as he staggered away." She laughs out the last few words.

"It was actually quite beautiful," I rasp. "You scared the hell out of him. His face just... I mean, I was kind of too in shock at the time to appreciate it, but... lil' mouse" —I smile at my bestie—"you're a fucking queen."

Emilia clears her throat, obviously not appreciating my language, while Mikayla starts to laugh. It's a quiet snicker at first but then turns into a loud burst of sound that's maybe tinged with a little crazy. Yeah, she's still in shock too.

We all are.

Because of me.

# CHAPTER 26
## LIAM

Rachel can't seem to stop crying, which is killing me.

Her tears are silent now, trickling down her cheeks while Mikayla laughs like a hyena. I share a worried frown with Ethan. He gives me a small nod, and as always, I'm grateful he can read my mind.

Sweeping Rachel into my arms, I murmur our good-byes and head toward the privacy of our suite. Ethan will be following shortly, but I just want to get Rachel somewhere safe and secure. I know that's what she's waiting for—a chance to really fall apart.

And it happens as soon as her bedroom door clicks shut. I lay her down on the bed, and her silent tears turn to gut-wrenching sobs.

It's torture watching her, but there's no way in hell I'm leaving.

Lying down beside her, I rest her head on my chest and hold her tight while she lets it all out.

She talks through her tears, words wobbling out of her in barely coherent spurts.

*"I just stood there while he hit her."*

*"Why couldn't I help her?"*

*"I was useless."*

I try to comfort her. "You called us. You did what you could to help."

"I should have done more," she whimpers. "Mick's face. That bruise on her cheek. It looks so painful."

Brushing my lips across her forehead, I run my fingers into her hair, noticing her flinch.

"You sore?" I lighten my touch as I investigate the back of her head.

"He pulled my hair pretty hard."

Rage rockets through me.

"It's just a bit tender." She tries to play it down.

I stop touching her scalp, forcing myself to bury my anger. She doesn't need to see it. She doesn't need to know how thick these vibrations are. They pound through my body—a medley of indignation and fury.

How dare that fucker touch her again.

How dare he hurt her. Scare her. Make her cry this way.

"I should never have taken that money." She rolls onto her side, turning her back to me.

I follow, wrapping my arm around her waist and spooning her. Kissing her shoulder, I murmur what I can to make her feel better.

"Those assholes don't deserve that money. You have nothing to be ashamed of."

"I'm a thief, Liam."

"Fuck that," I can't help snapping. She tenses, and I let out a soft sigh. "You're no thief. Not in my eyes. I don't give a fuck what that asshole called you. And I don't care what the law says either. Like they can even trace the money back to you. They have no way of proving you took it."

She goes quiet, the shudders in her body starting to slow as her sobs ebb.

"Where is the money?"

"Under your bed at Hockey House." She sniffs. "I've only used a bit of it. And I haven't touched it since getting that job at the diner. I never want to touch it again." She squeaks out the last few words, and I softly shush her before she starts crying again.

"It's okay. It's all gonna be okay." I kiss the back of her head. "I'm not gonna let anything bad happen to you."

I keep saying that promise until she drifts off to sleep in my arms.

Lying awake beside her, I try to relax but can't. My brain and body are humming. I need to get up, move, punch Matt in the face. Anything to expel whatever the hell is working through my chest right now.

Easing my arm out from under Rachel, I carefully get off the bed and sneak out the door.

I'm thinking of heading to the gym for a workout when I spot Ethan in the living area. He's slumped on the couch, nursing a beer and staring at the dancing flames in the fireplace.

"Hey." I take a seat on the adjacent couch, studying his deep frown and figuring he's wrestling with all the same emotions I am. They're dark and toxic. Shit, I feel like they're eating me alive.

"I don't know if I've ever legit wanted to kill someone..." Ethan sniffs, clenching his jaw before continuing.

211

"But if I ever see that Matt shithead, I can't say that I wouldn't try."

When he turns to look at me, his gaze is bright and intense. Shit. He means every word.

"I hear ya, man." I nod, feeling it with the same ferocity.

"That fucker hurt my girl," he growls.

"And she fought. She hurt him right back." I try to offer what comfort I can.

He snickers and nods, the edge of his mouth tipping up for a moment.

"How's she doing?" I ask.

"Monster headache. We've given her some painkillers, and now she's trying to sleep it off."

I nod.

"Ray?"

"Yeah, she's, uh..." I glance over my shoulder at her bedroom door. "She's cried herself to sleep." My smile is glum when I turn back to face him. "She's really cut up over how it all went down. Blames herself for everything."

Ethan's lips purse and twitch, and it makes me wonder if he blames her too.

I sit forward with a frown, ready to put him in his place.

"Don't look at me like that," he mutters. "I'm not holding her responsible. Sure, taking that money was stupid, but she already knows that."

I huff. "She deserved it after what they put her through."

"I know." He shrugs. "But it put a target on her back. Maybe if she'd just slipped out the door, then they could have let it go more easily. But she took their money, and now..." Ethan shakes his head as I let out a heavy sigh.

"I know." I lean back on the couch, stretching my arm along the back of it and staring at the flames. "But I'll protect her. I'm not gonna let her out of my sight."

Ethan snickers. "And how are you gonna do that?"

I whip back to scowl at him.

"What? It's a valid question and you know it." His eyebrows pull together. "You can't watch her twenty-four-seven. What, you gonna quit hockey and school to be her personal bodyguard?"

I hate that question. Clenching my jaw, I look away from him, my scowl deep and heavy as I glare at those orange flames. They dance like they don't know what went down today, partying away in the fireplace, oblivious to the ashy taste in my mouth and the venom spiking through me.

"You need to teach her how to defend herself. If this ever happens ag—"

"It *won't* happen again," I snap.

Ethan takes a breath. "*If* this ever happens again, she needs to learn how to throw a punch. Mick said Ray froze up. Maybe if she'd had more confidence, the two girls could have taken him out together."

"Fuck that!" I squirm in my seat. "I don't want her feeling that kind of fear again. I don't want her anywhere near that asshole."

"Obviously." He gives me a pointed look when I finally turn to face him. "But that doesn't change the facts. I'm guessing this Matt guy is not gonna let this go. And he'll tell her ex, and who the fuck knows how he'll react. Not to mention all the other sleazebags out there."

I growl in my throat, fisting my hand on the back of the couch.

"You can't always be there, man."

Throwing a glare in his direction does nothing. He meets it head-on, his eyebrow arching.

"Teach your woman how to defend herself. Give her the confidence to face whatever the fuck's gonna come her way. At least give her a fighting chance until you *can* get there."

"Mick can fight... and she still got hurt."

"Yeah, but it could have been so much worse. My little Black Widow left her mark." His eyes glitter with pride before he runs a hand through his hair. "Fuck, I hope his balls are aching for weeks."

Closing my eyes, I resist the urge to tell Ethan he's stupid and his idea is dumb. The very thought of Rachel throwing a punch doesn't compute with me. She's like a gentle lamb or something.

A gentle, terrified one.

Shit.

I hate that he might be right.

And I hate even more that I can't be there for her whenever she needs me.

My woman.

Ethan called her that, and it sits in my chest like a promise. The idea doesn't even scare me. Because she is mine, and I'll do everything in my power to protect her. I'll be her knight in shining armor. I'll be her tightest hug. I'll be a shoulder she can cry on.

But do I really want to be her coach?

I don't ever want her to have to defend herself like that. I want to do the punching for her.

But shit... what if I'm not there when Theo and Matt come after her again?

The idea makes me want to lock her up safe.

*Just the way Theo did?*

Thumping the couch with my fist, I bolt off the leather, mumbling that I'm taking a shower. I would normally go for a run, but I don't want Rachel waking up only to find me gone.

Because even if Ethan's right, the thought of leaving Rachel's side right now is killing me.

# CHAPTER 27
## RACHEL

I have no idea what time it is. The room is dark, the heavy black-out curtains making it impossible to know.

Liam's beside me.

We fell asleep spooning after a subdued meal. We ordered room service, and the four of us sat in numb silence, nibbling our club sandwiches and watching, but not really seeing, a movie. It was a sticky-sweet Christmas movie with zero violence and the cheesiest lines ever. But none of us could even muster the will to make fun of it.

I shuffled off to the shower, soaking under the hot spray before crawling into bed. Liam was already waiting for me, reading a book on his phone. I couldn't talk, so I just rolled onto my side and let him hold me.

His arms around me are bliss and comfort, warmth and security.

But how can I ask this of him?

I've known him long enough to understand that he's the kind of guy who would stand between me and whatever threat might be coming my way.

Ethan would too.

And Mick.

They're fierce warriors, and they'd fight my battles without me even having to ask.

But I can't expect that from them.

I need to get out of here. I need to return Theo's money and be done with it. I can't give him any more reasons to hunt me down. He can have every penny back with interest if that's what it takes.

Slipping out of the bed, I tiptoe into the living area in search of my phone. I think it's still in my bag from yesterday. I really don't want to do it, but maybe I can call Theo and we can sort this whole thing out. I'll offer to transfer the money into his account. I haven't quite earned enough to cover it, but I can deposit his cash, or I have Dad's investments I can draw off. I'm not supposed to touch those until I'm older, but scraping a couple grand away won't do any harm, and then I can be rid of Theo for good.

Rummaging around in my bag, I let out an irritated huff. My phone's not here. *Dammit. Where is it?*

Emptying out the entire contents onto the couch, I pick through my lip gloss, packet of tissues, wallet, and mound of old receipts. No phone.

Shit, I must have left it in the parking garage. When Matt grabbed me, I dropped it... and then forgot all about it.

I'm such an idiot sometimes.

Looking up to the ceiling, I shake my head.

*Seriously. What the hell does Liam even see in me?*

*Why is Mikayla even my friend?*

Yes, I'm very aware that I'm currently boarding the *I*

*Hate Rachel* train, but the door's sitting wide open. The whistle is blowing, and it's too easy to jump right on.

I've screwed up so royally, and they shouldn't have to put up with my shit.

I should go.

Just get out of here.

They can return to Nolan and get on with their lives trouble-free.

I don't know what the hell I'm gonna do, but I don't want to be a burden anymore. Maybe I should go down and hang with Mom.

*And take your problems down to her?*

With a heavy sigh, I gaze at the door.

The urge to walk through it and disappear is overwhelming. So I do it. I turn that handle and swing the door back. In nothing but my pajamas and bare feet, I start padding down the concrete walkway.

It's only just dawn, the sky barely light as the sun starts to rise over the hill behind the resort. Goose bumps ripple over my skin, the cold air making me shiver.

*You're being ridiculous.*

Logic tries to tap me on the shoulder, but I keep walking. I don't know what the hell I'm doing. All I can manage is one foot in front of the other.

I can see the outdoor pool coming into view. I'll walk around it, maybe head out the back to avoid reception and—

"Rachel." Liam's gruff morning voice jerks me to a stop.

My toes curl into the concrete. I can't turn and look at him, but my legs seem to have stopped working, so I just

219

stand there, listening to his feet running to catch up with me.

"Where are you going?" His hand trails down my arm, feather-soft and undemanding.

I dip my chin. "I don't know."

"Are you...?" He takes my face in his hands, lifting my chin so he can look at me. "Are you sleepwalking or something?"

"No," I squeak, trying to avoid his gaze. "I just needed to go."

"Go where?"

"Away," I whisper, my voice catching as I suck in a shaky breath.

My gaze skims his face, and I catch a flash of his confusion before I'm staring at the ground. My long feet look so skinny next to his broad ones. They're large and stable on the pathway, like strong tree roots that can't be moved. I want to lean against him, cling to his solid torso and never let go.

But that's not fair.

I can't keep relying on others all the time. I can't keep burdening them with my crap.

"Ray." His soft voice curls through me. I love the way he says my name. He holds it like a precious gift. "What do you mean?"

My jaw quivers as I try to explain in a way he'll understand. "It's not fair."

His hands cradle my neck, his thumbs skimming my jawline as he gives me a minute to explain.

But I don't want to explain. I just want to go.

*Except you don't!*

I close my eyes. "I can't burden you guys with this. I

need to go and let you be, and you can go back to Nolan trouble-free."

"What?" His shock has my eyes popping open. He gapes at me like I've lost my mind. "You think leaving me will make my life trouble-free?"

I swallow.

"*Cariña*, that's not true." He kisses my lips, a soft peck before crouching just a little so we can be eye to eye. "I would miss you. I would... *ache* for you."

The air in my lungs goes still.

"Can't you already tell?" His brown eyes shine in the dim light, a smile forming inside them. "I told you... you were gonna burrow. And you've burrowed deep, *mi amor*. You can't go leaving me now. You'll break my heart."

Tears pop onto my lashes before I can stop them. "But what if they try to find me? What if they hurt you trying to get to me?"

His eyes flash with something dangerous, his expression turning hard. "They can try, but they will fail. I will always stand between you and them. I'm your wall, Ray. I'm your rock."

"I don't want you to have to do that for me. I don't want you getting hurt. I don't want anyone getting hurt because of me." I wriggle out of his grasp, putting a few paces between us. "All you'll do is worry about me."

"And you don't think I won't if you're not around?" He stretches his arm, pointing behind him. "You're walking out here wearing practically nothing. You're shivering. You have no plan. And you're expecting me not to worry about you."

I sniff, wiping my nose with the back of my trembling finger. "I don't know what to do, okay? I just..." I shake my head, crossing my arms and trying to stop the shivers from working through my entire body. "I want to rid myself of Theo and this fear and this feeling like I'm useless. Like everyone has to fight my battles for me because I'm not strong enough to do anything. Why would you want to be with someone like that? I'm doing you a favor by leaving."

I close my eyes, not wanting to look at him.

For a second, all that exists is our breathing, my quaking puffs next to his heavy exhales. My heart is thundering, and part of me is expecting to hear a soft "You're right" just before he walks away.

But then he draws near. His breath brushes the side of my cheek as his strong arms wrap around me.

"You are stronger than you think," he whispers into my hair. "You left him. You stole his money, and you walked out that door. That makes you strong."

I'm about to argue that it also makes me a thief, but he keeps talking before I can.

"And I want to be with you because you're kind and you have a beautiful soul. You're gentle and sweet, and I love that about you."

"Gentle and sweet can get my ass kicked."

"So find your inner boss bitch," he counters.

I pull back, gazing up at his face. He's so confident and sure, and I'm just... "What if I don't have one?"

"You do." He grins, his eyes sparkling in the early-morning light. "And I'm gonna help you find her." His lips purse as he looks away from me. But then he lets out this dry laugh and shakes his head. "Shit, I didn't want to, but... I'm gonna teach you how to fight. Throw a punch, kick some ass. Defend yourself."

My chest flutters, a sensation I don't recognize whistling through me.

"You can do that?" *Why am I fighting a smile?*

"Yeah." The look on his face tells me it's not bullshit. I can believe him. Trust him.

That flutter in my chest gets a little stronger. I don't know what it is, but I like it. And so my smile grows.

Liam brushes his nose across mine. "So... you gonna stay?"

"Yeah." I breathe the word against his skin.

"Can I take you back to bed now?"

My lips quirk. "Yeah. As long as you promise that we won't be sleeping."

"Oh, I can definitely promise you that." He scoops me into his arms with a growl.

A squeal punches out of me as he starts running. I wrap my legs around his waist, laughing as I cling to his shirt, which I strip off as soon as the door clicks shut behind us.

Throwing me onto the bed, he pulls at my pajama pants, yanking them off my feet while I make quick work of his boxers. Our kisses are fast and ravenous, my wet core aching for him as he sucks my nipple into his mouth, then paints pictures on my skin with his tongue. His fingers circle my clit until I'm a panting mess on the bed.

I reach for his rock-hard shaft, but he stops me, pinning my arms above my head.

"You're close, *cariña*."

"Yes," I gasp.

"Tell me when," he murmurs against my mouth, still

teasing my clit while an energy made of light and fire expands throughout my body.

I cry out, the start of the build taking over. Light spreads from my core and down my limbs as I curl my fingers around his hand. He squeezes my wrists, sucking the tip of my earlobe between his lips as I groan, "Now. Now, now, now!"

And then just as the orgasm starts to rocket through me, he plunges inside me.

It's impossible to keep my scream in check. The noise coming out of me is all pleasure as I ride this orgasmic wave with him pumping inside me—sure, slick moves that set a heady rhythm I can barely comprehend.

As soon as the orgasm fades, a new one starts to build, his thick shaft working magic as it pumps and pleasures. It's intense and—

"Oh shit, I forgot to suit up," he groans.

"It's okay, I—"

He whips out of me, and we whine at the agony of pulling apart so abruptly. If his body is anything like mine, it's humming with an unquenched desire that makes me feel like I'll combust if it doesn't get met.

I should tell him I'm on the pill, that it's probably safe enough, but he's already launching off the bed, scrambling around in the bathroom, knocking things over in his haste. He returns moments later, his dick properly dressed.

Kneeling between my spread legs, he rests his hands on my knees. "What do you want, Ray?"

The question always makes me shy, but I smile, willing myself to tell him. "I want you inside me again."

"Yeah?" His hands trail up my legs and over my naked

torso. They round my breasts, massaging them while my nipples sing in ecstasy. "Anything else?"

My heart starts to dance. "I want you to hold my wrists."

He grins. "You like that, huh?"

Trailing his fingers down my arms, he curls them around my wrists and lifts them over my head. Our breaths mingle together as he stares into my eyes and slowly, exquisitely slides back inside me.

I can't take my eyes off his heated gaze as he starts to move, slow at first. Almost painfully slow. In, then nearly all the way out, then all the way in. My breaths turn shaky, my lips parting as he stares into my eyes with an intensity that's so incredibly beautiful. I've never felt more seen... and I've never felt more vulnerable either.

Closing my eyes, I tip my head back with a sweet gasp. His lips hit my chin, sucking the end of it as he plunges even deeper still. His pace starts to increase, his breaths growing ragged. As his fingers thread between mine, he pumps even harder and we cling to each other, rising on this glorious wave together.

I come first, my cries euphoric as he hits my G-spot and sends my body into sweet chaos. Then he's crying out, too, an uncontrolled sound that makes me feel like the queen of sex as his body shudders, jerking into me with two hard thrusts. His muscles strain as he buries himself deep—a heady satisfaction that I never want to get used to.

He fills me in ways so mind-blowing that I can't even put it into words.

So I tell him with a kiss instead. The second he releases my hands, I thread my fingers into his hair and pull him on top of me, sucking his tongue into my mouth and pouring everything I'm feeling for him into this moment.

His body covering mine is pure bliss.

And I never want to even think about walking away from him again.

# CHAPTER 28
## LIAM

The rest of our California vacay is on the sedate side. We chill at the resort, Rachel not wanting to venture out past those thick gates. Ethan and I play a round of golf while the girls get some much-needed TLC at the hotel spa. We play board games and sports with Mick's stepsiblings, gorge ourselves on too much delicious food, and end up leaving relaxed yet unsettled.

Mr. Hyde arranges his father-in-law's jet for us again, and we go for an early-morning flight rather than waiting for the evening like we'd originally planned. There's not the same excitement as we fly home in the lap of luxury. On the way to Cali, it was all buzz and laughter; this trip is quiet and broody. Mick, with a baseball cap low on her head, is curled up against Ethan, not saying much as she stares out the window. I do the same, playing with the ends of Rachel's hair as she reads a book.

Ethan drives us back to Hockey House. The snow has piled up, and our driveway needs digging out. Rachel's car is practically buried. I can just see the back corner of it. I frown at the deep white mess while Ethan parks along the curb with a growl.

Traipsing through the thick snow, we finally reach the door, out of breath and irritated. The TV is blaring with gunfire, and when we open the door, Casey starts yelling, "On your left! Your left!" He laughs. "Nice save, Warrior Chicken. Now cover my ass while I make a run for the door."

We dump our bags in the entrance and walk into the living area, Rachel's mouth dropping open as she takes in the carnage.

Casey's still oblivious, shouting into his headset, while my eyes slowly scan the piles of dirty dishes on the dining table, the take-out trash covering the floor like confetti, and the wafting odor of burnt coffee and I don't know what the hell else.

Baxter's head appears as he strolls in from the pool room. Jolting to a stop, he blinks, then points at us like he's confused. "Aren't you due back tomorrow?"

"No, you jackass," Ethan snaps. "It was always today. And what the fuck?" He spreads his arms wide, indicating the mess. "Asher's gonna lose his shit."

"Asher's not due back until Sunday."

"Which is tomorrow, dumbass," I snap, backing Ethan up.

"Yes! Trojan boys for the win!" Casey pumps his fist in air. "Let's go, McFrognuts. Up to the castle for—"

A cushion smacks him in the back of the head.

Spinning around with a surprised blink, he takes us all in for a second before his mouth stretches into a wide grin. "King Puck out," he murmurs into his headset before ripping it off and jumping over the back of the couch. "Hey, family! Welcome home." Spreading his arms wide, he goes in for a hug, but Mick stops him with two raised hands.

"Don't even think about it, you gross pig. This place is disgusting!"

"Oh." He jerks back, scratching his mussed-up curls while he looks around. "Oh, yeah. We had a bit of a kegger the other night and... well, you know we're gonna clean."

"When?" she barks.

"Oh, well..." He looks to Baxter, a silent plea for backup, but the goalie just shrugs. "When you guys got back?"

Mikayla's hands ball into two little fists, her nostrils flaring. "You were waiting until we got here so we'd do all the work for you!"

"No." Casey and Baxter shake their heads in unison. "But you're welcome to help." Casey winks down at the feisty little mouse. She growls, ripping off her baseball cap and glaring up at him.

His mischievous grin disappears the second he gets a look at her face. "What happened to you?"

"I'm not in the mood to tell you right now, you foul slob."

"Lil' mouse, you can't come in here with a shiner and not spill the tea. Come on, girl, you're—"

"No, Queen Pissed Off out!" She whips around to Rachel. "Come on, we're out of here."

"Okay." Rachel glances at me with a helpless shrug.

I give her a quick kiss. "It's good. You go. We'll make sure this place is spotless by the time you get back."

"Why are you kissing her?" Casey's asking. "Why is he kissing her? What the hell happened in Cali, you guys?"

I ignore all his questions until Rachel and Mick have walked out the door. Gazing through the kitchen window, I watch them clomp through the snow and wait until they're safely in Ethan's truck before spinning to face the argument erupting between Baxter and Ethan.

"Before the girls came along, you didn't give a shit." Baxter throws up his arms.

"That's total crap," Ethan barks back. "I never would have been happy walking into this. It's next level. No wonder the girls don't want to stay here!"

"They don't?" Casey looks crestfallen, his shoulders slumping as he tries to catch up on all the news.

Ethan's tone softens, turning into a mix of grunts and grumbles while he reminds them how this situation was always supposed to be temporary and maybe finding an apartment nearby for Rachel and Mikayla is the right move.

This puts Casey in a foul mood, and the next two hours is organized chaos as we clean and tidy this dump site. The time is peppered with arguments, outbursts, and the occasional story from Casey about the quality of the puck bunnies and how there were so many more to go around without us here. Even Baxter grinned at that. I think the shy goalie actually got some. Good for him.

When the girls return, the place is close to spotless.

Casey wraps Mick in the longest hug. She endures it like a pro, slapping him on the back and comforting *him* while he laments what happened to her. The hissy fit he had when Ethan told him about it has faded from his system, and he's simmered down to a low boil.

Rachel gives me a sweet smile as she helps me dry the last of the dishes and put them away.

"You guys have worked hard." Her nose wrinkles. "You shouldn't have had to do any of it."

"Yeah." I nod. "But sometimes it's easier just to pitch in." Tucking the hair behind her ear, I lean against the counter and grin at her. "Did you guys have a good time?"

She nods. "We just went to the diner and shared a slice of pie. Talked... a lot."

"Good stuff?"

Her shoulder hitches. "Trying to figure out what I'm going to do."

"Oh yeah?" My heart hitches, my fingers curling around the countertop as I brace for whatever she has to say.

"Don't worry." She grins, leaning forward to peck my lips. "I'm not going anywhere."

Relief washes through me, but I'm still kind of tense because her smile is fading fast.

"I need to give that money back to Theo, though. And I'm just trying to work out a safe way to do that. I don't want to give my location away or leave any kind of digital trail."

"Why do you have to give it back?" I take her hands in mine. "Just keep it. Use it."

"I can't." She shakes her head. "It makes me feel gross even having it. I want to rid him from my life completely. And as long as I don't return that money, he still has a hold on me, you know?"

Her eyes are so green right now. Shining emeralds, sparkling under the kitchen lights.

"Okay." I pull her against me. "We'll figure out a safe

way to do it."

"Thank you."

"Any talk about you looking for a place together?" I murmur against her neck. "Mick looked pretty riled when she left."

"Yeah, she's keen. I just..." She pulls back, putting on a smile.

"You just what?"

She swallows and shakes her head. "Nothing."

I want to ask for more, but she pulls away, walking out of the kitchen and straight into Casey's arms.

She kind of jolts as he wraps her in a hug.

"Your ex and his friends are fucking assholes." He rubs her back.

"Uh..." She pats his shoulder. "That's true."

Casey pulls away, his face the picture of sincerity. "If that fuckface ever gives you trouble again, you call me, okay? Any of the Cougars will be there for you in a heart-beat. You got that?"

She nods.

"I've gotta hear you say it, kid. *Them Cougars got my back.*"

"Um." She lets out a soft giggle. "Them Cougars got my back."

"Now shout it."

"Them Cougars got my back."

"Shout, sweetie, shout. I want to hear you roar that shit."

"Them Cougars got my back!" She screams the words and gets a hearty "Puck yeah!" in return.

I stifle a laugh, watching my woman go bright red and loving my bros for taking such good care of her.

# CHAPTER 29
## RACHEL

So, Mikayla did talk incessantly about finding a place while we were sharing pie at the diner. I nodded and softly agreed, but I'm really not sure if that's what I want to do. Hockey House was a pigsty when we returned, and yes, I get that living with boys can be super gross... but there's a safety to it, you know?

The house is filled with big, muscly guys who will defend me at the drop of a hat. Do I really want to leave that?

Liam's no longer sleeping on Asher's jacking-off couch, so I don't feel bad about that anymore. In fact, he slept in his own bed last night. With me. And that was divine.

I'm not sure I want to leave.

*Great, so you're gonna do exactly what you said you wouldn't. Fall hard and fast for a guy, then move in with him after mere weeks.*

Shit. I don't want to think about the fact that I'm repeating history.

Taking a tray of used dishes from the diner and through to the kitchen, I dump it down for the dishwasher and manage to give him a distracted smile. I think he says something to me but I'm not sure what, and I rudely ignore him as I head back out to do a final coffee round before finishing my shift for the day.

Liam's picking me up. Just the thought of that is a huge comfort, and... Crap, I'm totally relying on him. I'm acting the exact same way I did with Theo. Making my every thought and breath revolve around this new man in my life.

But Liam's different. He's nothing like Theo. Relying on him is a safe bet. And his friends are amazing and protective too. I know Mikayla's looking for a roomie, and getting an apartment together makes sense in so many ways, but...

I don't know if I can handle living without Liam.

Ugh. Does that make me pathetic?

The question circles my brain as I refill coffee mugs and try to be the polite, attentive waitress I'm supposed to be. I'm pretty sure I'm failing, and it's with a huge sense of relief that I return the coffeepot to the burner and head for the break room.

"Evening, Ray," the night manager greets me as I gather my things to leave. "How'd the afternoon go?"

"Yeah, pretty good. No drama. They're at the tail end of the dinner rush now."

"Got it." Her salt-and-pepper curls bob as she ties on her apron. "You have a good night."

"Thanks. You too."

Pulling on my coat, I feel that rush of anticipation, knowing Liam will be out there in Ethan's truck, waiting to take me back to Hockey House where I'll be safe and warm.

And that doesn't make me pathetic. Wanting to feel safe is a good thing. And there's nothing wrong with needing someone... is there?

But when I step out of the diner and don't see him, the fear that clutches my belly is so intense, I nearly buckle. I should wait inside. My heart hammers as I walk backward and end up bumping into the wall. My gaze darts to the snowy street as shadows quickly turn into lurking creeps and the laughter echoing around the corner sounds high-pitched and manic. My vision goes wonky as I fight the sensation of stepping into my own horror movie.

A car horn blasts, making me flinch.

I whip around, ready to flee back inside when I spot Ethan's truck pulling up.

"Hola, bella." Liam grins at me through the open window.

"Hey." I wave, trying to catch my breath as I jump up into the truck.

"Sorry I'm late. Practice went a little over tonight."

"No problem." I smile, desperate to hide the mini meltdown I was experiencing just before he pulled up.

Gunning away from the diner, Liam heads to the intersection and turns left instead of right.

"Where are we going?" I point out the window. "Hockey House is back that way."

"I know." He grins. "But I promised you we were going to work on some self-defense moves, and I figured we could start tonight."

"Self-defense." I nod, trying to look more confident than I feel.

This is good. I do need to learn how to throw a punch. Whether I feel capable of doing that is beside the point. The least I can do is learn, right?

Nerves skitter through me as we drive the darkened streets, then pull into an empty parking lot.

"This gym belongs to Hank. I work here when it's not hockey season."

"But it's all closed up right now." I throw a dubious glance out the window.

"Yeah, Hank closes up early three nights a week for family time. I've got a key, though, and he's already given me permission to use it tonight. We just have to lock up and alarm the place when we leave."

I swallow, slipping out of the car and following Liam.

The gym is a big, airy space. The lights clunk on, and the ominous mass of black becomes an invite to get fit and live your best life. Behind the counter is a basic gym with all the typical gear you expect to see—treadmills and weight machines, a wall of mirrors lined with free weights and bands. On the other side is a boxing ring, and behind that are a bunch of bags hanging from the ceiling.

This place must be humming when it's open.

"Come on." Liam takes my hand, pulling me toward the ring.

Unlocking a cupboard against the wall, he pulls out some gloves.

"Take off your coat and boots."

I do as I'm told, nerves making it hard to function properly. I'm seriously not sure if I can do this. Ugh. Liam will work out that I was always picked last in gym class soon enough. I'm the gangly kid who dropped the ball or fumbled the pass. I was the slowest kid at any running event, puffing over the line red-faced and ready to pass out.

"Here we go." Liam lifts the cords around the ring so I can crawl under.

Standing up in the middle, I brush my hands along the back of my leggings. My palms are sweaty.

"Okay." He walks into the middle of the ring. Having shed his outer layers, he's now standing there in sweats and a loose tank that hides nothing. His rippled muscles move beneath the fabric, and he looks sexy as all get-out. How the hell am I supposed to concentrate on anything he's saying to me?

"Let me see those fists of yours." He takes my hand, curling them into a fist and showing me where my thumb should be sitting before demonstrating a few basic moves.

I follow his instructions, punching through my body, twisting the way he was, relishing his praise when he tells me I'm doing good.

"That's it." He smiles. "So, if I was coming at you like this..." He slowly does the move, and I throw up my arm to block him.

"Yes, that's it. But strong, okay? Don't be hesitant. I might be stronger than you, but with the right technique, you can bring me down."

I'm boosted by that, so I give my next few moves a little more effort. It pays off, my confidence starting to build as we work up a sweat.

He takes me through blocking, how to get out of a

hold, what to do if someone attacks me from behind. I even manage to flip Liam over my shoulder.

Landing on his back with a thud, he lets out a soft "Oof" while I stand over him with a gaping mouth.

"Holy shit, did I just do that?"

"Yes, you did, *cariña*."

"Oh my gosh!" I squeal, jumping on the spot with a surprised laugh before straddling his waist. "I just threw you—Mr. Muscles—over my shoulder!"

He laughs along with me, the sound rich and delicious. Throwing my head back in triumph, I lift my arms and whoop. I seriously can't get over how good this feels. I did it. I fucking did it!

"We'll keep practicing until you feel totally confident with all this stuff." Liam rests his hands on my thighs, smiling up at me. "You're a sweaty mess, Miss Beauford. I kinda like it."

I grin down at him. "You like making me sweaty?"

His eyes heat with a look that makes my insides sizzle.

Poking my tongue out the side of my mouth, I join him in the eye sex we're currently having, my V-jay getting instantly wet. I'm so turned on right now I can barely see straight. Is it the empowerment of throwing a punch and flipping a large human over my shoulder? Or is it the fact that Liam is the sexiest man on this planet?

"Careful." His husky voice warns me.

"Of what?"

"That tongue."

"My tongue?" I tip my head, my eyes glinting as I lean over him.

"I know just what I want to do with it."

The constant ember in my belly—the one marked Liam—ignites and sends tendrils of pleasure racing down my legs as I softly glide the tip of my tongue over his bottom lip, then whisper, "Show me."

# CHAPTER 30
## LIAM

She doesn't need to ask me twice.

Cupping the back of her head, I pull her down and deepen the kiss, wanting to bury my tongue inside her... along with other parts of my anatomy.

She groans, slashing her tongue against mine with the same fervor.

Rolling over, I pin her to the floor, lifting her arms above her head and trailing the tip of my tongue along her salty skin. Finding a spot near her collarbone, I start to suck her soft skin. It's gonna leave a hickey, so the world can know she's mine.

A gasp escapes her mouth, her hips jutting against my already-pulsing dick.

"You're so hot," I murmur, trailing my lips over her jawline and pulling her luscious tongue back into my mouth.

I want to take her right here, but the thought that I'm not the only person with a key to this gym stops me.

Popping up to my feet, I ignore her whine of complaint, grabbing her hand and pulling her out of the ring.

Picking up my pace, I run us into the locker room. We stumble through the darkness, still making out like horny teenagers, until the automatic lights buzz and flick on. When we reach one of the shower stalls, I slam it shut and flick the lock, then turn on the spray while Rachel's tongue licks the sweat from my skin. Turning with a grin, I start stripping the sticky clothes off her body.

I drop to my knees and tug at her leggings. They're clinging to her skin, and I wrench them off, urgency pounding through me. I've never felt this kind of desire. She's all-consuming. Yanking them off her feet, I press her back against the cold tiles and lick my way up to her panty line. She's murmuring her consent, begging me to touch her.

The shower is heating up, the warm spray pounding my shoulders as I grip her delicate panties with my teeth and tear them away from her skin.

She lets out a surprised gasp, then stares down at me with wide eyes. When her teeth sink into her bottom lip with a heated, sexy grin, I nearly blow on the spot. She's so fucking beautiful.

Reaching up, I cup her breasts until she moans, then pinch her nipples, loving the way her fingers plunge into my hair. I'm still on my knees, water streaming over me as I lift her knee and dive for her pussy. Her heel hits my back when she drapes her leg over my shoulder. I grip her ass, sucking her clit until her moans create a symphony. The acoustics in this shower stall are comparable to Carnegie Hall, and her cries of ecstasy are fucking music to my ears.

I plunge two fingers inside her, marveling at her hot, wet core.

"Yes!" She's coming, her limbs quaking as an orgasm rocks her so hard, she nearly loses her footing.

I hold her steady, rising to my feet and supporting her against the wall. I kiss the last of her fading moans from her mouth, then whisper against her skin.

"Tell me what you want, Ray."

She tips her head back, her chest still heaving as she slowly comes down from her high. "I want..." She groans.

"Say it. I'll do whatever you want, *chica*."

She groans again, panting against my cheek as she grips the back of my neck. "I want you to fuck me hard and fast."

I grin, loving her abandon. The searing look she gives me when I check to make sure sets me on fire. With a wolfish growl, I spin her around, planting her hands on the wall before grabbing her ass. She tips forward, thrusting her butt into the shower spray.

"Fuck, I don't have a rubber."

"Don't worry. I'm on the pill anyway."

"You sure?"

She peeks over her shoulder at me, her lips rising into the sexiest smile I've ever seen. "You gonna give me what I want?"

"Fuck yeah." I grin, lining myself up and plunging into her.

"Oh!" The perfect sound pops out of her mouth, and fuck, I am in heaven right now.

Her hot, wet oasis has me pumping like my life depends on it. The hot water rains over us as my fingers dig into her soft skin. She leans her head against the wall and takes each pounding thrust with cries of glee. A new song starts between us, our skin slapping together as I take her just the way she wants me to. Her ecstasy spurs me on, and I can feel myself coming apart in record time.

The sensations coursing through me are hotter and more intense than anything I've ever experienced. I'm blinded by the orgasm that takes me out, releasing a strangled cry when I explode inside her. Slapping my hands over hers on the wall, I clench my butt, going as deep as I possibly can.

She moans, but it's not her usual scream that I love so much. My job here isn't done. Staying deep, I pinch one of her nipples, rolling it between my fingers while finding her clit with my other hand.

"No, Liam, it's too much." She starts to tremble, then groans, "You feel too good."

"I'll stop if you want me to." I tease her, lightly scraping my teeth over her shoulder, then nibbling her skin with my lips.

"No," she moans. "Don't stop. Don't..." Her voice is swallowed up by panting moans that quickly give way to a lusty scream.

Her inner walls contract around me, sending a new wave of luscious pleasure firing back through my body. My dick wants to stay inside her for decades. I can't fucking move, so we just stand there together, shuddering and panting in unison while hot water rains over us.

I've never come inside a woman before. Not without a shield in place. When I'm finally ready, I pull out of her and our juices flow together, trickling down her inner thigh. The shower quickly cleans it away, but it's the sexiest thing I've ever seen.

Gently turning her around, I then soap up my hands and wash my woman from head to toe.

"My woman." I kiss her lips with a smile, our slippery bodies moving together as we slow dance in the shower stall. "My sexy boss bitch."

# CHAPTER 31
## RACHEL

His sexy boss bitch. Well, that's a title I could get used to.

I'm not sure I'm quite there yet, but oh man, I want to be. Ordering him to fuck me hard and fast made my insides flush with humiliation, but then he grinned and spun me around. I've never been taken that way before, and holy hotness, it was fucking amazing.

So, if that's what being a boss bitch gets me, I'll take it. All of it.

The phrase seems to drive me in a way I didn't think was possible. It has me getting up at the same time as Liam every morning and doing a workout downstairs in front of the TV while the guys all troop off to the hockey arena gym. I work up a Zumba sweat, then head to the diner if I'm on the morning shift or do stuff around the house. I'm on my feet all day, yet still find the energy to head out for a late-night training session at the boxing gym.

It's been nearly two weeks, and I know this sounds ridiculous, but I swear I'm already stronger. I know I have hours of more work to do. I know I have a thousand more punches to throw and body flips to pull off, but even what I've done so far is addictive.

Liam makes it addictive.

He wants me to succeed.

He praises my efforts, my style, my determination. And he seems to genuinely mean it.

I've never felt so empowered. I even took on Asher the other day. He's fast, and I know he was going easy on me, but it made me feel pretty awesome that I could spar with him and not completely embarrass myself. He even told me I was pretty good at the end of our session.

The Nolan U Cougars are quickly growing on me. There's something kind of charming about each of them. Even though I don't love the way they treat women and relationships so casually, it's hard not to fall for their sexy winks and cute smiles. They laugh loud and live big. It makes me want to stay at Hockey House, but Mick has already started looking for apartments, and I know I need to be on board with that.

Living with her will be awesome.

We've always wanted to be roommates, and it would be nice to have a little space, although I'm going to miss Liam in my bed.

*"He can sleep over. Ethan's planning to."*

Mikayla's arguments are always so sound and confident. And it's not like I can admit that the thought of not living right beside Liam scares me. She doesn't think it's healthy to *need* someone. And she's probably right. I should *want* Liam, not be fueled by this desperation to be near him. Even though he's teaching me how to kick ass, that doesn't always dull the fear when he's not around.

Sometimes I get this sense like someone is watching me, you know? It's just old demons lurking in the shadows, trying to torment me. Logically I know this, but it spurs me to work harder at the gym, and it makes me want to be with Liam any chance I can get. Not only do I love his company, but he makes me feel secure.

Shit. I really do *need* him.

"Here we go." Mick pulls me down beside her, and I gaze around the overflowing stadium. It's the Cougars' first home game back after the winter break, and the crowd is electric.

"Hey, hockey buddy!" A friendly redhead gives Mick a quick high five before landing her bright blue gaze on me.

"Hi." I wave, my long fingers tinkling in the air.

"Hello." She kind of sings the word. She's so chipper, her smile so wide, her eyes so big and dazzling, it's like watching a real-life cartoon character. "I'm Caroline. I don't know if Mikayla's told you about me, but I'm the hockey nut who talks her ear off during most of the games. It's a miracle she still sits next to me, really." She laughs, a tuneful sound that matches her voice.

"It's nice to meet you. I'm Rachel."

"Yeah, I know." She grins. "Mick told me you're staying with her at Hockey House." She tips her head back, her red curls spilling over her shoulders. "You guys are so freaking lucky! Hockey House!" Her blue eyes bulge. "You get to hang with these guys all the time. I have to be jelly. There's no other option. What I wouldn't give to just walk in the door and meet these guys."

"You should." Mikayla shrugs, keeping her eyes on the ice.

"Yeah, right!" Caroline snorts and shakes her head.

Mikayla shares a quick look with me before giving her a dry smirk. "They're not gods, you know. They're messy and loud, and they stink sometimes. Like seriously. I had no idea smells that bad could come out of a human being."

I suppress a giggle behind my fingers.

"And Casey is the worst, by the way. I don't know if it's the green stuff he puts in his shakes or the stupid amount of bacon he eats, but that guy has got odors that are next level."

A loud laugh bursts out of me because it's true. I had the misfortune of waltzing into the bathroom after him the other day, and I swear my eyes started watering. My gag reflex kicked in, and even lighting a candle and dousing the room with air freshener didn't clear the evil stench. Asher was nice enough to let me shower in his en suite that day.

For a six-bedroom house, it seriously lacks bathrooms. I would have added at least another full one downstairs and not just an extra toilet.

"So he stinks. That doesn't change the fact that he's sexy as all get-out and still my favorite player on the team. You know he scored a—" Her fact is cut off by a loud cheer as she jumps to her feet and starts applauding the boys. They skate onto the ice, looking focused and fired up for a good game.

I stand beside Mikayla, clapping and looking for Liam.

It doesn't take long to find his number, and I can't help a buzz of electricity. *There he is! My man!*

I haven't made it to a game yet, so I'm both excited

and nervous to watch him play. I know he's part of the defense and that's about it. Sports isn't really my thing. I don't mind watching a little Olympics or something—usually gymnastics or, if it's winter, the figure skating—but that's about as far as I'll go.

The game begins, and it's a frenzied display of skates cutting through ice, sticks firing every which way, and men moving like bees as they whip and swerve around each other.

Liam gets slammed against the plexiglass, and I gasp.

"He's okay." Mick pats my thigh. "He's all padded up."

"But shouldn't that be a foul or something? That guy just totally pushed him."

"It's all part of the game, Ray-Ray." She turns with a twinkle in her eye, leaning in and whisper-shouting over the noise of the crowd. "If you like, we can swap and Caroline can chew your ear off. She's an expert in this game. That's how I learned all about it."

"Uh..." I lean back with a tight smile. "I'm good."

Mikayla laughs, squeezing my knee in a quick horse bite before turning her attention back to the game.

I continue watching, still kind of lost but also enjoying how skilled these guys are. The Cougars are up by one goal as they head into the final period. It's been a chaotic game against the Lennox Bears. They're a tough team and apparently famous rivals. Lennox College is only an hour or so away from Nolan U, so it makes sense. Plus, they seem well matched. They're definitely not giving away the game without a fight.

Sipping the hot cider Mick just bought me, I watch Liam skate off for a break and start scanning the crowd like I've been doing all night. They're just as pumped as they were when the game started. It's awesome to see the guys get so much support. They work so hard, training for hours, working out, honing their bodies, building muscle and skill with constant practice. They deserve this kind of encouragement.

Mikayla tenses beside me. "Go, go, go!" She jumps to her feet as Ethan makes a shot at goal. I hold my breath as he flicks his stick, and then Mikayla starts screaming, "Yeah, baby! Woo!" She pumps her arm in the air, and I'm pretty sure Ethan spots her because he lifts his stick in our direction, and Mick and Caroline start jumping around like crazy people.

I smile up at them, enjoying their antics until I feel a prickle along my shoulders.

It's the weirdest sensation and I rub at it, glancing behind me to see if I can figure out what this tingling means. Or what's causing it, at least.

Two large guys grunt in my direction, but they're focused on the game. I give them a polite smile, and they don't even notice. Next to them is a father with two kids who are only half watching. He's fully invested, and I can sense his frustration at having to split his attention between the game and the kids. Behind him is a line of students who are just having fun... so why do I feel creeped out right now?

Shuddering, I spin back around, focusing on the rink. Liam's jumping back onto the ice, and I pour all my attention onto him, trying to shake off this feeling like someone's watching me.

No one even knows me here.

I'm safe. Liam is keeping me safe.

I haven't used any of my credit cards. I've bought a new phone.

There's nothing for me to worry about, right? Theo has no idea where I am. If he did, he would have shown up by now and demanded his money back.

*No one's watching you, Rachel. Just get over yourself.*

Hunching my shoulders, I narrow my eyes on the game, trying and failing to follow the puck.

Trying and failing to shake off this chill along the back of my neck.

# CHAPTER 32
## LIAM

It's Sunday. The one day of the week I don't have anything to do. The one day I should be relaxed and happy and lying in bed with my woman, giving her orgasms or drawing lazy pictures on her skin with my fingers.

But nope.

We're out in the cold, the tip of her nose bright red as she stomps her way down icy streets looking at apartments.

She's getting colder by the minute, and I've quickly learned that a cold Rachel leads to a grumpy Rachel.

I need to stop and get her a hot coffee or something. Anything to warm her up, because this stubborn woman is refusing to call it quits.

It's pissing me off.

Why does she have to look at apartments today?

Why does she have to look for apartments at all?

I like having her in my bed. I like waking up beside

her, her warm, soft body cozying up against mine. It's my happy place right now.

I usually love it when the air has an icy bite to it. Being out in the snow always makes me feel like I'm home. But Rachel warm in my bed... that's my new home. And I want to be back there right now.

Shoving my hands into my jacket pockets, I follow Ray and Mick into a building lobby and immediately check out the security. There's a camera above the line of mailboxes and, from what I can tell, another one pointing at the elevators, which look as though they need a keycard to access. A leasing agent stands there smiling her Colgate smile and cheerfully greeting us.

"Third floor. Apartment B."

"Thanks," Rachel murmurs, pressing up against me when we crowd into the small space with another family.

Nothing is said as we ride to the third floor, but we exchange glances and polite smiles.

Rachel's quiet today. Actually, so is Mick. Probably because Ethan's not here. He had to go down and help his dad with a plumbing job. He offered to take Mick with him, but she said she'd better stick around and help Ray. I got the look and was silently told by my best friend that I was apartment hunting for the day. Whoopee.

Holding my sigh in check, I try to keep my foul mood under wraps.

I don't even know why I'm so grumpy.

*Yes, you do.*

My frown deepens as I step into my fourth apartment for the day and immediately know it's wrong.

For one, it's too small. And the layout is totally impractical. The sparse amount of furniture that comes with the apartment looks antiquated, like the owners hit up a few charity stores and bought the cheapest shit they could find. I take one look in the pokey kitchen and start shaking my head.

"It's in our price range," Rachel mumbles.

"I don't care. It's not the right place for you."

She gives me a curious frown, obviously picking up on my thinly masked mood, before walking ahead to check out the bathroom. Mikayla's standing in the tiny space, and if she stretched her arms wide, I bet she could touch both walls at the same time. And that's Mick we're talking about. Rachel could probably lay her palms flat against each wall. How the hell is she supposed to dry herself after a shower without bashing her elbows on the hard tiles?

"Nope." I shake my head. "This isn't the one."

"It's not your decision," Mikayla quips. "I don't even know why you're here."

I narrow my eyes at her as Rachel lets out a soft gasp. "Mick."

"What?" She spins to look up at her best friend. "It's not like he's going to be living with us, and all his grumpy ass has done all day is reject everything we've looked at!"

Clenching my jaw, I give her a stiff nod before easing out of the bathroom. "I'll wait for you guys outside."

Rachel lets out a soft tut, eyeballing Mikayla while I walk through the building, taking up post just outside and kicking at the snow.

There's no point getting into it with Mick. She's like a pit bull when she's fired up, and I can't deny that she's right. I have rejected everything we've seen today because their budget is going to have them moving into a piece of crap.

I can't stand the thought of Rachel coming home each night to anything that isn't half decent. She deserves warmth and security. So does Mick, for fuck's sake!

Scowling down at the snow, I wrench out my phone and try Mama again. I usually call her on Sunday and we have a decent catch-up, but she hasn't answered her phone today or replied to any of my texts.

When I messaged Maria to find out where she was, my sister gave a noncommittal answer about her being busy. Sofia was just as useless.

*Sofia: I'm sleeping over at Monique's. Would you stop texting me! It's embarrassing.*

I rolled my eyes and gave up with a huff.

And that's probably what's eating me so badly.

Mama always takes my calls... unless she's hiding something.

And the only thing she ever hides is the one thing I can't tolerate.

Which means she's probably with Dad right now.

I don't get it. After everything that asshole put her through, she still keeps letting him into her life. He has a restraining order, and she always lets him break it.

It fucking kills me.

The thought of him hurting her again is like a fist in the stomach. Like right inside my stomach, squeezing and making me want to hurl.

Part of me wants to drive down there and check that Dad hasn't knocked her out cold. He hasn't attacked her since getting out of prison, but that's not the point. We've put systems in place to keep our family safe when he's on a bender. But anything could trigger him, and it's like she's walking straight into a snake pit when she voluntarily goes to see him.

I don't get why she's so willing to risk her safety all the time.

It's like dealing with a stubborn child who just refuses to see common sense. It makes me feel like I have to be the grown-up. If only I could ban her from seeing him, ground her ass and make her stay away from the guy.

Kicking at the snow with a grunt, I nearly jump out of my skin when Rachel softly calls my name.

"Liam?"

Jerking around, I try for a smile, but it's probably a twitchy, grumpy-ass frown.

Her head tips to the side, her green eyes looking at me like I matter more than anything. Her sorrow makes my heart ache. She's worried about me, and I've given her no reason not to be. I'm acting like a dick.

"Where's Mikayla?" I ask, wincing at the way the words are snapping out of me.

Shit.

Rachel's expression is kind and patient, her eyes narrowing at the corners as she walks toward me. "She's still inside, asking the leasing agent if there are any other available apartments in the building."

I nod, scuffing my boot on the ground.

"What's wrong?" She stops beside me, wrapping her arms around herself. "Are you mad that I'm trying to leave Hockey House? Because, you know, I'm really torn up about it. Logically, I know it's the right thing for Mick and me and... probably everybody. But I hate the idea of leaving you."

My heart rate simmers down to a comfortable thud, and I manage to find my smile. Taking her gloved hands in mine, I give them a gentle squeeze.

"Of course I love having you live with me. I just want to make sure you find the right place."

"Yeah." She frowns. "Our limited budget isn't offering up the best options." She sighs. "But we'll keep looking. I'm just sorry it's upsetting you."

"Oh no, it's..." I never usually talk about my family, but Rachel knows enough, so I give in with a huff. "It's my mom. She's not answering my calls today, and I think she might be with my dad."

"What? Why?"

"I don't know." My voice pitches and I grunt, frustration coursing through me. "He's up to something, though. He's..." I shake my head, the cold air whistling through my nostrils as I try to take in a calming breath. "I don't trust him, and I wish she wouldn't. He always does this. He puts on the tears and this remorseful smile, and... and she just caves. Then he gets what he wants and inevitably fucks it up again!"

A mother walking past with her small children gives me a disapproving scowl.

"Sorry," I mumble as she rushes past us.

Rachel waits until they've moved on before stepping into my space and wrapping her arms around my neck. "I love how much you care about her."

My lips dip as I rest my chin on her shoulder.

"You need to tell your mom how you're feeling. You need to talk to her."

"I know." I squeeze Rachel to me, drawing from her comfort. "I've just got this feeling like she's not gonna listen. And I'm scared she'll get hurt again, and I'll be left to pick up the pieces like I always am."

Rachel presses her cold cheek against my ear, not saying anything.

What more is there to say?

Closing my eyes, I hold my girl and start wishing for this shitty day to be over already.

# CHAPTER 33
## RACHEL

Liam's mom finally called him back that night, but she was pretty hedgy. She wouldn't admit to being with her ex-husband, even when Liam outright asked. It really pissed him off, but he never shouted or raised his voice. I could just tell he was riled by the quiet way he conducted himself for the rest of the evening.

Thankfully, the guys were all home, and they provided the perfect distraction. Riley and Connor showed up with a board game that they forced everyone to play, and it was actually pretty great. It was dirty and hilarious—people had to form sentences from the cards in their hands, and the person with the funniest option won that round. Of course, the guys took it to the gutter and Mick was in her element, happily splashing around in the muck while I wrinkled my nose but ended up giving in to a few belly laughs.

Casey's one about his dream woman being found in a retirees nudist colony was freaking hilarious. The jokes went on for quite some time after that, and I had no idea what he meant when he pointed at Asher and said that was more his style, but Liam and Ethan lost it.

I shared a bewildered glance with Mick, who shrugged and started the next round.

It was the perfect way to end what had been a stressful day.

And once all the laughter had died down, things got one step better...

"How'd the house hunting go?" Casey shuffles the cards before passing them to Riley for stacking back in the box.

"Okay." I shrug, but Liam is shaking his head beside me.

"It was crap." He raises his eyebrows. "There's nothing decent around here."

"That one on Triton Ave wasn't bad," Mick argues.

"That's miles away. You'll have to buy a car."

"Rachel's got a car."

"You'll still have to get up stupid early to make it to class on time."

"So?"

Ethan starts chuckling. "Baby, your inner koala bear will die. She can't handle early mornings, you know that."

She huffs out her nose, crossing her arms and ignoring his common sense.

I wink at him, and we share a grin across the table while Mikayla sulks. She's just pissed because Liam's right. Nothing we saw today was good enough, and Mick hates losing.

"You know, I could always ask my aunt and uncle if they've got any listings you could check out. Maybe I could sweet-talk them into some kind of deal." Asher leans back in his chair, resting his feet on the back of the couch.

Mikayla and I bolt upright in unison. "Really?"

"Why didn't you offer that before, you jackass?" Ethan throws a card at his head.

Asher snickers, grabbing it off the table and flicking it back. "I only just thought of it."

"Can you think a little faster next time?" Liam grumbles. "Today was a suck-fest that could have been avoided."

I watch my grumpy boyfriend stalk into the kitchen, knowing this isn't the only reason for the suckiness of his day, but he isn't about to get into it with his hockey bros. It makes me feel kind of special that he shares those intimate details with me and not everyone.

We've really grown close since the Christmas break, and as we hit the middle of January, I'm feeling kind of good about how things are unfolding...

Monday classes have begun, and they've helped distract Liam from his family drama. Asher spoke to his uncle, who promised to see what he could find, which meant Mikayla and I could stop thinking about housing for a little bit and just get on with life.

Things are busy. Between hockey training and games, assignment work and my job, Liam and I have hardly seen each other the past few days, and I am once again home by myself after a dayshift at the diner. Mick's at the library with her study group, and I'm preparing a feast in the kitchen. The guys are always ravenous after practice, and on the nights I'm home, I try to have dinner basically on the table when they walk in the door. If they know I'm cooking, they'll pass up eating at the athletes' dining hall and come home, so I never mind putting in the effort.

The beef stroganoff is smelling pretty tasty. I give it a stir before putting the lid back on and turning to check on the cake in the oven. I've been researching healthy recipes for the guys and have managed to create a sugar-free zucchini chocolate cake that tastes amazing. It's moist and chocolatey, and the stevia gives it just enough sweetness to fool you into thinking it's a sugary treat.

I'm pretty proud of my efforts. I love redesigning recipes. It can lead to a whole lot of failures, of course, but when you hit a win, it's freaking triumphant. I've been compiling recipes and notes, storing them away for my future dream. Even though I don't know how it will ever happen, I can't seem to let go of the hope that one day I'll own a bakery. It's become a habit to file away my ideas... just in case.

The doorbell rings and I close the oven door, resetting my timer for fifteen minutes before wiping my hands on a towel. My stomach twists uncomfortably, the house suddenly feeling cavernous and empty as I shuffle into the entryway. Thankfully, there's a window right beside the door, and I take a quick peek.

I don't recognize the man standing on the steps. He's older, tall, but hunched over and looking kind of fragile.

The main thing is that he's not Matt or Theo or anyone I recognize.

When he bends over and starts coughing like he's sick, something in my chest gives a sharp tug and I'm reaching for the lock before I can stop myself.

"Hi." I greet the man. "Can I help you?"

He coughs into his fist again before eyeing me up with a slow nod. "I'm looking for Liam Carlisle." His voice sounds rough, like he's swallowed a glass full of gravel.

My eyes narrow slightly and I grip the wood, trying to figure out who this person is.

"Um... he's not home right now. Can I pass on a message?" I probably should invite him in out of the cold, the way Liam invited me in when I first got here.

But... I don't know this man.

He sighs, resting his palm on the doorframe. I take a step back, my polite smile getting a little tense.

"Tell him..." The man licks the corner of his mouth. "Tell him his father wants to see him."

"His father?" I jolt, then have to work overtime to pull my expression into line.

I don't think it works. The man's eyebrows dip together like he knows that I've heard of him. He's probably wondering what stories Liam has told me.

Licking my lips, I try to sound like my heart hasn't suddenly started hammering. "You're his father?"

Stupid question. Of course he is. Now that I'm looking at him with that knowledge, I can actually see some similarities. The shape of his face, the line of his nose.

"Yes. And I'm guessing from your expression that he's told you about me." His hazel eyes study me like he's trying to read my mind.

"A little." My voice goes soft and mousy. I can feel myself shrinking.

The man grunts. It's a scoffing kind of sound as he mutters something that I only catch the end of. "...

complains about me all the time, I suppose. His bastard dad."

"No, actually." I blink, my shoulders pinging back as the need to defend Liam rockets through me. "He never speaks badly about you to others. Even though he probably has every right to. I only know because I'm his girlfriend, and I've seen his pain."

The man's eyes flash, and I can't tell if I'm pissing him off or not, but I'm on a roll, and I think I'm quick enough to slam the door in his face if he tries to lunge at me. He looks like he can barely hold himself up, to be honest. He's hardly a threat, so I draw on what courage I do have.

*Be the boss bitch, Ray. You can do this!*

"You know... fathers are supposed to protect their families, not put them through hell. I understand that you had your struggles, but you could have gone for help. Instead, you chose a bottle and you... you tormented your children. Your wife." I can't believe I'm saying this stuff, but it feels so good to get it out. I want this man to understand how much damage he caused, what he's put my boyfriend through. What he *still* puts him through.

"Even after all this time, Liam still has moments of total grief. And he worries for his mother and sisters all the time. Why can't you just leave them alone? Can't you just let them get on with their lives?"

He's gone still before me, his breathing kind of shallow as he stares at the edge of the door. His chin is trembling as if he's fighting tears, and now I feel bad. Suddenly his fragility seems stark... and in spite of my indignant rage on Liam's behalf, this wave of sympathy courses through me.

There's something so broken and withered about

him. Standing under the porch light with this lost look on his face, he sways and looks ready to keel over.

"Mr. Carlisle, are you okay?"

Should I reach out to help him?

I'm moments away from inviting him in when he steps back and buries his hands in his pockets.

"You won't have to worry," he croaks, staggering away from the door. "I'll leave him be."

And with that, he clomps away from the house, snow reaching halfway up his calves as he navigates the front yard.

I stand in the open doorway, freezing air pouring into the house, while I watch him disappear into the darkness.

The engine of his car revs, and he putters away from the curb.

Liam always described his dad as this towering, formidable warrior. A soldier in the US Army.

But he didn't look very formidable tonight.

If anything, it looked like my lambasting just about broke him.

# CHAPTER 34
## LIAM

Practice was brutal tonight, and I shuffle into the house with aching muscles.

"Oh, sweet nectar of the gods, what is that smell?" Casey calls, kicking off his boots and leaving them in a haphazard pile by the door. "Thank God I didn't go to Offside." A soft squeal and laugh comes from the kitchen, and I wander in to find Casey lifting Rachel off her feet and spinning her in a circle. "Ray-Ray, I'm in love with you. I know you've got the hots for Liam, but seriously, would you consider—"

"No," she interrupts him before he can once again try to woo her to the Casey side. "Now put me down, Mr. Man Slut. We both know you're not a one-woman kinda guy, and I am most definitely a fan of monogamous relationships, so we could never work."

He gives in with a sigh, placing her on her feet so she can breeze into my arms. I wrap her in a tight hug, and she sighs against me.

"Maybe you could just live with me and be my

personal chef, then." Casey lifts the lid on the pot and takes a big sniff.

"No way." Asher walks into the living room with his hand raised. "I call dibs."

"Shut up, you can't dibs my woman." I throw my arm wide while tucking Rachel against my side.

"Ooo. Mr. Possessive." Casey waves his fingers in the air, then gives Rachel an emphatic look. "Do you really want that?"

She grins, wrapping both her arms around my waist. "I really want him, so..."

"Fine." Casey throws his arms up in jest. "I could make you scream louder, but whatever."

Rachel gasps, her cheeks turning beet red while I chase after Casey. His hoots echo through the house as I jump on his back and we scuffle on the living room floor, our antics turning into side-splitting laughter. Asher stands there, nibbling on green beans out of the bowl as Ethan walks into the room carrying Mick on his back.

"What the hell is going on in here?" he asks.

"They're just fighting over me." Rachel rolls her eyes. "Actually, not me. They're fighting over my cooking." Her eyebrows rise with a pointed look at Casey, who gives her his best smile before jumping up and pulling me off the floor.

"I would also love your body too." His gaze skims the length of her. "I feel like I need to make that clear."

I slap him in the stomach with the back of my hand, and he bends over with a dramatic "Oof."

Thankfully, Rachel starts serving up the meals, and we're soon camped around the table, chowing down on some kind of beef stew that I can't stop eating. Conversation flows easily between us, as usual. Even Baxter's come out to feed.

Riley's muscled in on our mealtime, too, and is sitting at the head of the table, laughing his way through a story about Connor, who's not even here to defend himself.

I stay quiet, checking out my girl as she sits there smiling along. But something's not quite right. She's nibbling on the edge of her nail... and her fingers are shaking a little. Something happened at work today. Did she have to face off with a shitty customer? Did she get scared being in the house by herself? It was daylight when she drove home, and I had a class I couldn't miss. As much as I hated it, I figured she'd be okay. But was I wrong?

Shit. We haven't been to the gym in a couple days. It was definitely making her feel more confident. Maybe I should offer to take her there right now. My assignment can wait. She needs this.

Leaning forward, I glide my hand over her thigh and give it a gentle squeeze.

"Hey." She turns into me so I can whisper against her skin. "Want to get out of here?"

She leans back, her green eyes studying my expression. She's worried about something; I can tell by the soft tremble of her bottom lip when she nods.

"I was thinking the boxing ring?"

Her nose wrinkles. "Actually, can we just go upstairs?"

"Sure." I nod, concern flickering through me as I brush the hair off her cheek and try to read her mind.

She looks away from me, gathering up the plates when she stands.

273

"Oh no you don't." Ethan stops her. "You cooked. We'll clean up."

"Thanks." She grins at him, then shares a look with Mikayla.

Her best friend sits up with a curious frown, but she mouths something I can't lip read, and Mick sinks back with a little nod, flicking a glance at me before resting her head on Ethan's shoulder.

I don't know what the fuck is going on right now, but I don't like it.

Following Rachel up the stairs, I rest my hand on her lower back as we walk into my room. I click the door shut and lock it as well. I'm sensing a need for privacy, and as soon as I turn to face her, I know this isn't a good kind of privacy.

"Liam." She sighs my name, then plunks down onto the end of my bed.

"*Cariña*?" I crouch on the floor in front of her, resting my hands on her knees. "What happened?"

"Someone came to the house today." Her eyes are big and scared, and it puts me on instant alert.

"Who?" I growl, my fingers curling into the fabric of her floaty dress. "What did they want?"

"They didn't want me." She shakes her head, her smile sad as she brushes her fingers down my cheek. "They wanted you."

I frown.

"Liam, it was your dad."

And my ears start ringing.

"He wanted to talk to you. He wouldn't say what it was about, but—"

"You opened the door for my dad?" I snap. I can't help

it. Rising to my feet, I pace away from her, palming the back of my head.

Rachel pauses, then softly explains, "I didn't know he was your dad when I opened the door. I checked through the window and saw this frail-looking guy, and I just... had to make sure he was okay."

"Frail?" My head jolts back before I start to shake it.

"Yes. He didn't look that well, to be honest, and then after we were done talking, he—"

"You talked to him?" I'm snapping again. Or growling. Whatever it is, I sound pissed.

I don't mean to be, but what the fuck? She opened the door to my dad?

"Was he drunk?" I spin to face her.

"I... I don't think so."

"How could you talk to him? You should have slammed the door in his face and called me."

"Liam, he looked like—"

"I don't care!" I flick my hand in the air. "You shouldn't have..." My voice starts to break apart. "If he'd hurt you, I..." I clench my jaw. Images of Rachel on her knees begging him to stop torture me. She morphs into my mother, then back again before my brain is terrorized by the idea of Dad's fist pummeling Rachel's delicate skin, his blinding anger wreaking havoc on her gentle soul.

Crumpling to my knees, I cover the back of my head and let out a shout before crawling toward her. My voice is fast and panicky. "Ray, please, you gotta promise me you'll never talk to him again. If he comes back, you can't open the door. You can't—"

"Shhh, Liam," she whispers, cupping my cheeks and gazing down at me. "He wasn't going to hurt me. He looked sad and broken. I think something's really wrong with him. I just got this overwhelming sense that—"

"Please, just promise me." I can't hear the rest of her sentence because I don't want her to tell me that I should give him a chance. I don't want to know that he's in trouble and I have to help him too.

I can't do that.

I can't.

"Liam."

"No." I shake my head.

Moving away from my woman hurts in a whole different way, but I refuse to sit here and watch her be sympathetic toward my father. Mama did that over and over again, and she was always punished for her kindness. Her care.

I won't let Rachel fall into that trap.

I want to protect her, but that's not going to happen if I let her entertain this notion that my dad's not all bad.

He is.

He's bad.

He's a wife beater. A child beater.

He never got help.

The stubborn bastard never got help!

Rachel watches me pace, wetting her lips before softly saying, "I can see this is cutting you up, but—"

"There's no *but*. This isn't a discussion. I don't want that man in my life, and I especially don't want him around you."

Her expression crumples like I've said the wrong thing, but I fucking haven't! I mean, what the shit? She has no idea. She wasn't there in that closet with me, all those times I had to listen to my mother get beat. She didn't hear the glass shattering or the knuckles crunching. She didn't have to walk back downstairs after the hurricane had stormed out to find the carnage—the upturned chairs and broken plates, the sobbing woman on the ground with blood dripping from her nose or mouth. She didn't have to see the way my mother cradled her ribs and flinched at loud noises and—

"Don't you at least think you should find out what he came here to say?"

"No!" I bark. "I don't want to hear one fucking word out of that bastard's mouth!" I move to the door. I feel like a bit of an asshole, yelling at her and not letting her finish any of her sentences, but she needs to understand that she's asking too much.

Standing from the bed, she crosses her arms with a heavy sigh. "I think you're making a mistake. You didn't see his face. I said some stuff that—"

"I don't want to talk about it." My voice is strained, stretching out the words and making them thin and quiet.

Rachel pauses for a moment, and the only sound in the room is me puffing like I've just run a marathon. My chest heaves as I wrestle my thudding heart into submission. It's not playing fair. My body is fucking vibrating, and it's only made worse when she softly tells me what she thinks.

"If you don't find out what's going on, it'll eat at you."

"I disagree." Wrenching the door open, I give her one more pained frown before turning my back and walking away.

# CHAPTER 35
## RACHEL

So it turns out when Liam's really wrestling with something, he goes super quiet. I guess that's better than yelling, but after two whole days of super quiet, I'm over it. He's not ignoring me per se, but his answers are the shortest they can possibly be, and I can tell he's still annoyed that I spoke to his father... and that I want him to find out what's going on. Even if he just calls his mother, surely she'll know something.

I'm tempted to call her myself, but I'm certain meddling in this one could end my relationship with a guy I'm falling pretty hard for.

This hiccup between us is a little disconcerting, but he's not being mean to me. He's just... processing, I guess. How long does it take a guy like Liam to do that?

It's impossible not to feel a sick sense of foreboding. Is this the beginning of the end for us? I don't want it to be, but I also don't want another Theo situation. Not that I think Liam would ever hurt me physically, but I thought Theo was pretty perfect until we moved in together. I never would have expected him to behave the way he did. What if Liam has some ugly surprises up his sleeve too? What if this whole "I'm gonna shut you out" thing happens more frequently than I expect?

A pain I can't describe tugs at my chest when I glance Liam's way. He's so beautiful, and shit... I think I love him. Like I'm *in love* with him. I don't know when it happened exactly, I just know it's true.

I don't want what we've got to putter out or end, but is this love? Feeling all these wonderful things for someone only to realize they're not as perfect as you thought they were?

Do you still keep going in spite of that, or do you break it off before things get even harder later on down the line?

Break it off.

The idea is like a boulder in my stomach.

Slipping my hand into Liam's, I cling to him and am grateful when his fingers curl around mine. We walk into the sorority party together, looking like a united couple. He's my big guy who will keep me safe. I shift a little closer to him, so our arms are bumping as we walk.

This is my first college party since arriving in Nolan. I've been to Offside a couple times, but these student parties have a different vibe. The alcohol is flowing freely, the antics on the lawn are already to the point of crazy, and I'm sure they'll only get worse as the night goes on.

The Cougars won their game and tomorrow is Sunday, which means no practices and no school. It's put everyone in high spirits.

A bunch of spectators walked straight from the stadium to the sorority house where the Gamma Sig sisters are putting on quite the soiree for the conquering heroes.

High-pitched squeals greet us the second we step through the door.

"Liam!" A sexy blonde with pigtails and a skirt that looks more like a belt jiggles up and down, her boobs bouncing as she waves at him.

He gives her a closed-mouth smile, then tugs me a little closer before letting go of my hand and wrapping his arm around my waist.

I can't stop my grin. Brushing my lips across his cheek, I'm relieved to share a smile with him before he's distracted by a massive guy called Wily. Turns out the football player is a gentle giant, and he shakes my hand like I'm made of glass.

As the guys talk sports, my eyes wander the room, and I spot the redheaded hockey fan standing beside a dark-haired beauty who looks like she could be on a billboard advertising relaxing getaways to exotic islands. All she needs is a grass skirt and a coconut shell bra. They're whispering together the way only best friends can while eyeing up some hot guy. I wonder who their target is.

Ten minutes later, I find out.

Caroline—that's her name—is tucking a red curl behind her ear while she chats up an interested-looking Casey. Poor girl, I hope she's not after something serious. He laughs at whatever she just said, and she grins up at him. Her starstruck gaze is one for the books, and I can't help watching the exchange.

Soon they're tapping their drinks together.

And a short while later, his hand is threading around her waist.

Yep, she's gonna get herself some Casey lovin'.

That's what she wanted. After all, he's her favorite player. His hand glides down to her butt, which is wrapped up tight in a sexy blue dress. He gives it a squeeze as he buries his tongue in her mouth. Her cheeks flush pink, and she presses herself against him... and now they're disappearing up the stairs.

I turn back to Liam and try to catch up on his conversation with Wily, but it's some football stuff I don't understand, so I start looking for Mick. Moving away from Liam, I strain to spy around the corner and check out the living room, which has been turned into a dance space. She loves to shake her booty at these kinds of things. Maybe we can shake together.

Liam's hand brushes down my back. He's still talking to Wily, not really looking at me, but it's nice to feel that connection. I'm about to shift back to his side when my heart catapults into my throat.

I freeze for a second, my stomach dropping as my entire body floods with adrenaline.

*Theo?*

*What the hell is he doing here?*

I can't breathe.

Is he...? Oh no, wait. That's not him.

Still can't breathe, though, can I?

My heart is thundering as I watch the guy I could have sworn was my ex turn to talk to a girl on his right. They look so similar, it's freaking me out.

"You okay, *cariña*?" Liam asks.

I spin with a smile that I hope he can't see through. "Just looking for the bathroom."

"Oh, there's one down the hall and to your left." Wily points, and I nod.

"I'll show you." Liam, obviously not wanting to leave my side, guides me down there, his hand on the small of my back. I appreciate it, but it makes it harder to hide my unrest.

I should tell him, but I can't.

He's had enough on his plate this week. I don't want him feeling like he has to play bodyguard and spend the entire party scanning faces to ensure Theo isn't, in fact, here. It'll ruin everyone's night.

Stepping into the bathroom, I lock the door and rest my hands on the shiny white vanity.

"Of course he's not here." I stare into the mirror. "He doesn't know where you are. You're safe. Even if Liam wasn't here, you'd be safe, because... because..." My frenzied brain scrambles for some logic. "Because you're at a party full of people, and he wouldn't be stupid enough to try something in public." My stomach jitters. "Plus, he's *not* in Nolan. He doesn't even know where you are. He doesn't know where you are. You're safe, you're safe, you're safe," I mutter, then go on to remind myself that I know how to punch back now. I know how to block and defend myself. I could flip that asshole over my shoulder if I had to.

Rising to my full height, I stare down my reflection, lifting my chin and forcing myself to feel strong and capable. "I could." I raise my eyebrows. "I could kick his ass, because I am a fucking boss bitch."

*Then stop hiding away in the bathroom and go enjoy the party.*

Closing my eyes, I brush my bangs to either side of

my eyebrows and do just that. When I slip out of the bathroom, Liam's waiting for me.

"You good?" He scans my face as if checking for signs of distress.

I put on a bright smile. "I'm great. Wanna dance?"

"Sure." He nods, and we head for the living room.

Ethan's on the edge of the room, watching Mick dance while sipping on a beer. Liam sidles up to him, and they start chatting while I bop my way to Mikayla's side. She jumps up and hugs me when I'm near, and then we start moving to the beat.

It's fun to let loose. I love this music, letting it carry me away, moving my body in sync with Mikayla's. We make each other laugh and belt out lyrics when we know them. My voice is hoarse after only two songs, but this is the best.

Spinning around, I look for Liam, getting ready to drag him into the dance space with me when I see he's on the phone. His eyebrows dip into a sharp V, and I wish I could read lips.

Or maybe I don't need to read them.

Maybe I just know that whatever he's hearing right now is freaking him out, because his face has gone the color of whipped cream.

I move off the floor, wrestling my way through bodies as I try to reach him as fast as I can.

# CHAPTER 36
## LIAM

I can barely hear Mama over the music, but I can tell from her tears that this is bad. My immediate thought is that Dad's been on a rampage again, but her tears have a different quality to them this time. Even over the thumping music, I can tell she's not panicked but more... distraught.

"He's in the hospital."

"Who?"

"Your father." She sobs. "Liam, he's dying."

The words sink into me, slow and heavy. Or maybe like a toxic gas.

I don't know what to feel as I inch my way outside, bumping into bodies and trying to swivel around them.

Dad's dying.

Mama's weeping.

And I can't feel anything.

As soon as I step outside, I move to a quiet spot around the corner and rest my head back against the outside of the house.

Mama's talking in Spanish now. "He just dropped to the ground, so I called an ambulance and—"

"What were you even doing with him?"

She huffs. "Liam, your father is very sick!"

Closing my eyes, I feel sick myself, bile surging in my stomach as I know what she's going to ask me next.

A soft hand lands on my arm, and I glance up. One look at Rachel's worried frown nearly does me in. She's so beautiful and kind, and she's been a total trooper as she's put up with my sullen mood the last few days. I've hated myself for it, but I can't seem to shake off this heavy, ugly feeling either.

Ever since Dad came knocking on my door, I've been restless, and now...

"You need to come see him, *mijo*. We're at St. Bart's. Fourth floor." The rest of her words fade as my stomach twists into a knot so tight, I wonder if I'm going to throw up.

Rachel's still staring at me, her long fingers squeezing my shoulder as she mouths, "What's wrong?"

She's looking really worried, and I have to tell her. But I can't just hang up on Mama in this state either.

In Spanish, I gently reply, "It's okay, Mama. I'll be there as soon as I can."

I hate those words coming out of my mouth, but what the fuck else am I supposed to say? She needs me. So I'll go.

Hanging up with a heavy sigh, I pull Rachel into my arms and bury my head in the crook of her neck.

"Liam, what's the matter? You're scaring me."

My shaking arms squeeze a little harder as I mumble

into her neck, "My dad's in the hospital. Mama wants me to go see him. She thinks he's dying."

Rachel pulls away from me, her gaze darting all over my face before she softly answers. "Let's go, then."

"No, I don't want you coming." I shake my head.

She huffs, looking uncharacteristically irritated. "It's not a discussion. I'm coming. So let's go." Taking my hand, she starts pulling me back inside.

It's a weird show of strength from her, and I'm initially so taken aback by it that I just let her drag me along. But once we've explained the situation to Ethan and have his keys in my hand, I finally find my voice again.

"Seriously, Ray, you need to stay here. Ethan can come with me."

"Yeah, sure." My friend nods, but Rachel is shaking her head.

"I'm going with both of you, then."

"No," I growl. "I don't want you anywhere near that guy."

She takes my face in her hands, her green eyes studying me with a look so calm, I can't even find my voice. "He's sick. In a hospital bed. He can't hurt me. And you need support right now. So I'm coming."

Working my jaw to the side, I try to conjure up a few more arguments, but she snatches the keys out of my hand with a huff and starts heading for the door.

My only choice is to muscle my way through the crowd and chase her.

"Good luck, man!" Ethan calls after me. "Keep in touch."

I give him a thumbs-up without even looking at him. Rachel's thin body is finding gaps in the crowd, and she's pulling away from me. I grunt and try to be polite, but in the end, I just start jostling bodies apart so I can reach her before she takes off without me.

Not that she would, but shit...

"Ray, wait up!" I call as soon as I make it outside.

She looks over her shoulder and slows her pace so I can run and catch up to her.

Sliding my hand down the back of her jacket, I ask for the keys, but she shakes her head. "You can be the nav man."

"Come on, let me drive." I wiggle my fingers for the keys.

"No." She gives me a pointed look, then mutters, "I don't want you leaving me behind."

I huff and shove my hands in my coat pockets. "I wasn't going to."

"Well, I'm sorry, but I can't be sure of that, so I'm driving."

"You don't have much experience driving in the snow. I'm just trying to—"

"I'm driving!" she snaps, stalking to Ethan's truck and easily jumping in behind the wheel.

Clenching my jaw, I buckle up in the passenger seat, and we don't say a word to each other as I set up Maps on my phone and put it into the holder so Siri can tell Ray where to go and I don't have to say a fucking word.

I can't believe I'm taking this beautiful woman down to see my dad. What a way to meet the family, huh?

Fuck. I hate this so much.

The car ride is slow and stifling. She wisely takes it easy, although Ethan's truck is like a tank, so I'm not too worried. We finally reach the hospital after an hour and eighteen minutes of zero conversation. It's been the worst trip ever, and I still don't know what to say to her.

As we slam out of the truck and walk toward the hospital reception area, I can feel my insides vibrating.

*I don't want to do this. I don't want to do this.*

"Hey." Rachel grabs my hand, pulling me to a stop just before we reach the sliding doors.

I can't look at her, so I keep my eyes on the ground as she steps into my space and softly says, "I know you don't want to be here, and I understand why. But if your dad really is dying, you'll regret it forever if you don't say goodbye. Trust me on this..." Her voice starts to quiver. "Not saying goodbye is the worst."

Her eyes are glassy, and I lightly brush my fingers down her cheek, feeling her pain as if it's my own. She never got to say goodbye to her dad. By the sounds of it, he was a good, kind man, not a drunken asshole like mine, and I'm sure she still misses him. When my dad goes, I won't miss him at all. It'll be a relief.

But is she right?

Will I regret it if I don't at least say goodbye?

My insides clench, rebelling against the thought, but I nod tightly. I force my feet to walk through that hospital door and take the elevator to the fourth floor.

"She's probably overexaggerating." I'm playing this down for reasons I don't even understand.

Rachel threads her fingers through mine, her smile patient as we walk down the corridor and find Dad's room.

Sofia is hovering in the doorway, keeping an eye out for me. When she sees me coming, she rushes forward, burying her face in my chest as she holds me tight. I rub her back, resting my chin on the top of her head.

"It's horrible," she mumbles. "Mama's a wreck."

"Yeah, she sounded pretty bad on the phone." I'm still frustrated at her, hating how much love she has for a man who used to beat her black and blue. I don't get it. I never will.

"We'd better go in, I guess." *Get this over with.*

Sofia pulls out of my arms and blinks. Then a sweet smile tugs at her lips. "Are you Rachel?"

"Yeah, hi." Rachel extends her hand and Sofia takes it, her eyes sparkling.

"Wow. You really are pretty."

"Oh." Rachel starts to blush. "Thank you."

"I'm glad you're here." Sofia looks between me and Ray while my girlfriend gives her a meaningful smile.

"Me too."

It still sits ugly in my gut that she's gonna be seeing my dad again. I've never really wanted to let anyone into that part of my life. Ethan's always known, but that's different. We grew up together. I wanted Nolan U to be untouched by my father's bullshit. But he's been to Hockey House now. He's tainted the doorway. He had a conversation with my girlfriend. The woman I'm falling in love with. He could have hurt her. He could have—

The curtain swishes aside, and I spot Dad in the bed.

He looks half his normal size, his cheeks sunken in, his skin tinged yellow. My lips part in horror before I blink and pull myself together with a thick swallow. He's declined so much since that night I took his drunk ass home. That was only a month or so ago.

"*Mijo.*" Mama gives me a teary smile, letting go of

Dad's hand and moving around the bed. "You came." She pulls me down into a hug, and I pat her back, murmuring gentle words in Spanish.

She nods and sniffs against my shoulder, then steps away, wiping her face with a balled-up tissue before putting on a polite smile. "And who is this?"

"Oh, this is Rachel." I rest my hand on Rachel's lower back as she smiles at my mother.

"*Hola*, Mrs. Carlisle."

"*Hola*." Mama looks between us, her lips quirking into a soft grin of approval. At least I think that's what that is.

But then Dad groans from the bed and her attention is diverted back to him. She rushes around to his side, taking his hand and asking what he needs.

"A new body," he grumbles.

I stand at the end of the bed, staring down at him. "What's wrong with your body?"

"Liver cancer," Maria says from behind us.

She walks into the room, her boyfriend hovering nearby. Polite introductions are made, and then an awkward silence descends. Mama's crying again, rubbing her thumb over the back of Dad's hand while the rest of us linger around his bed, not knowing what to say.

Sofia eventually plunks into a chair on the other side of Dad's bed. He turns to her, his lips rising into a glum smile. There's a softness in his gaze that I'm not used to seeing, and then his eyes start to glisten with tears.

"I'm sorry," he rasps.

"I know." Sofia gives him a half smile. "You've already said that."

Dad sniffs, nodding and then searching the room for Maria.

She steps forward, her voice feather soft. "I know, Dad. I forgive you, okay?"

I look at her, unable to hide my disbelief.

She mirrors my expression for a second, then sighs. "He's dying, Liam. Just... forgive him."

*I can't.*

The thought hits me like a bullet.

I guess I didn't realize how thick and unrelenting my feelings were.

But how can Maria just stand there, casually handing out forgiveness like it costs nothing?

Was it because Dad never got a fist on her?

She still had to hear our mother's tears and wails. She still curled up in that closet shaking with her own tears as we listened to the carnage downstairs.

"Do it for Mama." My older sister gives me a pleading look, and my eyes are drawn back to the bed, to the sallow man who's lying there not even looking like the father I once revered, then feared, and now hate.

Rachel's hand slips into mine, and she gives it a gentle squeeze.

"The doctor told me there's nothing more we can do other than make Dad comfortable," Maria keeps going. "The cancer wasn't caught in time. Dad left it far too late before seeking help. He's riddled with it."

"Why didn't he get help?" I mutter.

"I didn't want to be a bother," Dad rasps.

I can't help a scoff.

*No bother. Dad didn't want to be a bother.*

*What the fuck does that even mean?*

After torturing us for years, coming back and knocking on our door, being a complete pain in the ass, he didn't want to bother anyone with the fact that he was dying?

I can't compute this shit.

I can't make sense of what's happening right now.

Sofia was so scared of our old man, she'd lock herself in her room whenever he was around. Now she's sitting next to his bed, sharing little smiles and telling him it's okay.

No. It's not okay.

It'll never be okay.

I back away from the bed.

"Liam," Dad calls to me, his voice weak and pathetic.

"No." I shake my head and start walking out of the room.

"Liam!" Mama shouts, but I can't do this.

Slipping out the door, I head for the elevators. Rachel's quick steps are just behind me, followed swiftly by my mom's. She's still calling out to me, and I'm forced to stand by the elevator and wait while it rises to our floor.

"*Mijo*." Mama's voice has lost all its tenderness as she steps in front of me and looks up with a fierce frown. Her Spanish is fast and clipped as she tells me off. "You need to forgive him. You need to let him apologize."

"Why should I let him do anything?" I argue.

"Because he's your father! And you will regret it if you don't."

I scoff and shake my head.

The elevator arrives with a ding, but we stay put, staring at each other in huffing anger, until Mama eventually tuts. "I expected more from you. You're a better man than this, Liam Carlisle. A better man."

She clips away from me, and I remain still, glaring at the buttons on the wall. The elevator has disappeared again, so I slap my hand against the down arrow with a growl.

Rachel's fingers trail down my back, her sad sigh ringing in my ears.

"I can't do it, Ray. You don't know what he was like."

"It's okay." She slips her hand into mine. "I get it."

But I'm not sure she does.

I curl my fingers around hers, and we step into the elevator together and ride to the bottom floor.

I feel like crap.

Like an asshole.

Maybe it's justified, but shit... why the hell did Mama have to tell me I was better than this?

# CHAPTER 37
## RACHEL

The car ride back to Nolan is as quiet as the one to the hospital, but the feeling is completely different. The energy on the way there was sparking with underlying anger and unrest. The energy on the way back is heavy and sad.

Liam spends most of the time staring out the window.

I put music on, something quiet to break through the silence, but I don't know if it helps. I guess it gives *me* something to focus on.

When we pull into the driveway, the door pops open and Ethan runs out. He's obviously been worried about his friend, and I leave them to it. Maybe he can tend wounds that I obviously can't.

Walking into the house, I find Mikayla at the dining room table. Her blue-gray eyes give me a sad smile. "How was it?"

Plunking down with a heavy sigh, I rest my head in my hand. "Not great. His dad's really sick. He looked awful the other night when he came here, but he looked so much worse at the hospital."

Mikayla's lips pull into a frown. "How'd Liam take it?"

I shake my head. "He's not in a good space. His family wants him to forgive his father, and it just feels like too much. His mother's annoyed with him, I think, and his sisters don't understand why he can't do this one simple thing."

"Forgiveness is not simple," Mikayla murmurs, and I know she's thinking about her mom right now.

"Yeah." I bite my lips together. "But my parents always taught me that it sets you free, you know? Like, if you can forgive, then it doesn't burden you anymore."

"I know." Mikayla shrugs. "It's just not always that easy. And Liam's dad..." She shakes her head with a sigh.

"Yeah."

We leave the rest unsaid, then stare at the table until I hear footsteps in the entranceway.

Ethan walks toward Mikayla. His smile is glum as he wraps his arm around her shoulders. "Wanna go to bed?"

"Yeah." She stands and he takes her hand, tugging her up the stairs.

I slowly rise from the table, glancing at the microwave clock in the kitchen: 1:36 a.m.

Thankfully, everyone can sleep in tomorrow. Hopefully. If Liam *can* sleep. If he's anything like me, his brain will be a whirlwind of worry.

He's hovering in the living room doorway, staring at me with this lost expression.

My heart aches in a way it never has before. He's hurting. And I feel his pain.

Is this love?

When I know I would do anything on the planet to take that sad look off his face. I'll do anything to make him feel better, to take this burden from him.

I pad toward him, lightly resting my hand on his chest. "What do you need, Liam?"

His hand slowly curls around my arm, and he tugs me to his chest. "I need you." His words are muffled by my hair, but I feel them throughout my body. My heart expands and pulses—a beat that's for him alone.

"Come on." Taking his hand, I lead him up to his room.

As soon as the door clicks shut behind him, I unzip his jacket and get him ready for bed. He quietly stands there, watching me as I slip the clothes off his body. He's now standing in his boxer briefs, exposed and bare. His raw power is entrancing, and I skim my lips across his shoulder.

"What do you want, Liam?" I whisper against his skin.

"I want..." He nuzzles his lips into the crook of my neck. "I want you. All of you. I want to feel you all the way to my core."

Swirling the tip of my tongue along his collarbone, I kiss a line up his throat, over his chin. His stubble scratches my lips, and his soft tongue is a sweet contrast when I reach his mouth. He moans deep, his arms wrapping around me before he lifts me off the floor and moves us back to the bed.

His knees hit the edge and he flops down. I catch myself before I smack into his chest, standing back up so I can strip off my clothes.

He's watching me, so I slow down, enjoying the heat in his gaze, how distracted he is. Slipping my clothes off one piece at a time, I let him look. His eyes travel up and down my body as I work through my layers. Eventually I'm swaying in front of him in absolutely nothing.

He reaches for me, and I step between his legs. His hands curve around my naked ass, giving my cheeks a squeeze as he kisses my belly button. I breathe in his masculine scent, let those trills of pleasure race down the back of my legs.

But I want this moment to be about him and his pleasure. I want to make him come in new ways. I'll do anything to take the sting out of his sadness, to wipe away the angst he's been carrying for the last few days. Even if it's just for a moment.

He's not asking or demanding this of me, but I want to give it.

Because I love him.

Inching down to my knees, I let his tongue brush over my left nipple before I hit the floor. Skimming my knuckles down his rock-hard torso, I reach the band of his boxer briefs and slip my fingers beneath them. He leans back with a satisfied sigh, lifting his hips so I can let his impressive manhood spring free.

I slide his underwear off, then trail my tongue up his thigh while wrapping my fingers around his cock.

He groans, flopping back on the bed and covering his eyes with a murmured "Fuck, that feels good."

I grin, pumping him a few times before licking him. I start at his balls and work my way up. When I reach the tip, he moves, perching on his elbows so he can watch me. We maintain eye contact as I suck his cock into my mouth. There's something so erotic about this, like our eyes are fucking too.

Squeezing the base of his dick with my fingers, I lick and play with his tip, then take him into my mouth as far as I can handle.

He likes it. I can tell by his groans, by the way his fingers dig into my hair and curl at the base. His hips start to pump, and I match his rhythm.

"Oh fuck." He keeps saying it over and over again, his voice pitching as he starts to climax.

I've never taken a guy's cum into my mouth before, and I have a silent freak-out just before he expels a sexy wail and starts spurting.

I drink it in, swallowing down the salty tang when it hits the back of my throat.

It's not so bad, and I take it all, knowing how much pleasure this is giving him. He's still making uncontrolled noises that set my lady parts on fire, and when he's done, he flops back onto the mattress, his chest heaving.

"That was…" He can't even find words.

I bite my bottom lip, grinning as I slide up his body, enjoying the feeling of skin on skin when I straddle his legs and lie over him. My soft breasts squish against his hard chest, my sensitive nipples weeping at the heady rush.

Tucking my knees up, I nestle my wet center over his recovering cock and am pretty sure I could fall asleep this way. Liam's hands trail up my naked back, painting circles and sending tendrils of pleasure running down my spine.

He's getting his breath back, and much to my delight, his cock hasn't gone completely flaccid; if anything, it's growing harder again already. A thrill races through me as I tickle his neck with my lips.

Cupping the back of my head, he finds my mouth and we sink into a deep, languid kiss that is all goodness.

His cock twitches beneath me, and I start to rub against him, my hips pulsing as the idea of his long hardness sliding into me is almost too much.

"You're so wet," he murmurs against my lips.

"It's hard not to be." I sit up a little so I can smile down at him. "You have no idea how sexy you are, do you?"

He smiles back at me. "You're the sexy one, Ray. I always want you. Always."

His husky voice is the one I know he only uses on me, and it sends another wave of love crashing through me. I need him inside me, like right now.

Rising up, I grab his hard cock, placing it between my folds. For some reason, I want to be looking into his eyes as I sink onto him. And that's just what I do. As he slides into my wet center, our gazes are locked, and it's the most intimate thing I've ever done. This time I won't close my eyes or look away. This time I run headfirst into the vulnerability.

Taking his hands, I thread our fingers together, raising his arms above his head as I ride him. It's a slow, languid ride, but I feel every inch of him inside me. It's like he's taking over my entire body, owning me from my toes to my heart to my soul.

Our faces are aligned, and we're still drinking each other in as I pump up and down—a slow but steady dance we've never done before. It all feels so different tonight.

A breath whistles out of me as my body is taken over by those tingling sensations, the ones that usually make me scream his name or cry out like a porn star. But I don't want to release those sounds just yet.

I want to keep staring into his eyes, reveling in that deep look of... adoration.

My chest squeezes as I realize the depth of his emotion.

"I love you." I say the words before he can. I need him to know how much I'm feeling it. How I mean it with every fiber of my being. "I love you," I say again, tears building on my lashes.

He lets out a breath, like he's surprised I'd say it.

But then his eyes start to smile. I sense gratitude and wonder. And then he wriggles his hands out of my grasp and cups my face, holding it with a tenderness that is all Liam Carlisle.

"I love you too," he whispers, tugging me down to meet his lips.

We kiss deep and long, matching the slow strokes of our bodies.

This is an unhurried affair. There's no rush, just deep pleasure.

As our tongues tangle, the heated prickling starts to spread with more urgency, but still we don't hurry. His hands eventually slip over my shoulders and whistle down my body.

"Sit back up, *cariña*." He nudges my body so I'm perched right on top of him. The angle changes his depth, and a groan oozes out of me. Tipping my head back, I linger in it for a moment. Linger until it starts to hurt.

And then I begin to ride him.

I pump up and down, sinking to his hilt, feeling him all the way through me.

He holds my breasts and starts murmuring in Spanish, rubbing my nipples as he whispers words I can't understand. I assume he's telling me I'm beautiful. His endearments are a husky tune of love. I hear *bella* and *amor*. I sense wonder and adoration.

My body is blooming with the onset of an orgasm, and I pick up my pace, unable to help myself.

"My girl," he coos. "*Mi chica bella.*"

And then his thumb is on my clit, massaging that pulse between my legs and accelerating that blooming to a burning fire that's all-consuming.

I tip my body back, resting my hands on his thighs and pumping a little harder.

His breath catches. "I'm gonna come. I'm gonna come." His words are strangled, like he didn't expect it to hit so fast.

I get it, because the moment the orgasm starts to fire through him, I lose it as well, a cry punching out of my chest that seems to echo across the room. It bounces back to us as I sink onto him, trembling and jerking like I have no control over my body.

Maybe I don't.

I definitely don't.

Shuddering and moaning, I try to memorize each sensation as he sits up, sinking his fingers into my ass and holding me onto him. He bends his head and sucks my nipple into his mouth, and I can barely contain what's happening inside of me right now.

It's too much, so I nudge his head back up, wrapping my arms around his shoulders and clinging to him. My legs curl around his hips, and he holds me tight as the last shudder passes through him.

After that, he goes still, his arms still holding me close against his chest.

And that's how we stay for I don't know how long.

On his bed, him still inside me, panting together... as one.

One couple.

One unit.

One love.

# CHAPTER 38
## LIAM

I held Rachel close that night. There was no rolling away, no separation. We crawled under those sheets and clung to each other, like if we woke up in the morning, it might all have been a dream.

But it wasn't.

When I opened my eyes, she was still there.

I lay there listening to her breathe until she stirred and rolled over in my arms. As her sleepy green eyes began to clear, a smile bloomed on her face.

"Good morning."

"Morning."

We gazed at each other for a long beat, and then we both said, "I love you," at exactly the same time, as if we both had to make sure it was true. After a little laugh, she rolled on top of me with an indulgent smile, cupping the top of my head and kissing me deep and slow again.

*Shit, I could get used to this.*

Palming her ass, I kept her in place so she could feel

me growing hard beneath her. It never takes long with this gorgeous girl.

Her giggles of appreciation were licked away by my tongue, and then I ensured that every inch of her body was thoroughly tended to before burying myself inside her.

I took her on her stomach, covering her with my body and whispering words of affection in her ear, lifting her leg to change the angle and bury myself that much deeper when she started to pant and moan for more.

Just before I was about to lose it, I flipped her over, needing to look into her eyes again. Needing to watch her face as I drove her over the edge and then tumbled right down after her.

It's a feeling I never want to take for granted.

Rachel makes my heart race in a way no one ever has.

She makes me forget. And that's all I've wanted to do for the last few days. Forget.

Forget about the fact that I have a dad who's dying and a mother who keeps texting me.

Forget about the fact that my sisters could forgive him so easily when I could barely think about him without feeling an overwhelming rage bubble through me.

Shit. Maybe *I'm* the one who needs help.

I always accused him of never going to counseling. Am I being a hypocrite by not going myself?

*You've never hit anyone who didn't deserve it.*

I've barely thrown any punches at all. At least not at humans. I've beat the living shit out of my share of punching bags, and I worked up a pretty decent sweat waiting for Rachel last night. She drove over after work, and we did another session in the ring. She's getting good, more confident, although I still worry that if the guy is too big or strong, she'll be flattened. I have to keep reiterating that I'm only teaching her this stuff so she has enough time to get away and run for help.

She always nods and agrees, but I'm never 100 percent sure if she means it. She gets kind of fired up, and as much as I love seeing her confidence grow, I can't shake my fear completely.

I guess that's my upbringing, though, right?

I've been wired to always fear the next fist, the next whimper, to try and read a room in minimal time and pick up even the slightest hint of tension.

It's impossible not to blame Dad for all of it.

And now I'm supposed to somehow forgive him.

Walking into the locker room, I fling my bag down and try to shed my angst as I get ready for practice. I don't want to take that shit onto the ice with me. As I pull my phone out of my pocket, I wince at the line of notifications from my mother.

*You're running out of time.*

*When are you coming back to the hospital?*

*You need to see your father before it's too late.*

Two days' worth of messages and missed phone calls.

It's starting to wear me down, which I'm sure is

Mama's plan. I can already feel myself beginning to cave, knowing that after practice, it'll only take one offer from Ethan to drive me down there and I'll say yes, or one sweetly whispered hint from Ray and I'll give in with a sigh.

I don't want to, but... I hate letting people down.

"Aw, fuck." Ethan wrenches his locker open, staring at his phone screen with a frown.

"What's up?"

"The girls have found an apartment they love."

"Really? When?" I jerk forward, looking around his arm to read the screen as well.

*Lil' Mouse: Asher's uncle came through! We've just checked out the perfect place! Two bedrooms, clean, fresh, bright, and... you wanna know the best part?*

She leaves us hanging because she's a pain-in-the-ass tease. I share a quick look with him.

"Do I fucking want to know?" he grumbles.

"Ooo! I do!"

"Casey, would you fuck off and stop eavesdropping!" Ethan snaps while Casey lets out a loud laugh.

"Ash, I think you're in trouble, man. Looks like the girls have found a place." Casey announces that news to the entire locker room, and now every pair of eyes is staring at us.

"So..." Riley spins his finger in the air. "Where? What type? When are they moving?"

Ethan relents with a huff, typing back a quick query, while Asher gives me a guilty smile.

"I didn't think he'd work that quickly."

I shake my head, trying to feel happy for the girls. It's what they wanted, right? But shit, how am I gonna wake up without Rachel in my bed?

"Oh." Ethan's eyebrows pop up.

"What?"

"Their new place is only five doors down from ours." His smile starts to grow. "You know that apartment building with the orange brick and—"

"That line of trees along the front," Asher finishes for him. "That place is awesome! They got a unit in there?"

"Yeah, a two-bedroom one. Well, I mean they're putting in an application for it."

"Sick." Asher grins.

Ethan joins him, and I have to give in to a smile. Five doors down isn't so bad. We're basically neighbors.

Thank fuck for that.

I let out a relieved sigh, grateful for the small win.

After the shit-fest of a week, I need it.

"Okay, ladies. Enough with the chitchat, let's go!" Jason barks, clapping his hands together.

I roll my eyes at our captain's orders, but I really should pick up my pace. I'm not even dressed for practice yet. The locker room clears out pretty fast, and I'm left alone to throw on my jersey and lace up my skates. Coach is gonna yell at me, make me stay late to run extra drills, but—

My phone starts ringing. I glance at my open locker, wondering if I should ignore it, but as soon as it stops, it starts ringing again.

Grabbing it with a sigh, I see Mama's number, and for reasons I can't even explain, I answer the damn thing. "*Hola*, Mama. I can't talk right now. I've got practice. I'll call you back after—"

"He's gone, Liam." She sniffs. "He died about twenty minutes ago."

I slump back against the lockers, my brain going dead for a second.

*He's gone?*

I have no words. I try, but every time I open my mouth, nothing comes out.

Mama cries quietly into the phone, and I just sit there, trying to find my voice. Trying to form a complete thought.

Trying to figure out why I feel like I've just been punched in the chest with a mallet.

"Sofia's already here. Maria's coming. She's going to help me with all of the arrangements, but I thought you should know."

I blink, then swallow.

Everything is moving in slow motion.

"Let, um…" I lick my lips, dragging the wooden words out of my throat. "Let me know what you need me to do."

"I did, but you ignored me."

I wince. "Mama."

"He's gone now, and you lost your chance." Her voice starts to wobble. "I'm so sad for you, *mijo*."

My eyes start to burn.

"But I'll let you know when the funeral is going to be. And Maria will call if she needs anything. Okay?"

"Okay," I croak.

"Okay. *Te amo*." She murmurs the last two words

before hanging up. They're fast, and I'm not sure how much she's feeling them.

Of course she loves me, but... fuck.

My arm flops to my side, the phone slipping out of my hands and clattering onto the floor.

I don't move to check if it's cracked or broken.

I just sit there.

Staring at the locker room wall.

I can't move.

I can't lace my skates. I can't—

A dry sob punches out of me, my chest heaving.

I don't know what the fuck is happening right now, but suddenly my burning eyes start to overflow.

My stomach jerks and I hunch over, resting my elbows on my knees and whimpering.

For what feels like an eternity, the only sounds in that lonely locker room are my childlike sobs as I cry for a man who I didn't even think I loved anymore.

But I weep.

I sit there all alone and fucking weep like a part of my heart has just been broken all over again.

# CHAPTER 39
# RACHEL

Mikayla and I arrive at the funeral, two girls dressed in black with a horde of hockey players in their wake. I'm glad Liam has so much support, but we draw a lot of attention as we slip into the small chapel where the service is being held. It's connected to the funeral home, and only a smattering of people are in attendance.

Mr. Carlisle's boss is here, although he looks as though he doesn't want to be. And there are two men dressed in military uniforms. Then it's Liam's family and... us. That's it. My heart weeps for how sad and lonely Liam's dad must have been. I know he brought a lot of it on himself, but that doesn't make it any less heartbreaking.

I eye up the soldiers, looking unemotional and almost regal in their dress blues. I wonder what their connection is to Bobby Carlisle. Were they friends? Did they keep in touch over the years? Try to help him?

Should the man in the coffin be having a military funeral? Why isn't he?

"Mrs. Carlisle. I'm so sorry for your loss." Mikayla gives the woman a sad smile, and I follow suit, lightly kissing her cheek before taking a seat beside Liam.

His mother is trying to remain stoic, but her chin is bunching and trembling. I can't even imagine what she must be going through. She obviously loved this man with all her heart, but I'm sure there were moments when she hated him. Moments when he was hurting her and she didn't even recognize the man she married.

Liam swallows, the muscles in his jaw ticking as he stares at the coffin ladened with flowers and a handsome photo of his father. He looks nothing like the man who visited Hockey House just a short time ago. He has a vibrant smile on his face. He looks happy and confident. That must have been taken before he enlisted. Before his life was destroyed by an IED that took out his entire unit. How do you reconcile with something that horrific?

I guess you don't... especially if you try to find solace in a bottle of Jack.

Liam's staring at the photo now; I can tell by the way his chin bunches and trembles.

Threading my fingers between his, I try to offer what comfort I can.

He squeezes back but doesn't look at me.

Sofia is sitting on his other side. She looks sad but not devastated while Maria sniffles into a tissue. Her boyfriend has his arm tightly around her, murmuring soft things into her ear.

I glance over my shoulder and share a pained look with Mikayla and Ethan.

This is going to be a hard service.

It brings back memories of my dad's funeral, and my gut drops as thoughts I'd long buried start to surface. Mom was a wreck. I was numb. The minister spoke about my father, and then three of his friends got up to talk about what a great man he was. There was laughter despite the tears. And there was love. So much love. The church was bursting with it as we celebrated my dad. He was taken too soon, but the years he was on this earth, he lived his best life.

My heart thuds with a sad beat as I compare it to the feeling surrounding me now.

Bobby Carlisle made some bad choices. His life—especially the last ten years of it—was not the best. So how do we laugh and celebrate? What do we even say to commemorate this man who left so much destruction in his wake? He hurt the people who loved him the most. He turned his son against him.

My throat swells with the onset of tears as the chaplain steps up to the microphone.

He has a soft, lilting voice. It's calm and clear as he goes through the process. Everything feels so formal and wooden. His eulogy is brief but interesting. I didn't realize Liam's father was captain of his football team in high school. He was a motivated and driven man. A romantic.

My eyes dart to Mrs. Carlisle, and she's staring up at the chaplain with a tumultuous smile. He must be talking about the guy she fell in love with. The one who brought her flowers and serenaded her. The one who proposed at a baseball game, asking her to marry him on the big-screen TV. She said yes while the crowd cheered and whistled.

This man he's talking about doesn't sound a thing like the one Liam described. War transformed him.

The chaplain rushes through the latter part of his life. Of course there's no mention of beatings and rampaging through the house. That truth can't come to light in this small chapel. It must remain buried and secret. Part of me wishes it'd come out. I don't want people judging Liam for not visiting his father in those last few days of his life. People don't understand what Bobby put his family through, and a big part of me thinks they should.

"And now I'd like to take a few moments to allow people the opportunity to share any stories or memories they might have of Bobby. If you'd like to speak, please come up now."

The room goes silent... and not the pleasant, peaceful kind.

A heavy stillness settles over all of us, and it's more than awkward.

No one's getting up.

I glance around me, stealing a look at Liam's mother, whose expression is crumpling. She knows. She knows that the freshest memories are the most painful. She knows Bobby spent the last decade of his life driving people away from him.

Rubbing my thumb over Liam's hand, I try to give him some comfort, but he pulls away, his jaw clenching tight as he glares at the photo on the coffin, then glances at his mother.

With a heavy sigh, he stands up, buttoning his suit jacket and walking toward the microphone.

*Oh no.*

I whip around to send a silent SOS to Ethan.

His brows dip together and he shuffles to the end of the row just as Liam clears his throat, the ominous sound echoing throughout the room.

# CHAPTER 40
## LIAM

I don't know why I'm standing up here.

For a second, I think about telling the room what an asshole my dad was. That eulogy painted a very different picture than the life I experienced after he returned from Afghanistan.

But as I gaze out at the rows of people, at my mother's desperate expression, I can't bring myself to say any of that shit.

So what the fuck am I gonna say?

I got up on impulse, and now I'm standing here, every eye in the room on me, Rachel's anxious frown making my gut twist, Ethan hovering at the end of the row, ready to jump up and intercept me.

Clearing my throat again, I shift my eyes to the coffin. To that photo I can't see anymore because I'm at the wrong angle. Dad is smiling like a man who could take on the world. Smiling like he loved life.

And he did.

My mind fires back to a memory I'd totally forgotten about.

"Uh…" I sniff, begging my voice not to shake. "So, it's no secret that my dad and I weren't too close these past few years."

My mother sucks in a breath, her look of pure desperation making me feel kind of bad. Fuck. She has so little faith in me right now. Probably because I turned my back on a dying man who wanted to apologize.

Closing my eyes, I pull in a breath and conjure up that memory again.

"But I remember this time… when I was seven." My chin starts to tremble, so I pinch it. "Dad was home on leave. It was the summer and hot as hell. I can't remember where Mama was, but Dad was in charge, and we were bored and restless. I think Maria and I were fighting or something." I glance at my sister. Her eyes are glimmering, and I wonder if she remembers this story too. She nods, and it gives me the strength to keep going. "So, he… he made us go outside. And I remember being so mad that he was banishing us out in that killer heat, but then… he came out too." My lips twitch as I hear our giggles and screams. "And he turned on the hose, and he chased us with that thing." This watery laugh punches out of me, my eyes starting to burn as I picture the scene. Two kids running around the lawn like crazies while this bear of a man chased them with a hose, growling and laughing. "We ended up having a massive water fight, and… and it was the best." I swallow, trying to control my voice. "Then we walked down the road together, soaking wet, and he bought us popsicles." My voice cracks as tears start to blur my vision. "And it was so hot, they were melting all over us, and Dad just sat there laughing. Like, it wasn't just the best day for us but for him, too, you know?" I sniff and rub my eyes, trying to clear my vision. "He loved us. He couldn't always show it, but he did. He loved us."

Mama's breath catches again. I gaze at her through my tears as she covers her mouth and dips her head. She's weeping as Sofia jumps up from her place and wraps an arm around her, resting her head on her shoulder. Tears slip from her eyes, gliding down her rounded cheeks... and I'm done now.

Stepping away from the mic, I stop by Dad's coffin and lay my fingers on the edge. Looking at his photo, I summon what I can from deep within and softly whisper, "I forgive you." I don't feel like I truly mean it yet, but I say it for Mama. I say it because maybe one day I will feel it. Maybe one day the only memories I'll have left are water fights in the sun and melting popsicles.

Rachel's waiting for me when I return to my seat, her fingers threading between mine as soon as I sit down. I soak in her tearful smile and feel her love and pride all the way to my core.

As I lean back against the pew, this weight I didn't even realize I was carrying seems to lift off my shoulders, and I let out a long sigh. Ethan squeezes my shoulder, and I get a few pats on the back from my teammates. I'm grateful for my family. My brothers who are here to support me on my darkest days.

Just like I'll be there for them.

Family.

I gaze at my dad's coffin and know I can't keep denying that he was mine. There were moments when he was a good dad. I guess I just have to focus on those and let the rest go. He can't hurt us anymore... unless I choose to hold on to the crap. I need to let that shit go and move on with my life.

And remember the good times.

Only the good times.

# CHAPTER 41
## RACHEL

By the time we get home from the funeral, I'm exhausted.

The guys have a game in two hours, and they'll be heading off to warm up soon. The fact that they had two weeks of home games in a row was like this little miracle. It means, of course, they'll be away the following two weekends, but thank God they're home now.

I'm not sure how Liam will focus on his game tonight. There's no way I could give my all on the ice after such a draining day, but he kisses my lips and heads off. I can tell he's itching to get on the ice, and he plays like a demon.

The Cougars annihilate the visiting team, and it's a heady triumph for them all. The celebrations in Hockey House tonight are loud and raucous. It's like the guys are all trying to burn off the sadness from the funeral. They need to party and let loose. The house is bursting with people I don't know. The entire team is here along with a plethora of puck bunnies, friends, and college fans. Music is pumping, liquor is flowing, random people are making out with each other, there's a dangerous-looking game of darts happening in the pool room, and I'm standing against the wall, trying to turn myself into an invisible ornament.

Sure, I laugh at some of the antics going on around me and can't help grinning as Liam—the only guy not drinking—monitors the room, diverting disasters in the nick of time. He's a good man. I should be out there helping him, but I'm too tired to move. I just want to go to bed. I'm seriously exhausted. It makes me feel like an old nana, but I don't care.

Eventually I give in and slip out of the room, heading upstairs to hide myself away on Liam's bed.

I call my mom and update her on how the funeral went today.

Seeing her face on my screen brings tears to my eyes. She smiles at me, and we talk about Dad, remembering the good times. The ache in my chest pulses away, matching the beat of the music downstairs.

"Sounds like it was a tough day, sweetie."

"It was," I murmur, curling my knees to my chest. "But I'm grateful I was there for him."

"You seem to really love this guy." She tips her head, studying me carefully.

I bite my bottom lip and end up nodding. "I do. I... I guess I've been kind of hesitant to give my heart to someone else, but he makes it an easy offer, you know? He's kind and gentle and giving and... He's just a really great guy."

"And you're not worried that things are going too fast?"

I sigh and nod. "Sometimes. I don't want to make the

same mistakes I did with Theo, but... Liam's different. He's good to his core, and he's got great friends. He's a man of honor. He's protective. He wouldn't just sit by and let someone beat me up, you know?"

I catch my breath, realizing what I just said and feeling my cheeks instantly heat.

Mom's eyes narrow. "What does that mean?"

My chest squeezes as I wince and look away from the camera.

"Ray-Ray. Is there something you're not telling me? Did someone... beat you up?" She looks horrified by the very thought of it. And this is one of the reasons why I didn't want to tell her.

But I let my guard down and went and stuck my foot in it. Damn my tired brain.

I lick my lips, shaking my head and refusing to look back at my screen while my mind scrambles for a way out of this.

"Baby, what happened with Theo? You've never really told me, and every time I try to bring it up, you change the subject. Why are you hiding the truth? We always tell each other everything. What are you not saying?"

I steal a glance at the screen. Mom's eyebrows are puckered, her mouth stretched into a thin line.

"You're not gonna like it," I mumble.

"Tell me anyway."

So, I do. I tell her everything. From the ugly way Matt and Theo treated me to the fact that I took his money. I cry my way through an apology for not listening to her when she warned me against moving in with Theo.

And she does exactly what any good mother would.

She tells me that she's proud I left him. She tells me

that she loves me. She cries with me and wishes she could give me a hug.

"I'm sorry I didn't tell you before. I was just... so ashamed of how it all went down and what I did. And I was worried you'd freak out or be disappointed in me."

"Aw, baby. I definitely would have freaked out." She laughs, but it's a shaky one that gives away just how much she's fighting her emotions. "But I'm not disappointed in you."

I give her a closed-mouth smile, appreciating her kindness.

"Where's the money now?"

I sigh. "Still under Liam's bed. But I haven't spent any of it since I got my waitressing job."

She tuts. "You know what you should do?"

"What?"

"You should invest that money."

"Huh?"

"I know you took it, but technically that money was in a house you were sharing with Theo. You could argue that it was *your* money too. He had to start the game with something, didn't he? And you were working like a little slave—two jobs, double shifts, your wages going into *his* pocket. I don't see why you can't simply use what you took for a greater good."

I can't help a soft laugh. "And what greater good would that be?"

"Well, you always dreamed of opening a bakery. Remember—Sunshine and Cupcakes?"

I grin.

"You made a logo for it and everything. Baby girl, I would love to see that happen for you. Dad would too."

I cringe and groan. "What do you think he'd say about the money?"

"Once he was finished beating Theo to a pulp, you mean?"

"Mom, come on."

She gives me an aggrieved frown before mulling it over. "He'd probably call it dirty money, and he'd want you to burn it. But I say that's wasteful. You've got the smarts and talent to make your dreams come true, Ray. That money could be put to good use."

"But then a part of Theo would always be attached to this great, wonderful thing."

"Well, use the money to pay for the toilets, then. Every time you pee or take a dump, you can imagine it landing on his head."

Laughter bursts out of me. "Mom. You're so bad."

"He deserves much worse, believe me." Her emphatic expression fades away to a soft smile. "I don't judge you for a second over taking that money. I'm proud of you for walking away. I'm proud of you for making a new life for yourself. And if this apartment works out for you and Mick, then that's another step in the right direction. You're a strong woman, Rachel Josephine Beauford. You don't need a man to succeed, you hear me?"

My lips part. Is she about to tell me to break up with Liam?

Her smile lights up the screen. "A man in your life is a bonus. It's a pleasure, not a necessity. You know what I mean?"

I nod. "Yeah."

"So, you enjoy being with Liam, but you carve out your own life too. Don't settle for being a waitress when you want more. Go for your dreams. I know you can do it."

Biting my lips together, I try to speak past the lump in my throat, but I can't.

"I believe in you. And I love you."

"Love you, too, Mom."

She blows me a kiss, and we wave goodbye.

As soon as the screen goes blank, I drop the phone, swiping at my tears and flopping back onto the pillows.

The party continues to thump beneath me as I close my eyes and picture myself behind a glass cabinet filled with beautiful cakes designed by me. The sign above me sparkles as happy customers walk in my door, oohing and ahhing over my creations.

*Sunshine and Cupcakes.*

Maybe that dream *can* become a reality.

# CHAPTER 42
## LIAM

I don't know when Rachel slipped out of the party, but I spent over half an hour looking for her until I finally thought to check my room. She was asleep on my bed, curled up like a cat, blissfully unaware of the world around her.

I covered her with a blanket and crept back downstairs, hanging around to keep an eye on the guys. I drove a bunch of players back to their dorms around two, since I was the only guy sober enough to do it.

Sunday comes around slowly, people staggering out of bed late.

Rachel is already up when I open my eyes, her patch on the bed cold and empty when I brush my arm over it. I instantly miss her. Pulling on a sweater, I pad downstairs to find her cooking up a storm in the kitchen. She's in leggings and my hockey jersey, making it nearly impossible not to hitch her up on the counter and take her right there.

But Baxter is nursing a coffee, perched on one of the

stools and watching her work. His hair is mussed, his expression more curious than grumpy. I give him a silent smile, enjoying the mouthwatering smell of freshly baked muffins before wrapping my arms around my woman and burying my nose in her neck.

Her scent is richer and more beautiful than anything she could ever cook.

"Good morning." She giggles the words, burrowing back into me while continuing to mix up another batch.

"Are you cooking for an army?"

She laughs. "I'm making you all a carb-heavy breakfast. I'm guessing the guys still have plenty of liquor sloshing around in their systems, and they need the starch to soak it all up. I've got muffins and scones, and this mixture here is for cinnamon rolls."

"You are an angel." I kiss the curve of her neck, running my hands down her body, pressing my semi into her back so she knows how much I want her.

She peeks over her shoulder, her eyes dancing with amusement, and I'm tempted to scoop her into my arms, princess-style, and carry her back upstairs. But then a timer starts ringing and she's back into baker mode.

The delicious smells draw everyone out of their rooms, and we're soon piled around the table, munching on the best food in the world. Like seriously. The best.

Conversation flits from the game to the party. Ethan asks me how I'm doing, and the guys all look genuinely interested in my answer. I keep it light, not wanting to drag the mood down. I do actually feel better.

Mama hugged me before I left the service, thanking me for what I said. Things are gonna be okay between us, and I don't have to worry about Dad showing up drunk anymore. The relief is huge, although it carries a weight of sadness too. It's gonna take time for old wounds to heal, but we'll get there. Somehow, we'll all get there.

Mikayla's phone starts ringing, and Casey leans back in his chair, snatching it off the counter before she can even rise from her spot on Ethan's knee.

"Mickey Mouse's phone, how can I help you?" Casey puts on a Mickey Mouse voice that cracks Asher and me up.

Ethan's dying, trying to contain his laughter, while Mick lunges across the table, snatching the phone off a laughing Casey.

"Hello? Sorry about that. I live with a bunch of morons." She wiggles on Ethan's knee, jabbing him with her elbow when he tries to tickle her. "Yes... uh-huh..." Her eyes dart to Rachel, her face lighting with excitement. "Really? Thank you so much... Yes." She laughs. "I know, right? That is so awesome. Thank you. Thank you!" Hanging up, she drops the phone with a whoop, then points across the table at Ray. "We got the place!"

Her little arms punch into the air while Rachel's smile grows wide. "Aw, yay."

The rest of the guys slump back in their seats with frowns of varying degrees.

Mikayla's oblivious as she chatters on. "We need to pop into the office tomorrow morning to sign the paperwork, and now that I know just how loaded my dad is, I didn't have a problem asking him to cover the first and last rent, plus utilities." She laughs. "It also helps that Asher's incredibly amazing uncle is giving us the deal of a lifetime! Seriously." She shines Asher a grateful smile, and he beams back like he somehow orchestrated this whole thing. "Oh, and we can move in next weekend."

Ethan's mouth falls open as Rachel's eyes go wide. "That fast?"

"Yeah, they're keen to get tenants in ASAP. They'll give it a final clean, and then we're free to start moving in on Saturday."

"That's amazing." Rachel blinks like she can't quite believe it while my heart starts burning up in my stomach acid.

Next weekend.

That's so soon.

She glances at me, resting her hand on my leg. "It's only five houses down."

How does she read my mind like that?

Dammit, I love this girl so fucking much.

Standing with a little growl, I pluck her out of her chair and start walking for the stairs.

"What are you doing?" She grins, her legs swinging back and forth as I carry her just the way I wanted to.

"You're leaving soon. There's no time to waste."

Her head tips back with a laugh and I look down at her beautiful face, love pulsing through me in waves so thick I can barely contain it.

She stays in my arms as I flop back on the mattress. We bounce together, laughing into each other's mouths as we kiss and tease. She leaves my jersey on as she rides me with sexy little moans that make me come at speed.

I hold her and kiss her lips, drinking her in as I recover, then stripping her naked and teasing all her sensitive spots until she's coming again, then begging me to take her. With her legs wrapped around my hips and her heels digging into my ass, I give her all the pleasure I can, filling her until she's screaming my name. Our flesh slaps together, a heady, fast rhythm that careens us over the edge.

"Oh fuck," I groan in her ear. "Fuck, you're sensational."

With a few quick jerks, I come deep, letting out my own cries of pleasure before my muscles go lax and I flop onto her.

She lets out a little "Oof," and I quickly take my own weight, my body trembling as it tries to revive after that mind-blowing orgasm.

"I love you," she murmurs against my lips.

Rolling onto my back, I pull her close. She's a snug fit, molding into my side perfectly.

Playing with the hairs on my chest, she paints circles and lines while we talk in hushed tones.

The day slips away from us as memories are shared and dreams are built.

She tells me about the bakery and what her mom said.

I agree and start getting all excited for her, picturing her talents on display for all of Nolan to enjoy.

"You'll have a line around the block for your food."

She giggles, kissing my shoulder before finding a perch on top of me. I rest my hands on her ass, loving the way it curves and molds beneath my fingers.

Her green eyes drink me in like I'm special, her wide lips rising into a cautious smile. "You sure you're okay about me moving out? You get it, right?"

"Ray, you don't need my permission. It's your life, and you can do what you want with it." I brush her bangs to the side with the tips of my fingers. "I'm just grateful I get to be on the ride with you, you know?"

Her eyes start to glisten.

"Sure, I love waking up beside you, but I can still do that at your place, right? And you can stay here sometimes too."

"Definitely." She kisses my chin.

"I'm not saying I won't miss you or that I'm not sad over you leaving, but it's a good thing. You and Mick will have some space, and I'm just down the road if you need me."

"I know." She sits up, showing off her perfect tits.

It's impossible not to reach for them.

I cup them, giving them a gentle squeeze as she nestles her pussy over my cock. It's already getting hard, the thought of round three making the guy all excited.

"Truth is, I've been a little scared to leave you." Her lips twitch into a quick frown while something in my chest swells. "Even though you've taught me how to fight and defend myself, I still sometimes get these moments of total fear, where I think I can't do this without you. But... Mom says I'm strong and capable, and logically I know she's right. But I have to move out to prove to myself that she *is* right, you know?"

"Ray," I whisper, cupping her cheek and making sure she's looking right at me. "You are strong. And you can look after yourself. You've already proven that. But if you need me, I'll be there in a heartbeat. I'll fight any battle you need me to. I'll fight *with* you."

I wanted to say I'd fight the battles *for* her, but I caught myself in the nick of time.

Thank God.

Because it's true. She needs to know that she's capable of anything and that I'm not her master or the guy who's better or stronger than her.

We can beat the odds together.

That's what I want for us.

I want to protect her just like she'll protect me.

I want to be her strength just like she'll be mine.

# CHAPTER 43
## RACHEL

A day of sex in bed is good for the soul.

I think I already knew that, but it was proven to me yesterday. I don't even know how many times we did it, but my tender V-jay is telling me to take it easy tonight.

So worth it, though.

Liam inside me is bliss.

Liam telling me I'm strong and that he'll fight with me... holy crap. My heart just about flew out of my chest.

He's so freaking amazing.

I love how quietly confident he is. I love that he knows just what to say to make me feel better... stronger.

He believes in me with the same tenacity my mother does.

And that's why I can trust that this relationship is gonna last.

Theo always made me second-guess myself. I never noticed it back then, but looking back, I can see all the times he tried to control me or make me feel bad when my opinion wasn't the same as his.

He always made these suggestions, which were really just veiled commands. And I did exactly what he told me because I was afraid of losing him. Then I was afraid of upsetting him.

But Liam doesn't make me feel that way.

I don't want to lose him. I love having him in my life, but our relationship isn't tied to this desperate need, like I'll stop breathing if he's not there.

I can move in with Mikayla. We're gonna set up an awesome apartment, and it's gonna be great. And I can survive without Liam right by my side. In fact, I might even flourish in this new setup.

My mind swirls with possibilities as I imagine Liam sleepovers, then baking in that beautiful new kitchen without guys constantly coming in to interrupt me and steal taste tests. Once the food is finished, I can walk it down to Hockey House, and they can devour it there.

It'll be great to have some quiet, less human traffic, fewer gross smells and disgusting burps at the table. It's made easier by the thought that we're welcome at that table anytime, though. We can come and go between the two places. Seriously, we're getting the best of both worlds, and it's going to be awesome.

A smile tugs at my lips while I sit on the bench seat, watching Liam's hockey practice. I'm not technically supposed to be here, but one of the assistant coaches saw me loitering outside and recognized me.

"Just stay quiet and try to be invisible." He winked at me, ushering me through the door before disappearing down a corridor that led who knows where. I know this arena is decked out with offices, training rooms, physio rooms, gyms, lockers—the works. I'd love to take a tour sometime, but for now, I'm happy just to "hide" in the stands and watch my boyfriend.

In spite of trying to be subtle, he spotted me in the stands a few minutes ago. I didn't tell him I was coming because I wanted to surprise him. I've planned a special date night for the two of us. Mikayla helped me pull it together in between classes today. I'm borrowing Ethan's truck and taking Liam to some lookout point on the hill. Mick's already programmed the directions into my phone for me. We'll sit in the truck, eating treats I've baked, then hopefully making out like horny teenagers.

All I have to do now is wait for practice to end and for Liam to shower up.

Checking my phone, I send a text to Mom, letting her know about the apartment. She gets back to me within seconds.

*Mom: Best news ever! Send me pics as soon as you've moved in.*

*Me: I'll do you one better and give you a video walk-through.*

*Mom: Bring it on, baby girl. Love you bunches, sunshine!*

I grin. Dad used to call me sunshine. It was his pet name for me, and when he died, I couldn't tolerate anyone ever calling me that again.

But Mom's been trying to reinstate it for a while now. I

haven't wanted to be bitchy about it and demand she not use it, but maybe I'm ready to acknowledge the fact that she's said it. So I grin down at her text, then give it a heart and send back a GIF of a smiling sun.

She hearts it, and I can just picture the delighted look on her face. A warm feeling buzzes through me and I tuck my phone away, feeling this newly acquired strength continue to blossom inside me.

I like this new Rachel. In fact, I'm kinda falling in love with her.

"Okay, guys, good job today." Coach Bergenon starts slapping the boards, grabbing everyone's attention. "Shower up and let's get the hell out of here. Looks like some of us have ladies waiting on them." He frowns at Liam, and I wince, shrinking in on myself.

The guys start laughing and hassling Liam as they skate off the ice. He whips his helmet off, grinning at me like he's the lucky one and doesn't give a rat's ass what anyone says. Me showing up at his practice just made his day.

And there go those warm fuzzies all over again.

Coach shakes his head and wanders off, no doubt muttering about how I got in and whose butt he needs to kick.

I hope that assistant coach doesn't get in trouble. He was just being nice.

Resting my chin in my hand, I watch the Zamboni clean up the ice after practice. The driver ignores me like I'm not watching him, obviously wanting to finish up quickly. I get the sense that home time is looming because no one else is in the rink area, and I bet once Mr. Zamboni is done, he'll be cutting out for the day. People are probably in offices and the various rooms around the arena, gathering their things and getting ready to go.

As soon as the red machine lumbers off the ice, the silence that descends is almost unnerving. I get up and wander down the steps, standing by the plexiglass and staring at the smooth ice.

I wonder if I should go wait outside the locker room, but I'm already not supposed to be in here, and I don't want to bump into the head coach or anything. Maybe I should go wait outside. But what if Liam comes looking for me in here?

I amble along the edge of the rink while I wait, not even looking up until I feel that prickling sensation on my neck. The fine hairs stand to attention under my collar, and I jerk still.

Rubbing at the spot, I tell myself to stop being so stupid. There's no one around to give me these creepy chills right now. Even so, I can't help looking over my shoulder... and that's when my blood runs cold.

Standing two steps above me, his hands shoved into his jacket pockets and a dangerous glimmer in his eyes, is the guy I never wanted to see again.

"Theo," I rasp, stumbling back as if he's real. Surely he can't be. I'm hallucinating or something, right? Because it's impossible that he'd be here right now.

Even so, I keep walking backward until I hit the door leading out to the ice. It swings open behind me... and Theo's still standing there with this look on his face that's cold and terrifying.

I freeze, my insides turning to concrete when my ex-boyfriend slowly walks down those stairs.

He's moving.

He's real.

*Shit, shit, shit!* This nightmare is actually happening!

"Hey, cutie."

"Wh-What are you doing here?"

"I'm here for you, of course."

My breath hitches and I inch back, my hip hitting the low wooden doorframe. "How'd you find me?"

"You dropped your phone in the parking garage. You know, when your shitty little friend mutilated Matt's balls."

I swallow, my hands sweaty as I fold my arms and grip the edges of my jacket.

"It took us a while to finally unlock it, but we got there in the end, did some research, and figured out you were in Nolan."

My belly starts to shake, jumping and skittering when he stops right in front of me.

"I've been here for a little while, looking for you, trying to spot you in the crowds, asking around until finally someone pointed me in the right direction. Then I decided to follow you, get a glimpse of what you're up to." His dark eyes take on a look of malice as he growls, "So... you're fucking a hockey jackass, huh?"

"Theo."

"What about us?"

"There is no us," I manage. "We ended the second you let Matt beat the shit out of me."

He scoffs. "You were being difficult."

"And you were being an asshole."

That insult scores me a cracking slap across the face. I gasp, my head whipping to the side as fear skitters through me. Matt must be rubbing off on Theo. I can just imagine what he's filled his head with, spurring him on, encouraging him to teach me a lesson when he found me.

*Shit. Shit! He's gonna hurt me. He's gonna—*

*Stop it. Don't let him treat you this way.*

*Be a boss bitch and put him in his place!*

"Where's my money, Rach? Huh? You spend it all?" He reaches for me again and I slap his arm away, shoving him back with as much force as I can.

The move catches him off guard, his eyes bulging before he launches himself at me again.

I jump back from him, forgetting the door to the rink swung open before. Tumbling onto the ice, my boots slip on the frictionless surface, and I land with a thump. Pain rockets up my elbow, but I ignore it, struggling back to my feet.

My boots skid on the ice as I try to balance myself.

I need Liam. I want to shout his name, beg him to come rescue me.

But he's not going to hear me out here. His head is probably under a shower spray, warm and oblivious to my peril. And Mr. Zamboni is already out the door.

Oh man, what would he say if he saw us messing up his perfect ice? I need to get out of here. I need to run and find help.

Struggling to get a grip on this ice, I totter away from Theo, but it's a pointless escape. He's on me before I get three steps, wrapping his arms around me like a python.

"Ah!" I struggle against his hold, fighting the urge to freeze up and start begging like I normally would.

"Did you think you could get away with what you did

to me?" he seethes in my ear. "You're gonna pay, Rach. You're gonna pay hard."

"No," I grit out, acting on instinct and driving my heel into the top of his foot.

He howls while I snatch his arm, throwing my butt back and heaving him over my shoulder the way Liam taught me to. Despite my slippery grounding, the technique works, and Theo lands with a smack onto the ice, letting out a feeble groan as he tries to get his breath back.

*Holy shit, I can't believe that worked!*

Ignoring Liam's warning to run as soon as I can, I take advantage of this spike of rage and plant my knee on Theo's chest, driving my fist into his face.

"You bastard." I'm tempted to spit on him as well.

But the blood around his lips is enough satisfaction for me. At least I made him bleed.

I feel so fucking empowered as I take a step toward the door. I'm gonna run to Liam and tell him what I did. I'm gonna—

"Ah!" The sound pops out of my mouth when Theo's fingers wrap around my ankle, giving it a hard tug.

My knees smack into the ice, sending shock waves down my legs while my stinging hands feel like they've just been burned on a stove eye. The harsh ice sears my skin, and I hiss at the pain.

"You fucking bitch!" Theo spits. Bloody saliva hits the white ice, making my stomach lurch.

I start scrambling on all fours, ignoring the burning sting as fear claws at my stomach. It's like being back in his house again, when I was desperate to get away from Matt, but he wouldn't let me go. Just like then, Theo yells and drags me back. With no way of countering his pull, I slide across the slippery surface and feel like I'm heading for the edge of a cliff.

"No. No!" I plead, grappling for a hold that doesn't exist.

Dragging me under him, he straddles my hips, firing a fist at my face.

I manage to partially block it but still feel the sting when his knuckles connect with my cheek. Bucking my hips wildly, I scuffle with him when he tries to capture my flailing arms.

"Lemme go!" I scream, bucking with more force and tipping my body at the same time. He crashes sideways onto the ice, and I kick with my legs, crawling away from him as soon as I have enough space.

"Get back here," he growls, snatching at my ankle again.

I spin around, launching my foot at him before he can get a hold of me. I manage to clip his nose with my boot heel. He lets out an indignant wail, cupping his face while I scramble in a panic, clawing at the ice like a crazed person until I reach the side of the rink and haul myself through that door.

"Liam." I rasp his name, taking off at a run toward the locker room as Theo lets out another roar and chases after me.

# CHAPTER 44
## LIAM

The shower is bliss, and the only thing to get me out from under the hot spray is knowing that Rachel's waiting for me. It was the coolest surprise seeing her sitting in the stands. I have no idea how she got in, but I'm not complaining.

With a grin, I grab a towel, patting down my face and chest before wrapping it around my waist. The mood in the locker room is light and jovial, probably thanks to Coach ribbing me about my girlfriend.

I grin as more hassles are fired my way, whipping off my towel and flicking it at Riley when he gets a little too mouthy. The kid's grown in confidence so much this year. It's great to see him coming out of his shell.

But he still needs to know his place, and it's with much satisfaction that I hear his yowl when I snap the edge of my towel on his bare thigh.

"Fuck, Liam." He spins with a scowl that's already breaking into a grin as Ethan gives his shoulder a light shove.

"Watch your mouth, kid." He laughs, mussing up Riley's wet hair.

The volume in the locker room rises as we throw a few friendly insults Riley's way, but his comeback is cut in half by a terror-filled scream just as the door bursts open.

"What the hell?" someone yells. "Hey! You can't go in there!"

"Liam!" Rachel shouts, bolting into the room and running at me like she's being chased by a pissed-off polar bear.

"Ray." I try to capture her in my arms, but she moves around me, cowering behind my back. She's wet and shivering, her clothes icy cold as they brush against my bare skin.

What the hell happened to her?

I'm about to ask when there's a scuffling sound outside the door, followed by a grunt and then a roar. "Rachel!"

"What the fuck?" Ethan murmurs, moving to block her from whatever's coming.

He's not the only one. As my hands reach around behind me, pulling her against my back, a wall of hockey muscle forms in front of us.

Whichever asshole is shouting her name barges through the door and comes up short as he's met with a mass of riled testosterone.

Half the guys are still naked from their showers—wrapped in towels or just standing there all bare, completely bare.

"Can we help you?" Asher growls.

The guy stumbles back a bit, wiping blood from his nose before pointing a shaking finger at her.

"She owes me," he snarls. "I'm just here to get what's rightfully mine."

"Fuck off, peewee," Casey warns him, but the little shit doesn't listen.

"She's mine! Hand her over. Now!"

"I am not yours," Rachel mutters against my shoulder, then huffs and moves out from behind me. It's an effort to let her go and do that, but she flicks my arms off with surprising force, her head popping up between Riley's and Baxter's shoulders. "I am not yours, Theo."

*Theo?*

*Well, fuck me.*

My hands curl into fists before I can stop them.

"I don't belong to anybody. You can't own me." Rachel lifts her chin. "And I don't owe you anything."

"That money was mine!"

"It was ours!" she yells back. "I earned that money too! I worked my ass off for us, and you just stood by while your friend beat the shit out me!"

Her voice rises to a roar as she muscles her way between Baxter and Riley.

"So I'm keeping that money. And you're gonna turn around and walk out that door. And you're *never* going to bother me again."

He pauses for a beat, like he can't believe she's saying this shit to him. That she'd dare to yell at him. He looks at her like he doesn't even know her before letting out a scoffing laugh that's all mockery.

*Motherfucker.*

I growl, pushing my way through the wall to stand beside Rachel.

"Get outta here." I point to the door behind him, my

voice shaking as I try to contain the volcano bubbling in my chest.

Theo's smirk is so fucking punchable, and I'm not sure how much longer I can hold out before unleashing a little hell on his ass.

"Don't give him the satisfaction," Rachel murmurs. "Theo, just go."

He scoffs again, shaking his head before pointing at her. "Fuck you." He leans forward with an arrogant scowl. "Fuck you, Rach! Fuck! You!"

"Oh, that's it," I snap, lunging forward and grabbing Theo by the collar. Smacking him against the door, I push my forearm into his chest and snarl, "You say one more word to her, you even look at her again, and I will end you. And *no one* will be able to save you from what I have planned, you understand me?"

His glare is dark and malignant. "Is that a threat?"

"It's a guarantee," I seethe, nice and slow so there can be no misunderstanding. I'm not sure what my face is doing, but it must be reflecting some of the anger pulsing through me, because finally he gets the fucking point.

A flash of uncertainty skitters through his eyes before he wrestles me off him and shoves the door open.

"Fuck you all!" he yells, raising his middle finger at us before disappearing into the hallway.

"Yeah, I don't think so," Ethan mutters, stepping past me and chasing after the guy.

I have no idea what he's got planned, but I can't go.

Right now, the only thing I have to do is turn and make sure my girl's okay.

My strong, brave, beautiful woman.

Her chest is heaving, and I can see a red welt forming

on her cheekbone. It makes me want to crush Theo's head with my bare hands, but I let that rage travel through me quickly before stepping into her space.

He can't take this moment from us.

I won't let him blacken a thing of beauty.

Lightly cupping her cheeks, I brush my thumb under the red spot below her eye and smile down at her. Her watery grin is gorgeous, and my chest swells with a mix of pride and adoration.

"Good girl," I whisper, sliding my thumb over her bottom lip. "You made him bleed."

# CHAPTER 45
## RACHEL

I did make Theo bleed.

Go me.

The thought fills me with pride but still doesn't eradicate the shakes. At least I'm steady on my feet, though.

Curling myself into Liam's embrace, I close my eyes and feel his heartbeat against my chest. He sprinkles kisses across my forehead and keeps telling me how proud he is, how strong and amazing I am.

I do feel kind of strong, actually. I stood up to Theo. I fought him.

And now I have an army of half-naked guys chasing after my tormentor. In fact, my actual boyfriend is butt naked, but he doesn't seem to care. He's too busy making sure I'm okay.

I love him so damn much. The emotion blooms and pulses in my chest until I think it might burst wide open.

I'm not sure what the Cougars are gonna do with Theo, but I'm just gonna stay in Liam's arms for a little bit longer, drawing on his strength and reveling in what feels like a triumph.

Despite my stinging hands and aching face, I triumphed.

Theo didn't get the best of me, and I fought him off like a boss bitch.

Badass Rachel Beauford. That's what Mick's gonna call me. And I could get used to it.

The door swings back open, and Casey returns with an update. "Asher's calling the cops. Your fuckwit ex punched Coach Renard too."

"What?" I jerk back in surprise. "Why... why's he calling the cops?"

Casey's forehead bunches with a frown. "Because he attacked you and one of our assistant coaches, and this time he's not going to get away with it."

I shrink against Liam, my heart pounding as I think about Theo's intimidating father and how he's going to react. It'll be my word against his son's. And I know we're in a different state and everything, but cops support cops, right? There's probably some kind of code or something. What if Theo spins some lie, accusing me of attacking him first?

"I don't want the police involved," I murmur.

"Ray." Liam always says my name with such tenderness. "It's gonna be okay."

"But it's my word against his."

"Actually, there are cameras all over the arena." Casey twirls his finger in the air. "None in here, of course, but I'm pretty sure wherever he attacked you will be caught on film. Where'd it all go down?"

"On the ice."

Two sets of eyebrows rise while I look down at my wet jeans and jacket. "I don't know how he got into the arena, but I was walking past that little door that you go through to get onto the rink. Maybe it wasn't shut properly or something, but when he lunged at me, I fell through it."

Liam tenses, and I check his face.

Now it's my turn to say, "It's okay."

"I just hate the fact that he hurt you again."

My lips twitch. "I got a few hits in this time."

"And now I have to see that video." Casey rushes to his locker, throwing on his jeans and a shirt. "Let's go, let's go!"

Liam pulls a pair of sweats on, going commando and not even bothering with a shirt before following Casey down to the security room.

Asher's already down there, on the phone with the police while sitting at the monitor next to a man and woman who I don't recognize. They glance over their shoulders at me, and I spot a security emblem on the man's shirt.

"Yeah, okay. Thanks." Asher places his phone down and turns toward us. "The cops are on their way."

"Where's Theo?" I cross my arms, wishing my voice didn't shake every time I said his name.

"He's currently face down on the floor in the main entrance with Ethan sitting on his back and Coach Bergenon going off on him."

Liam grins. His smile is broad and beautiful before his expression turns serious and he points at the screen. "You know how to work this thing?"

"Do I know how to work it?" Asher rolls his eyes. "Of course I fucking do, man."

Spinning back around to face the screen, he goes to show us just how amazing he is, but his hand is slapped away by the woman beside him. She gives him a scowl and mutters something about him not touching her equipment.

"Come on, Pats. Play nice." Asher winks at her.

She fights a grin, shaking her head and rewinding the footage for us.

I watch the black-and-white images of the rink in reverse, flinching when I see myself on the ice. It's so fast, it's hard to tell what's going on, but then we get to the beginning, and the lady stops rewinding and presses Play. I hold my breath as I watch myself face off with Theo.

Liam's hand glides around the small of my back, his breaths uneven as he watches Theo attack me.

"Ooo, nice!" Casey grins when I flip Theo over my shoulder, then pumps his fist in the air with a cheer when I punch Theo in the face.

"That's one hell of a thunder punch." Asher throws a grin over his shoulder.

"Thunder punch and sword dick." Casey laughs. "They're like the perfect pair."

Asher cracks up while I frown, looking to Liam for an explanation. "Sword dick? What does that mean?"

"Nothing," Liam growls, shoving Casey's shoulder.

But the guy doesn't even notice. His laughter has evaporated, his eyes locked on the screen as the rest of the video plays out. Things got messy and desperate near the end there. You can taste my fear as I scramble to get away from Theo.

When my boot smashes into his face, it's not as satisfying as I thought it would be. I'm starting to shake again, and Liam's hand curls around my waist, tugging me against his chest.

"It's over now," he murmurs. "It's over."

I close my eyes, exhaustion swamping me, while Casey and Asher have a quiet chat with the security man.

"It'll be enough to convict him. It's obvious he attacked first and she was just defending herself." Asher points his thumb at the screen.

Let's hope the police agree with him.

They arrive about five minutes later, and we walk out to the front entrance, where Theo is cursing up a storm and accusing Ethan of assaulting him. The head coach puts a quick stop to that before turning on the weeping woman behind him and barking at her for letting this moron in.

"He held the door for me. He was nice and smiley and helpful. I didn't even think about it when he followed me inside." She whimpers, dabbing at her eyes with a balled-up tissue. "He looked like he was supposed to be here."

The coach grunts, muttering something about security not being tight enough. His dark gaze sweeps over me, and I shrink back, knowing I'm included on his list of people who should not be in here right now.

It's a long evening as the police question everybody involved. They watch the video, and I walk through what happened all over again. The officer who interviews me is very kind, and I'm grateful for her calm manner. It's obvious that I was just defending myself, and as I watch them finally drive away with Theo in the back of their squad car, I feel this huge weight lift off my shoulders.

My surprise date with Liam is shot, and I don't have

the energy to go out now, so we head back to Hockey House, where Mikayla has been pacing.

She yells at Ethan for not keeping her in the loop.

She gives me a fierce hug, then tells me off for not calling her immediately.

Then she rants for a while about... you know what? I don't even know.

"She's hangry." I cringe, sharing a look with Ethan.

He snickers and pulls his phone from his back pocket. "Anyone up for pizza?"

A loud "Puck yeah!" echoes throughout the living room, Mikayla's voice among the loudest as her boyfriend places an order.

I grin, smiling around at these hockey men and my lil' best friend. I love them all so much... and it suddenly hits me that my life is in Nolan, Colorado, now. The girl who hates the cold and always dreamed of living by the beach is settling into a small, landlocked college town.

And the weirdest thing is... I couldn't be happier about it.

Flinging my arm around Liam's shoulders, I plant a kiss on his cheek, and as he gathers me against him, I know I'm exactly where I belong.

# CHAPTER 46
## LIAM

It's been nearly a week since Rachel was attacked on the ice. She's healed pretty fast, the bruising on her face light and barely noticeable. Thanks to her block, Theo's knuckles only skimmed her cheek. It still riles me when I think about it, but all I have to do is picture the way she defended herself and the angst is replaced with a glowing pride.

"One, two, three, lift." I stand with a grunt, the sofa bed that weighs a fucking ton in my hands. Ethan's on the other end, straining as we shift it to the other corner of the room, the way the girls asked us to.

We set it down, turning to check with them. Mikayla's nose is wrinkled. Rachel's lips are pursed.

"Actually, maybe it's better where it was." Mikayla crosses her arms, gazing around their new apartment living room.

"Are you fucking kidding me?" Ethan raises his eyebrows at her.

She stares at him for a beat, and then her lips start to twitch. "Actually, yes, I am."

Rachel laughs, pointing at Ethan. "We got you."

He shakes his head, sharing a dry look with me before stalking out of the room and slapping Mikayla's butt on the way past her.

She yelps but doesn't give chase.

The guy has been a grumpy ass all day, but it's only because he's sad Mick's leaving. Yes, she's just down the road, but he's still hating it. The guy likes having his woman in his bed every night, and he's gonna miss her.

I get it.

We've been working like Trojans this morning, helping the girls rearrange their new apartment and lugging up the few new pieces of furniture they bought. The place was mostly furnished, but they wanted to add a bookcase, and they fell in love with this coffee table when they were out shopping, so the one that was already here is going into storage. The girls have spent the morning putting the bookcase together while Ethan and I have hauled the rest of their shit up to the third floor.

There's a bunch of boxes to unpack. Rachel arranged for her old boss in Fontana to stop by Theo's place and grab what was left of her things. Thankfully, Rachel didn't have much there. She was half expecting to find out Theo had burned it all, but it was waiting in four boxes when her boss arrived, and she couriered them over to Colorado.

Only a few of the items were damaged. Her eyes welled up when she discovered her personally signed copies of her favorite romance novels had been ripped up and graffitied with permanent marker. Cartoon dicks and hairy balls were littered through the pages along with insults like "bitch" and "slut" in capital letters.

I took a photo of the covers and will contact the authors this week. There's no way that asshole is making my girl cry again. We're still waiting to hear what's gonna happen with the guy. Rachel's pressed charges, and we have the video evidence to prove it, but he's a first-time offender (sort of—there's no proof of his first attack on Rachel), and his uncle's an amazing lawyer with contacts for other amazing lawyers around the country, so Theo will be well represented. He'll probably get a slap on the wrist, which makes me livid, but at least we've secured a restraining order.

Once all the legal stuff is over, he'd better not even think about stepping foot in Nolan again.

I follow Ethan back downstairs and head for Hockey House. We've only got Mikayla's and Rachel's bags left, so we walk down the street to collect them, chatting about the new apartment.

The girls are gonna turn that place into a home, and it won't take much. It has a cozy feel already. I can see why they like it. The kitchen is amazing. Considering the size of the apartment, it's quite big, and it's all new and shiny. It was just redone last year, and the look on Rachel's face as she unpacked the new utensils and cutlery she'd bought was a thing of beauty. She's gonna love baking in there.

By the time we return, the bookcase is secured against the wall. Mick's packing up the tools while Rachel is loading up the shelves. She has a pretty decent collection of books. She obviously loves buying ones with pretty covers and spines. The look on her face as she arranges them like a rainbow is adorable.

"Looks cool." I point at it.

"Thanks." She beams.

Once again, I'm struck by her beauty. By the fact that she's my girl.

I love her so fucking much.

"Babe, would you quit sulking? You're killing my happy buzz." Mikayla tucks herself against Ethan.

He flops his arm over her shoulders, gazing around the apartment. "I'm gonna miss you, okay?"

"I'm just down the road, and I'm not planning on sleeping here every night. I'm kinda hoping we can take turns." She gazes up at him, nudging him with her hip until he turns to look down at her. "Would you just smile, please? I'm not leaving you."

His lips twitch with a barely there grin.

"Why don't you sleep at Hockey House tonight, then?" I suggest. "It'll give Ray and me a chance to christen every room."

My girlfriend gasps, whipping around to bulge her eyes at me. "You did not just say that."

Ethan's already laughing, lifting Mick off her feet and carrying her toward the door. "Have fun, you two. It'll be our turn next weekend."

"Ethan!" Mikayla complains, but it's all for show. The look on her face is electric as she dives for his mouth.

He stumbles back against the door for a second, moaning as they deepen the kiss to pornographic. Mikayla shifts in his arms, wrapping her legs around his waist while Rachel stands there blushing up a storm.

I share a bemused smile with her, my gaze softening

as I drink her in. She grins back at me, her eyes heating with a look I know all too well.

"Okay, you two, take that game of tongue twister somewhere else." I walk toward my woman as Ethan carries Mick out the door.

I swing it shut behind them, pulling Rachel against me as soon as the door clicks.

"Every room, huh?" She giggles into my shoulder.

"Every room." I suck her earlobe, then trail kisses down her jawline.

Her shirt is soon on the floor, her bra quickly finding a home on the edge of the bookcase. Her sweet moans fill the apartment as I take my fill of her gorgeous tits and she frantically scrambles to unbutton my pants.

We end up on the floor, where I ask her what she wants. She's getting better at telling me, and she's soon writhing with an orgasm before scrambling up to her knees and leaning against the sofa bed. She pokes her perfect ass toward me, spreading her legs and beckoning me like a siren.

I take her from behind, my knees rubbing against the plush rug as she screams my name. I suck her shoulder as she comes again, then wrap my arms around her, pulling her back against me and cupping her boobs while an orgasm rocks me blind.

And that's how we spend the rest of our day.

Chasing one orgasm after another.

We stop for food... and do it in the kitchen.

We take a shower... and do it against the bathroom wall.

We unpack some more boxes... and she sucks me off in the hallway.

Then we finally make her bed with fresh sheets... which we quickly dirty up with a romp that turns us into blobs of jelly.

I fall asleep with her locked in my arms, her ass nestled against my crotch, my hand tucked beneath her boob.

I'm not sure I've ever felt this happy before.

The girls were right. It's nice to have another space to go to. It's quiet and private—our own little oasis.

Just as I predicted she would, Rachel burrowed deep into my heart. If anything, she stole the whole thing, overtaking each ventricle and finding a home in my soul.

I love this woman.

And I can't imagine that ever changing.

A smile curls my lips as I slip into la-la land with the knowledge that I've finally found the girl I was looking for all along.

# CHAPTER 47
## CASEY

The end of hockey season is screaming toward us.

We have one month to go until The Frozen Faceoff, and the Nolan U Cougars are looking like strong contenders. We'll make the cut and go on to win the trophy for sure. This is our year. I can feel it.

I'm loving this season so far. We've got a solid team, and the guys are awesome. Hockey House is lit, and even though two of my favorite people moved out nearly four weeks ago, they still pop over all the time.

Lil' mouse is here right now, sitting on Ethan's knee and reading one of Asher's comic books. She arrived with a basketful of freshly made muffins from Rachel, who's off on some picnic with Liam. The guy is so whipped that he's almost impossible to be around. I caught him singing in the fucking shower the other day.

Singing.

In the shower.

It was some sappy love song, and I nearly gagged as I brushed my teeth and tried to block him out. Seriously.

As much as I adore Ray-Ray, she's brought out the sap in Liam, and it's kinda painful.

I'm never gonna be that guy.

I love women. I seriously do. Their bodies are awesome. I love laughing with them, turning them on, watching them orgasm, playing "hide the wiener." I love sitting with them in class and eating lunch with them.

Girls are fantastic.

But I never want to be in love with one of them.

I've watched guys around me change as a woman takes over his life. They get all attached and goopy. That's so not me. I will never fall hard. I'm just not wired that way.

Give me variety.

The special ones get a tat on my arm to remember them by, but I won't be calling them the next day. Or even a week later. I'm not going to let myself get tied down to anyone.

I brush my thumb over my latest tat—a little red heart with a Q below it. It sits just above my thick watch strap, and I can't help grinning at the memory of the ginger siren who it's in honor of. Shit, she was fire. Some of the best sex I've ever had.

It was tempting to use the number she gave me, but I'm not that guy. So when I got home from the sorority party, I washed the inky numbers off the back of my hand and thought instead about the shape of her body and how good it felt to be buried inside her.

Fuck, I'm getting hard just thinking about it.

Turning back to the fridge, I peruse the contents, wondering what I'm in the mood for. A monster sandwich could go over nicely... or those leftover nachos from Offside.

"Hey, anyone want the nachos? You've got point-five seconds to reply or I'm taking them... No answer? Sweet, they're mine."

Asher mutters something about me being an asshole just as the doorbell rings.

I glance over my shoulder, slapping the fridge shut as Asher walks through to answer the door.

"Hi there."

Shit, it must be a woman. His voice always goes soft and husky when he's talking to a hottie.

"Hey. I'm looking for Casey. Casey Pierce. He lives here, right?"

"Yeah."

I stiffen, wondering who the hell Asher is letting in to see me. I don't bring girls to Hockey House. Well, hardly ever. I've had the odd drunken whoopsie where we've ended up back here, but I've never let anyone stay the night, and no girls have ever bothered to knock on my door.

So why is—

*Oh shit, it's the Queen of Hearts.*

She walks in beside Asher, those red curls cascading around her shoulders and ending right on top of her luscious tits. The girl is stacked. It was one of the first things I noticed about her. Her funbags all snugged up in that tight blue dress she was wearing, smooshed together and just begging to be played with.

And play with them I did. Fuck, it was hot.

Images from that party run through my head, making it impossible to hide the fact that I recognize her. Those big blues eyes and plump lips. Holy fuck, she's gorgeous. No wonder I had so much fun banging her.

The second she spots me, she jerks to a stop.

I sense Mick moving off Ethan's knee and trying to catch her eye. She's grinning as if she recognizes this girl. Do they have classes together or something?

More flashes of the party where—fuck, what's her name?—and I had mind-melting sex in one of the upstairs rooms hit me, and I can't help a small grin.

Maybe I could make an exception and go for round two with this one.

She—

"Hey." Her voice is snappy, and my slow-ass brain suddenly registers that her blue gaze is lacking some serious warmth. She looks super pissed. "You remember me?"

I nod, pointing at her with my best smile. "I want to say Karen."

Mick lets out a soft gasp, then mutters something under her breath.

I don't catch it because I'm too busy staring down the female version of a bull ready to charge. Her nostrils flare, and she grips the strap of her handbag, her knuckles going white.

"Caroline. My name is Caroline."

"Oh yeah." My eyes run down her body. I can't help it. She's in these tight-ass jeans with this red-checkered shirt that makes her look like a sexy country girl.

*Sweet Caroline.*

Yeehaw. I wouldn't mind a ride with her again. She can keep the shirt on. As long as I can bury my fingers in those luscious curls and—

"We hooked up at a party in January."

"Yeah, I remember."

The leather bands around her wrists click together, the colorful beads spinning as she crosses her arms and practically growls, "You were gonna call me. I gave you my number."

I cringe, running a hand through my hair. "Yeah, I'm not..." I hiss, flashing her an apologetic smile. "I don't really do that."

She scoffs. "So, what, you just collect girls' phone numbers like little souvenirs? Is that it?"

I look to the ground, shoving my hands in my pockets.

"I thought we had a good time together."

"We did." I glance up, my eyebrows popping high. "I just don't... you know. I'm a onetime guy. Sorry. I thought everyone knew that about me."

Her chin trembles just the tiniest bit.

*Oh fuck, please don't cry. Please don't cry. Don't cry. Don't cry.*

Her eyes go vibrant blue, glistening a little as she clenches her jaw.

And this is why I don't do relationships.

"Men can be such assholes. Amiright?" Mikayla gives her a sympathetic grin.

Caroline's smile is kind of tumultuous and only curls her lips for a second as she shares a brief look with Mick.

Lil' mouse waves, mouthing, "Hey."

Caroline nods at her, then lets out a heavy sigh, tucking a lock of hair behind her ear. "Look, Casey, we need to talk."

*Oh shit.*

369

But to prove I'm not an asshole, I put on a smile and nod. "Sure, what's up?"

She glances around at Asher, who's still hovering behind her, then Ethan at the table, and finally Mikayla near the kitchen counter, before looking at me and raising her eyebrows. "In private."

No fucking way.

It might make me a coward, but I'm not walking out of this room. I can sense that I need some major backup. I have no idea what the fuck this is about, but if she's going to go off on me, I want witnesses.

"Truth? Whatever you tell me will get back to these guys anyway, so..." I shrug.

She stares at me for a long beat, a muscle in her neck straining as she grips her bag strap again.

"What's said in Hockey House stays in Hockey House," Mick tells her. "But we can go upstairs if you want."

"No, that's cool. She doesn't mind, right?" The words rush out of me. "I'm gonna tell these guys as soon as you leave anyway."

Shitballs. I am such a coward.

Her jaw works to the side, her nostrils flaring again as she mutters, "Fuck it." Unzipping her bag, she yanks it open and proceeds to destroy my life. "I'm pregnant."

My ears start ringing, and all I can do is blink at her.

She slaps a pregnancy test down on the counter, and I bulge my eyes at it. The pink cross is bright and terrifying.

"And in case you think that one was a mistake, it's not."

Turning her bag upside down, she gives it a shake and

about twenty tests tumble out of it, hitting the counter and the floor, bouncing off the stool. One of them does a flip, then skids across the tiles, landing against my pinky toe.

I snatch the test off the floor, gaping at it and wondering what happened to my heartbeat. It's either disappeared or it's going so fucking fast, I can't even feel it.

"It's yours, in case that's not already clear," Caroline snaps.

"How do you know?" I rasp.

"Excuse me?"

"How do you know it's mine?"

Mikayla hisses and starts shaking her head while Caroline glares at me like I've just insulted her.

"I know because I met you at a party and thought we had a connection, so I slept with you, and then you said you'd call me."

I wince. Her eyes are fire right now. An icy blue burn that's going to turn my insides to ash.

"And then I stupidly waited for your fucking phone call! So that's how I know it's yours!"

I gulp, still trying to overcome this numbing shock. It's hard to think straight. It's hard to do fucking anything.

Dropping the test on the counter with the others, I lean against it, needing the support to hold me up. "But we used... we would have used protection. I... I always wrap my dick."

She sighs, her shoulders deflating. "Those things don't always work. It says so on the box."

"It does?" My voice pitches. "Where? I mean, shouldn't that be in bold or something?"

Her fiery gaze starts to lose its energy, her blue eyes filling with a sorrowful look that breaks my fucking heart.

I want to say something to take that frown off her face, but I've got nothing.

All I can do is stare at these positive tests and feel my gut sink all the way down to my asshole.

*Shit.*

*Shit, shit, shit.*

"I know you don't want this to be your problem." She says the words so softly I nearly miss them. "But *Karen* thought you should know."

Her voice drips with sarcasm—a final blow to fuck up my day—before she spins on her heel and heads out the door.

I flinch when it slams shut, then flinch again when Mikayla smacks me on the arm.

"What are you doing?"

"Reeling. I think the word is reeling."

"Get your ass out that door and chase her down! You might be a whole lot of things, Casey Pierce, but you are not going to let the woman carrying your kid walk away without at least offering to help her out."

Images of my mom flash through me. When she told my dad she was pregnant, he just left her to it. That's one of the reasons I never wanted to become a father. My dad was a shithead. I've never even met the guy, but the way he treated Mom was...

My insides clench into a knot so tight, I think I might throw up. I hate so much that Mikayla's right.

"Fuck," I shout before slapping the counter and running after the Queen of Hearts.

Thank you so much for reading THE HEART STEALER. Liam and Rachel's story packed an emotional punch, but I love the depth of their romance. They're the sweetest couple and their HEA makes my heart sing.
And now it's time for a very different couple to get their happily ever after...

*Casey's the honorary kid of Hockey House, so when he finds out he's having one, he's thrown into adulting, and struggling to cope with it. But he's determined to support Caroline, and willing to do anything to help her through this pregnancy. Luckily for him, her hormone-crazed body needs a little Casey lovin'... he just didn't realize that jumping into a sexy affair would quickly turn into more. He's never fallen in love, and he never wanted to, but this queen of hearts is changing his life with a force he has no chance of fighting. Mr. One-Time Only is about to be off the market for good... unless Caroline's secret comes to light and destroys her one chance with the only guy she's ever truly wanted.*

*If you want to be the first to read THE GAME CHANGER, sign up for Katy's newsletter. You'll get an exclusive teaser of Casey and Caroline's sizzling first hook-up. You also get the Nolan U. Sports Digest filled with images and character interviews, plus a chat with me!*

### SIGN UP HERE:
www.katyarcher.com/the-game-changer-sneak-peek

# NOTE FROM KATY

Dear reader,

I hope you enjoyed Liam and Rachel's story. I was so aware when I was working on it, that I was touching on heavy topics, and I ended up crying a few times, especially at the funeral. I felt Liam's pain and his struggle to forgive. I felt Rachel's fear and her fight to become her own person—a woman who doesn't need a man to feel whole.

That took me way too long to figure out in my own life and I ended up in a relationship where I was emotionally beat up for a couple years before I found the courage to leave. But I learned so many things through that nightmare. I became a new person, someone who was strong. Someone who could love herself. So, as much as I'd love to erase that chapter of my life, it made me who I am now and I kinda like me. Actually, you know what? I fucking love me! 😉

And I love you too

You are awesome and worthy and beautiful and I'm so grateful for you. Thank you for reading my books. Thank you for making time in your life to escape to Nolan U, to hang out with these hockey bros. Being in Hockey House brings me so much joy and I hope it does for you too. I can tell you that writing Casey and Caroline's book put plenty of smiles on my face. He cracks me up and I can't wait for you to see these two together. They're sizzling and fun and chaotic and I love that about them.

If you enjoyed *The Heart Stealer*, I would so appreciate you leaving an honest review on the online bookstore where you got this book and/or Goodreads. Even just a star rating is helpful. You don't have to write anything if you don't want to. But star ratings and even short reviews really help validate the book, letting readers know it's worth a shot. It also tells online bookstores and Goodreads that this book is worth shining a spotlight on. I know there are a bunch of readers out there who love college sports romance just as much as we do. If you can help me reach them, then that would be freaking fantastic.

Thanks for the assist!

I'd also like to thank a few key people who have been instrumental in helping me get this book off the ground —Megan, Kristin, Beth, Rachael, Meredith, Melissa. Working with you guys is awesome. I'm so grateful for your input and your friendship. Thank you.

Maggie—you continue to inspire me. I look up to you so

much and am beyond stoked that you've welcomed me into your world and let me work with you.

Trudi and Nicky—my lunch buddies. Our monthly catch ups are the best. I always come away pumped to be able to do this amazing job and sharing our writing journeys together.

My husband—you make me laugh every day, you support me no matter what and you'd do anything for me. You seriously are the best guy a girl could ask for.

My sons—thanks for making life brilliant.

My creator—thank you for love and forgiveness. Thank you for being a part of who I am and teaching me that worthiness doesn't have to be earned, it's my birthright, because you made me and everything you create is good and beautiful. Thank you for gifting me this passion for story-telling. I will love you forever.

And last, but absolutely not least—my readers. Thank you for reading this book. Thank you for celebrating this Nolan U world with me. Your emails and comments on social media, your kind reviews and support, mean the world to me. You are the reason why I want to keep publishing for as long as humanly possible. Thank you!

xoxo
*Katy*

# BOOKS BY KATY ARCHER

### NOLAN U HOCKEY

Hockey House V-cards (prequel)
The Forbidden Freshman
The Heart Stealer
The Game Changer
The Love Penalty
*Bonus Epilogue novella (TBC)*

### NOLAN U FOOTBALL
*In development*

### NOLAN U BASKETBALL
*In development*

# CONTACT KATY

I love to hear from my readers, so feel free to email me anytime. You can also find out more on my website.

EMAIL: katy@katyarcher.com

WEBSITE: www.katyarcher.com

And if you want to connect with me on social and see pretty reels and teasers from the books, you can find me Addicted to College Sports Romance on...

INSTAGRAM
@addictedtocollegesportsromance

FACEBOOK
@collegesportsromancebooks

TIKTOK
@katyarcherauthor